Praise for *Promises Reveal*

"Few writers can match the skill of Sarah McCarty when it comes to providing her audience with an intelligent, exhilarating Western romance starring two likable protagonists. The fast-paced story line hooks the audience."
                                                                —*Midwest Book Review*

"Entertaining and kept this reader turning the pages. I've got a soft spot for Western historicals, with their hard times and smooth-talking cowboys. Ms. McCarty delivers on both of those fronts."
                                                        —*Romance Reader at Heart*

"I absolutely adored the chemistry and witty banter between these two spicy characters, and the sex, as always, was titillating, sizzling, and realistic . . . I don't know how she does it, but I want more and more and more. You will too once you read this fantastic tale."
                                                                —*Night Owl Romance*

"A must read . . . Enticing and erotic . . . I am already craving more!"
                                                                —*Romance Junkies*

"Highly entertaining . . . Plenty steamy . . . and a great compliment to the series."
                                                                —*A Romance Review*

"A delightful tale with lots of intense passion . . . Outstanding! Not to be missed by fans of historical Westerns who enjoy a strong dose of erotic fiction."
                                                —*The Romance Readers Connection*

Praise for *Running Wild*

"[Sarah McCarty's] captivating characters, scorching love scenes, and dramatic plot twists kept me on the edge. I could not put it down."
                                                                —*Night Owl Romance*

"McCarty . . . skillfully brings out her characters' deepest emotions. Three strong heroines and three mouthwatering heroes . . . will tug at your heartstrings, and the well-written sex scenes will not disappoint."
                                                                —*Romantic Times*

continued . . .

⊰⊹ THE SHADOW REAPERS ⊹⊱

REAPER'S JUSTICE

Sarah McCarty

BERKLEY SENSATION, NEW YORK

THE BERKLEY PUBLISHING GROUP
Published by the Penguin Group
Penguin Group (USA) Inc.
375 Hudson Street, New York, New York 10014, USA
Penguin Group (Canada), 90 Eglinton Avenue East, Suite 700, Toronto, Ontario M4P 2Y3, Canada
(a division of Pearson Penguin Canada Inc.)
Penguin Books Ltd., 80 Strand, London WC2R 0RL, England
Penguin Group Ireland, 25 St. Stephen's Green, Dublin 2, Ireland (a division of Penguin Books Ltd.)
Penguin Group (Australia), 250 Camberwell Road, Camberwell, Victoria 3124, Australia
(a division of Pearson Australia Group Pty. Ltd.)
Penguin Books India Pvt. Ltd., 11 Community Centre, Panchsheel Park, New Delhi—110 017, India
Penguin Group (NZ), 67 Apollo Drive, Rosedale, North Shore 0632, New Zealand
(a division of Pearson New Zealand Ltd.)
Penguin Books (South Africa) (Pty.) Ltd., 24 Sturdee Avenue, Rosebank, Johannesburg 2196,
South Africa

Penguin Books Ltd., Registered Offices: 80 Strand, London WC2R 0RL, England

This book is an original publication of The Berkley Publishing Group.

This is a work of fiction. Names, characters, places, and incidents either are the product of the author's imagination or are used fictitiously, and any resemblance to actual persons, living or dead, business establishments, events, or locales is entirely coincidental. The publisher does not have any control over and does not assume any responsibility for author or third-party websites or their content.

PRINTING HISTORY
Berkley Sensation trade paperback edition / February 2011

Library of Congress Cataloging-in-Publication Data

McCarty, Sarah.
   Reaper's justice / Sarah McCarty.—Berkley Sensation trade paperback ed.
      p.   cm.
   ISBN 978-0-425-23668-0
1. Werewolves—Fiction. I. Title.
PS3613.C3568R43 2011
813'.6—dc22   2010045392

PRINTED IN THE UNITED STATES OF AMERICA

10 9 8 7 6 5 4 3 2 1

To Linda, Isaiah's Woman of Radiance:
May the paths you travel be lined with all the love and
happiness you deserve. The best is yet to come.

⊰ 1 ⊱

THEY'D STOLEN HIS SANITY.

A hint of dawn watered the darkness to a pale gray, illuminating the doorway in a feeble wash of light. Isaiah Jones touched the piece of deep blue wool caught on the shattered wood of the door frame, a tiny, lingering fragment of the violence that had invaded the peace he'd found, tainted the haven she'd created. Touched *her*.

He pulled the scrap free of the splinter. It came easily into his grip, as if sensing his need. It was cold, devoid of the heat of her body, empty of that subtle scent he associated only with her. They hadn't taken her recently then.

He tucked the piece of fabric into his pocket and shoved the hanging door out of the way. He didn't go any farther into the kitchen than the first foot. This was her space, her world, not a place where a man like him belonged. Besides, he didn't need to go into the room to know when they'd taken her. The pink-and-white teacup on the table told the story. She was a woman of habit, going through her day in an orderly manner. No matter what chaos stirred around her, she handled everything with efficient competence, maintaining her balance through the rituals she cherished, sharing that balance with others who came into contact with her. She never looked deeper than a person's need, meeting it as best she could. It was one of her more foolish habits and one of the reasons he'd taken to guarding her. That and the fact that he owed her.

One of her nightly rituals—one he approved of—was to sit at the kitchen table every evening at nine o'clock with a book and a cup a tea. She read for half an hour then rinsed out her cup and put it back on the drying towel on the counter before going to bed. He knew because he came by her house whenever he was in town, drawn against his will to check on her, the ghost of his existence haunting hers. Except for tonight, the one night she'd needed him.

He forced himself into the room, toward the table where her teacup still rested, guilt driving his feet forward. The scent of sweet dough settled around him, drowning out the other smells, pushing against the inner walls that contained the beast.

One step, two steps. He made it one more before the walls closed in around him. *Shit.* He hated enclosed spaces. He blinked as reality wavered and the cheery, blue arbor rose wallpaper disappeared into the memory of damp, crevice-laden dirt walls, crawling with cockroaches. He breathed steadily as the slip between past and present persisted, gliding silently forward, roses and roaches shimmering one over the other. He stopped just short of the table, instinct carrying him through the confusion, and reached out to touch the cup. Her cup.

The room snapped back into focus. He traced the rim of the cup, experiencing the delicate fragility of the china against his rough fingertip. Beside the cup sat a smooth piece of gleaming amber. Her worry stone. It was hard to touch the small, flat sphere so loaded with her scent and the remnants of her energy. His connection to her was already too strong.

He forced his finger to the smooth surface. He pictured her as he saw her so often, head bent over a book, the stone in her slender hand, her fingers rubbing back and forth in an easy rhythm as lamplight shone on her hair, highlighting the blond streaks that glowed like lingering rays of sunshine. He picked up the amber and carefully put it in his pocket. She'd need her worry stone.

He turned to go and made it halfway to the door before he stopped. He glanced beyond the door, the anonymity of the night calling him. Behind him the cup and saucer sat, a ritual incomplete. The amber burned in his pocket. Rituals mattered, kept a body sane. He, more than anyone, understood that. He hesitated a moment, and then returned to the table. The sense of connection increased as he picked up the delicate china. Tea sloshed in the cup. A growl rumbled in his throat. She hadn't even gotten to finish her tea.

He rinsed out the cup and saucer and placed them on the drying towel, completing her ritual. He paused an instant, his fingers resting on the fine material of the lace-edged white towel. Even her mundane items were delicate and fancy, little tells of the vulnerable femininity she tried to hide because she saw it as weak. His dark fingers lay in stark contrast against the fragile needlework, the network of scars on the backs the opposite of beauty. The opposite of peaceful. And tonight that was good.

The sound of wind roared in his ears, but outside the window the branches of the willow tree didn't sway. The scent of blood blended with the scent of sweet dough. He blinked slowly.

Not real. It's not real.

Real or not, it didn't matter. He felt the icy lash of rain against his cheeks as if it were yesterday. Felt the pain as the scars split into gaping wounds that never healed, spilling blood until it stained the field of his vision. He blinked again and pulled his hand away. The towel slid off the counter, but it was white, unmarked by blood. Just another trick of his mind, heralding the split building inside as all the rituals he'd devised over the last three years to protect the world from himself tore off, layer by layer. He put the towel back to rights, but inside the destruction continued, and the beast howled to be so near its freedom. And this time he didn't fight it back.

He would have stayed invisible forever, blending with the shadows, enduring the cacophony of his life until something brought it to an end if they hadn't touched her. But they had. They'd slipped into his private sanctuary and threatened the only thing that mattered. The only good he knew. He turned on his heel, melting comfortably into the shadows of the room, heading out the door, no longer human. No longer anything but the deadly specter he'd been taught to be.

The early morning air took him into its cold embrace. The smooth leather of his knife grip settled into his palm with the familiarity of a trusted friend. He hadn't asked for this. The choice had been theirs. Foolishly and arrogantly, they'd ignored the laws of nature that called for balance, the laws that kept evil circling good, and with their actions had released the evil circling her. Him.

He knelt at the foot of the steps, his night vision illuminating the pattern in the dirt. The prints told the story. Three men. All wearing boots. The one with a tendency to roll his right foot to the inside held her. She'd fought. The scuff marks told that story. He followed the tracks back to the narrow alley behind the building. Dark splotches in the dirt drew his touch.

Blood. He brought it to his nose. Hers. The beast snarled and bared its canines. Inside, the hunger surged. Inhuman. Dangerous. The end to her struggles hadn't been painless. For that they would also pay. He scanned both sides of the alley. No bodies. They'd probably made it to their horses without notice. Which probably meant she was still alive. He grunted, pressing the sand between his fingers, holding on to the essence of her as if through sheer force of will he could keep her alive. She just needed to stay alive and he would find her. No matter where they took her, no matter how they tried to cover their tracks, he would find her. And he would bring her home.

His gaze was drawn to the remaining splotch of blood—growing, spreading until it swallowed the ground. Rivers really could run red because the ground wasn't always thirsty enough to soak up men's violence, and when that happened, there was no stopping the carnage. He took a breath and then another, fighting the urge to tumble into the growing vision, to accept the stain that was so much a part of him, to accept that there was no rebuilding a past that had been stolen so long ago.

The old anger rose, feeding the emptiness he'd lived with since before he could remember, before they'd taken away what little he'd had. With a snap of his teeth, he won the battle to stay in the here and now. At the end of the alley, between the rough wood sides of the buildings, the horizon flushed with the first hint of morning. A new day. One more night survived without succumbing.

Isaiah rested his forearm on his knee and formed a mental picture of the terrain beyond the town. The men who'd stolen Adelaide would likely be relying on their lead to get them through so it'd make sense for them to take the easier southwest route. If he cut through Ambush Canyon, he could make up a lot of ground. Assuming they continued southwest.

He stood. That was a pretty safe assumption. In his experience, men kidnapped a woman for only three reasons—money, lust, or revenge. This had the feel of all three, seeing as the woman was beautiful, salable, and of good family, with strong protectors.

5

Only someone mad as hell would risk setting the Camerons on his tail. There wasn't a more relentless or deadly force in the Territory, if he discounted himself, than the Cameron men. The fact that the kidnappers had targeted a member of their tight-knit clan made this personal. He'd figure out why after he brought Adelaide back. He didn't leave dangling threads from a threat any more than he left witnesses.

The kidnappers would likely ride through the night before they felt comfortable enough to stop. And when they stopped, the lust and revenge angle would come into play. His mouth set into a grim line. The thought of what that would mean for Adelaide hardened his resolve. They weren't going to touch her.

IF he touched her again, Adelaide was going kick to him between the legs, and to hell with the consequences. She tossed her hair out of her eyes. It fell back into her face immediately, blocking her field of vision. The even cadence of her breathing snagged on a moment of panic. The leader glanced over at her from where he knelt by the fire. His mustache twitched with his grin. She pulled her hands apart, using the pain of her bonds cutting into her skin to bury the emotions battling for dominance. Oh God, she wanted to scream, cry, throw herself on the ground and rage, do anything but stand here and pretend she wasn't terrified. But giving in to emotion wouldn't gain her freedom. She needed her wits about her to get out of this mess. A mess that had just gotten worse by the addition of the ten other men who'd joined her three kidnappers as soon as they'd forded the river.

The leader stood and approached, the cruel-looking spurs on his boots clinking with every step.

"You are a proud woman," he said as he drew even, reaching out. She jerked her head out of reach. He studied her defiance for an instant, his hand open, level with her cheek, the fingers drawn back in a threat. The split in her lip burned from where he'd struck her before. Fear rose, but she wouldn't cower. She didn't blink or look away, just stared at him as impassively as she could manage, giving herself a focus for calm through memorizing the details of his face. Her cousins would want to know what he looked like so they could hunt him down and kill him. When they asked for a description, she would like to have something to give them beyond "filthy and stank of horse and old sweat."

"I was raised to be a lady, no matter what the provocation."

The man looked to be in his thirties, with lank black hair and swarthy skin. From the dirt that was ground into his pores, he obviously did not believe in the saying "Cleanliness is next to Godliness." He was missing his right eyetooth and one of his lower front teeth. His face was broad, so much so that his eyes looked too small above his flattened nose. He had a thick, droopy mustache, which hid his lips but showcased the remains of whatever he'd eaten the last few days. She shuddered as everything else faded to unimportance. "Disgusting" was the description she came up with. Her cousins would not be happy with her.

"You're damn uppity for a prisoner," the man informed her, his rolling accent mellowing the threat inherent in the observation.

She waited one breath before answering. One breath in which she recovered from the shock of his stench. "I prefer to think of myself as composed."

His eyebrows went up into the shaggy line of his uncombed hair. "Composed?"

"Yes. Composed. As in not carrying on and giving into hysterics at the least little thing."

Like being kidnapped by the king of filth and his entourage of dirty minions.

The leader cupped her chin in his hand. She couldn't suppress her shudder. He didn't bother to hide his amusement. "I think you will find we're not such a 'little thing.'"

She refused to think of him as big. If she did, she'd lose all hope. His filthy thumb touched her cheek. "I'm sure."

His head canted to the side. "But you still intend to keep yourself composed?"

One of the new men, dressed in black from his hat to his boots, taller, leaner, *cleaner* than the others, looked up from where he hunkered down, rummaging through a saddlebag. His expression was blocked by the brim of his hat, but she knew he was listening. And he didn't approve. Whether of her or the situation, she wasn't sure. "Absolutely."

"Why?"

The leader's accent turned the question into two syllables. She motioned to the double row of ammo draped over his shoulders. "Why are you a bandit?"

His mustache twitched, either with a smile or a grimace. She couldn't tell beneath the overgrowth of hair. "It is what I do."

She shivered and hunched lower into the horse blanket they'd thrown around her shoulders. It stank but it was infinitely preferable to freezing. "Well, being composed is what I do."

His fingers slid down her jaw, toward her mouth. "One wonders if you would be so composed were I to kiss you." His thumb crept toward her mouth. "I think you would scream."

She shook her head. "No. I wouldn't."

Again, that twitch of the mustache. His head tilted back as he looked down his nose at her. Who knew bandits could be so arrogant? "You are so sure?"

"Yes."

He took a step nearer. She looked him straight in the eye, stopping him with two words that were the absolute truth. "I'd vomit."

She was about to vomit from his filthy hand being so close to her mouth.

"Then I would kill you."

She wanted to roll her eyes. He was probably going to do that anyway. Instead, she breathed steadily through her nose, trying to suppress the gagging urge as the wind swirled his odor around her. "Vomiting just happens. Threats will have no effect on my reaction."

The man in the black hat made a sound. Laughter?

The bandit pulled a big knife. He held it near her face. It was ten times cleaner than his hand.

"What do you say now?"

"I'm relieved to see you keep your weapons clean, at least."

He blinked. She couldn't blame him. She hadn't meant to say that out loud. She was just too nervous to think straight. The knife caught the sunlight, flashing the glare back over her face. "It will not matter if the blade that kills you is dirty."

It would matter to her. "That makes sense."

His eyes narrowed to slits. "I cannot determine whether you are very brave or very stupid."

Well, she wasn't brave. "Does it matter?"

His mustache spread and his eyes crinkled at the corners. The aura of friendliness was disconcerting. And wrong, because it didn't extend any deeper than his expression. His hand dropped away from her face. "No. Your value rests in other places. What is your name?"

"Adelaide. What's yours?"

The mustache twitched. "You may call me José."

Not "my name is" but "you may call me," which meant she didn't have any more to give her cousins when they came for her. They weren't going to be pleased. She'd have to do better or they'd chew her out.

"Thank you."

José touched the knife to the tip of her right breast through her dress, gauging her reaction before dragging it down to her stomach, lingering at her navel. When she didn't flinch, he slid it a few inches lower and poked it into the folds of her skirt between her legs.

She forgot all about memorizing details and focused on controlling her reaction. She hadn't expected this weakness in herself. She'd spent the whole afternoon going over in her mind all the possibilities about what might happen to her, and certainly being raped was number one on the list. She'd thought she'd prepared herself for the eventuality. Logically, she knew it wasn't going to be pleasant, but she was sure she'd survive it. Common sense said the act was survivable. Otherwise, the ladies at the White Dove Saloon would be disappearing faster than Miss Niña could replace them.

"Aren't you in a hurry?"

"Now, *sí*."

José pressed the knife until it dug into her skin. Much more and it would break through the protection of her dress and cut. She breathed slowly, hiding the panic inside.

Now.

The start of fear that went through her wasn't logical at all. She knew all she had to do was survive until help arrived, but still, when faced with the carnal intent of this filthy man, feeling his gaze crawl over her, she shook inside with a fear that went beyond rational to primal. José laughed, a mean, nasty laugh, before sheathing his knife. He didn't step away, just leaned in, overwhelming her with the reality of the threat as he sheathed his knife. "But we will have tonight."

Which left her no option but to come up with a plan before

tonight. She would not lie down, willingly or unwillingly, with a man who did not understand the concept of hygiene. It was a firm statement—rational, logical, decisive. It was amazing how little it did to make her feel better. José gave her another look.

"You are going to bring me a very good price."

She'd rather bring him a severe case of indigestion.

He turned and gestured to the men. "Mount up. The day is wasting."

The men stood in haphazard order, including the man dressed all in black. She met his flat blue gaze. His mouth set in a straight line and then he turned his back on her, grabbing the saddlebag and tossing it over his horse's flanks with more force than necessary. He acted for all the world as if he was mad at her. As if she'd asked for three men to break into her house and disrupt her evening reading. She could really work up to hating men.

She waited for someone to tell her what to do. The faint hope that they'd forget about her in all the hustle of getting ready to ride persisted against the logic that said they wouldn't. Still, when the leader turned his horse toward her, she couldn't prevent a shudder. In her dime novels, this would be the time for the hero to show up on a thundering steed, guns blazing, and bandits expiring under the hail of bullets.

She glanced around. No hero in sight. Just winter-killed brush and brown flatlands that rolled into distant mountains. She squared her shoulders and lifted her chin. She wasn't going to cringe, no matter how repugnant the thought of riding with the leader was. No matter how terrified she was inside. This time she wouldn't lose her pride. It was very hard to live without pride.

Another horse sidled up alongside the leader's when he was about three feet away. It was the disapproving man in black.

"I'll take the woman up with me."

José put his hand on the butt of his revolver. "Your sacrifice is not necessary, Billings."

Billings glanced at her as he pulled his makings out of his pocket. "I wouldn't call having my arms around a pretty lady a sacrifice."

"Then why should I give this pleasure up?"

He opened up the paper. "Because if her people come after her, we're going to have to split up and they'll follow whichever horse she's riding." He shook some tobacco into the paper. "Doesn't make sense to lose a leader over a piece of tail."

A piece of tail? Never in her life had Adelaide been referred to in that way. Never had she heard of any woman referred to that way. It was as shocking as it was disgusting.

The man didn't even look at her as she gasped and flushed. With efficient movements, he rolled the cigarette and struck a sulphur, lighting the tip. The acrid scent of cheap tobacco stung her nostrils as he snuffed the flame between his spit-moistened fingers. "It's up to you."

José looked at her, then back at Billings. He didn't take his hand off his gun. Tension thickened the air. The big man drew on his smoke. The end glowed a bright red. Adelaide reached into her pocket, automatically searching for her worry stone. It wasn't there. The glow of the cigarette faded. The tension remained. She rubbed the thick wool of her skirt between her fingers. It wasn't the same. It did nothing to stabilize her emotions.

The chill of the wind replaced the heat in her cheeks as José nodded and pulled his horse up. "The woman will ride with you."

Billings kneed his sorrel forward. He held out his hand. She took a step back, every muscle protesting the movement, instinctively shaking her head.

"You can ride sitting in the saddle or across it. Your choice."

It was a simple truth. She forced herself to accept it. And at least she had control of this, even if the choice was a tiny thing like how she would ride against her will. Control was good. It could be won and maintained in small measures. It should be held on to. She placed one of her bound hands in his. Her feet left the ground so fast she almost didn't have time to throw her leg over the horse's back. Her skirt wrapped in an uncomfortable knot around her legs as she struggled to find her balance.

She tugged at the heavy material, yanking it out from under her thighs, trying to cover the scandalous amount of petticoat and calf that showed. In the process, she kicked the horse's side. It did a little hop to the left. She grabbed the man's waist. Nothing but hard muscle met her touch. He swore and glanced over his shoulder.

"What in hell are you doing?"

She dug in her nails as the horse hopped again. She wiggled her right leg. The maneuver ended in another kick that generated another protest from the stupid horse. "My skirt is tangled."

"Well, cut it out. You're scaring Jehosephat."

She tried a tug-and-hop maneuver. This time the horse bucked. "Jehosephat needs some manners."

Controlling the horse with a shift of his weight and tension on the reins, Billings growled, "He's got plenty of manners. Now settle down."

The last rumbled out of his chest as more sound than enunciation. Too scary to ignore.

"I can't." She pulled at the hopelessly trapped material. "It's not decent."

He glanced down at her leg and then back at her over his shoulder, his mouth lifting in a sardonic twist. "Lady, showing a bit of leg is the least of your worries."

⇥ 2 ⇤

IT *WAS* THE LEAST OF HER WORRIES.

Eight hours later, sunburned, thighs chafed, frozen stiff, and tied to a tree while the men made camp, Adelaide had to agree with Billings's earlier comment. Showing a bit of calf was no longer one of her worries. It had long since fallen off the list. She was far more concerned with freezing to death and being raped. Well, and maybe that someone would make her eat the mess they'd pulled from their dirty sacks and were calling food.

She wanted to do nothing more than close her eyes and go to sleep, but if she did, she might not wake up. Or she might wake up to being attacked. Both options terrified her, so she forced herself to sit upright, and kept herself that way through sheer force of will. For how much longer she could maintain it, she didn't know, but it was going to be longer than this minute and definitely through the approach of yet another of the bandits.

It was the squint-eyed, dirty boy. He wasn't really a boy, he just had a youthful face and one eye that wouldn't open all the way, which gave him an absurd appearance of concentrating when she'd already established through observation that a high mental capacity wasn't his strong suit.

Let him walk by. Let him walk by.

The hope wouldn't die, even when his gaze locked with hers and a lecherous smile took up residence on his pimply face. After they'd retrieved her from the Comanche raids, her cousins had made her promise never to give up hope should she be stolen again, but they hadn't told her how hard it was going to be to hold on to that hope in the face of overwhelming numbers of the enemy, exhaustion, and the threat of death. They hadn't told her because they hadn't imagined it could happen. Not with them protecting her. But two years ago she'd managed to finagle her way to town, put down roots in her bakery, and take the first baby steps out of the past because even after all these years she hadn't given up hope that she could have the life she wanted. No. A body didn't give up hope. They held on to the possibilities that lurked around the corner. Just as she was doing now.

Squint-eye stopped in front of her and held out a grubby, half-eaten piece of jerky and smiled, revealing rotten teeth. "Want some?"

Keep your head down and keep your strength up.

Her cousin, Cole's, words this time. He'd taught her a lot of things about fighting and survival. The number one rule was not to become weak, so when her chance for escape came, she could take it. She forced herself to smile. It felt more like a pathetic twist of her lips, but it was all she had. "Thank you."

Squint-eye held the jerky closer. The rank odor of his body didn't cover the rancid odor of the meat. It was turning. Her stomach heaved as she thought she saw something moving in the jerky. The smile slipped out of her control, fading away. She forced her mouth open. She had to keep her strength up. The food was yanked away.

"Ask me to touch your breasts and you can have some."

The shock of his words, their meaning, froze her. No one had ever talked to her that way. She didn't even know men did talk to women that way. She didn't like it. She most definitely wasn't going to cooperate with such childish taunting. "No."

He waved the meat as if it were a special prize. "You're going to get mighty hungry if you don't learn to cooperate."

"Really?" She cocked her head to the side, meeting his gaze. "And here I thought you needed to deliver me alive to get your payment."

"Alive don't mean happy."

"No, but I imagine well fed means more money, and since your companions look like the greedy type, I imagine I will be fed regularly, which means your threat was not a very well-thought-out one, rendering it rather pathetic when it comes to persuasion."

The men nearest, having heard the exchange, laughed. Squint-eye's face turned red. "You think you're too good for the likes of me?"

She bit back an "absolutely," a cold, hard surge of pride giving her the control to keep the quaver out of her speech. "I'm merely pointing out that your threat lacks logic."

His face contorted into an ugly caricature. Before she even gathered his intent, he slapped her, his "Fuck you" joining the ringing in her ears as her head connected with the rough bark of the tree. A distant growl joined the rumble in her head. Lights flashed before her eyes and then the pain hit. She moaned. A shadow came between her and the firelight, rendering everything except the stars streaking across the inside of her lids black. A hand came under her chin, roughly jerking her jaw from side to side. "Damn it, Bob, if you broke her jaw, I'm going to cut your pecker off. A woman that can't suck ain't worth shit."

She didn't want to know what those words referred to. The right side of her face throbbed a protest as José manipulated her jaw up and down. She tucked squint-eye's real name away for future reference.

"I didn't break her damn jaw, just taught her some manners."

Adelaide opened her eyes and found the men staring at her with varying degrees of inquiry. José's gaze dropped away from her face as abruptly as he had grabbed it. José's profile was hard as he said, "Then next time choose a better way."

"Maybe he needs teaching on how best to discipline a woman," a voice she didn't recognize suggested.

José glanced over at Bob, disgust on his face. "You might be right. Pay attention, boy."

As if it were nothing more than brushing a crumb off his shirt, Jose's fingers closed on her nipple through her dress. She didn't have time to absorb the shock of being so intimately touched before agony seared up from her chest, driving a scream from her throat. If she hadn't been tied to the tree, she would have doubled over. Men laughed as she jerked upright. José merely continued his lesson. "You don't need to mark a woman, boy, to make your point. Just grab hold of her teats and twist a bit." Satisfaction edged the cold smile on his lips. "Works every time."

He let go, but the pain continued. As Adelaide reeled with the residual agony, she heard it again, that deep, unearthly growl that echoed in her mind. José's head came up. "You all hear that?"

Oh, dear Lord, it wasn't in her head. There was a wild animal somewhere behind her growling, and she was tied.

"Hear what?" someone asked.

"A growl."

"Probably wolves drawn by the food," Billings offered, rolling another smoke. "Winter's been a hard one."

José drew his gun. "I fucking hate wolves."

Adelaide yanked at her hands.

Bob pulled his revolver, too. "I'm not afraid of wolves."

Her estimation of his mental capacity dropped another notch. Wolf packs killed cattle, sheep, horses, and people when times got very tough. At the end of winter, times were their toughest. He crossed to the small fire and grabbed a stick, the slight swagger in his step telegraphing what he intended to do before he said it. "I'll check things out."

"You do that, boy, and when you get your frozen ass back here, you can tell us all about the wolves you didn't see."

Bob shot the speaker, the man she'd classified as "fancy-man" from his shiny vest and ornate spurs, a disgusted look. "Fuck you, Dempsey. If it's close, I'll find it."

"Don't no one find wolves," a man too nondescript to have earned a name yet said. He made the sign of the cross. "They are devil animals."

Adelaide made note of his reaction. Superstition could be worked with.

"It's just a damn wolf, Manuel," Bob said with disgust, lifting the torch. "Just let me get the gleam of his eyes in the light and I'll put an end to his growling."

Now, she had five names.

Sticks cracked and snow crunched as Bob moved out of her line of sight and headed into the night behind her.

"Stupid kid," Dempsey muttered.

José holstered his gun. "Eh, let him go. It matters not if he kills the wolf."

"It will matter a lot if the gunshot alerts the posse following," Blade stated logically.

"There is no posse." José made a dismissive motion with his hand. "The sentries have seen nothing."

Billings crushed out his smoke. "The Camerons aren't the sort to send sign ahead. And that older cousin of hers isn't called Ghost for nothing."

"They're men. We have the higher ground. If they were following, we would know."

The certainty in José's voice crippled Adelaide's conviction. The scoff in Billings's voice restored it. "That what you want me putting on your grave marker? 'We would know'?"

She couldn't see José's face, but the set of his beefy shoulders worried her. If the two men exchanged gunfire, she'd be in the path of the bullets. She tugged harder at her bonds. "I'm starting to believe you're chicken shit, Billings."

"Believe whatever the hell you want."

"You've been whining ever since we stopped in Dover's Crossing."

"Kidnapping women is bad business."

"You superstitious like Manuel?"

"Nah, just logical. Kidnapping a decent woman gets everyone who hears of it riled. Puts the kind of posse on your tail you can't shake."

There was a murmur of agreement from the men.

With the blade of his knife, Billings pointed at her. "Especially one with kin like hers."

"Her kin killed my brother."

"Guess it wouldn't do any good to point out he was killed during the kidnapping of another woman?"

"He was my brother."

"Thought not."

"I'm thinking you're yellow."

Billings cut off a piece of jerky. "You're welcome to test that theory anytime you want. But truth is, I signed on for a bank robbery, not a kidnapping."

There was another murmur of agreement among the men.

José seemed to square off. "You don't like the way I do things, you can ride out."

"I'll keep that in mind."

"Now would be good."

Billings went still and somehow all that nonchalance turned lethal as he held the slice of jerky balanced on the edge of his knife. "Morning will be soon enough."

"And if I insist you leave now?"

Billings rose to his feet. He was tall, standing a good six inches over José. He popped the piece of jerky into his mouth.

Adelaide wished she shared his nonchalance.

"Then you're going to have to go chase down Bob yourself."

José stared at him for a long minute. All Adelaide could see was his profile. It didn't tell her much. Then he grunted and jerked his thumb over his shoulder. "Earn your keep and fetch him back, Billings."

Billings sheathed his knife long before Adelaide would have. She didn't trust the leader as far as she could throw him, but Billings strolled by him as if he knew he was no threat. Or, she realized as José stepped out of his way, as if he were confident he could handle any threat José threw his way. She blinked and the man was gone. Disappeared into the shadows like mist into fog. One minute Billings was there and the next he wasn't.

"*Madre de Dios.*"

Dempsey stared at the spot where Billings had been and made the sign of the cross. José's hand came up. He stopped just short of completing the gesture others in the group were taking up. Adelaide tugged harder on her hands. Pain ground up from her wrists, traveling up her half-frozen arms in an unrelenting shudder. She gasped. José looked at her, evil in his eyes, and then turned back to stare into the darkness.

Something grazed her fingertips. Panic froze her more solid than the temperature. Dear God, the wolf! The next instant, a hand covered her mouth and nose, holding her pinned through her instant of panic. When she stilled, the hand moved down a fraction so she could breathe. The scent of leather filled her lungs on her first breath. A barely audible "Shhh" wrapped around her, more welcome than warmth.

She wasn't alone anymore.

"No noise."

The voice was rough, as if rarely used. The syllables flowed together, only skimming the consonants.

She nodded.

There was a rustle of cloth and then something heavy and warm covered her. She sank back against the tree as the coat enfolded her in blessed heat. The scent of leather intensified, but beneath it came another scent. Something masculine. Pleasing. A fragrance she thought she should recognize but couldn't. There was another rustle and then a piece of jerky prodded her lips.

The dark whisper came again, a near silent extension of the night. "Eat."

Her stomach rose, remembering what she'd seen earlier. Her stomach didn't care. It gurgled so loudly she feared the men would hear. But no one paid her any attention. Someone had pulled out a flask. They were passing it around, gaining courage. Gaining ideas. The jerky pressed against her mouth again. She took a bite of the tough meat and held it in her mouth as revulsion wove through her. For the possible condition of the meat, for the drunkenness of the men. For what it was all going to mean to her.

The unseen stranger's hand left her mouth. More rustling. Something creamy and cool smoothed onto her wrists around the bonds, burning and then soothing. Balm? Why was he applying balm? Why wasn't he untying her? She chewed faster. The meat was tough. To heck with it. She was just going to have to talk with her mouth full. "Untie me."

Instead of answering, hands cupped hers. They were large and strong, rubbing her fingers with brusque efficiency, his flesh catching oddly on hers. After a couple minutes in which she chewed and he rubbed, the feeling came back to her fingers in a burning ache. She gasped.

She froze as Dempsey looked in her direction. Oh God! He'd see the coat and it would be all over. That hand came back over her mouth, making her order of "Run" a puff of sound. Dempsey's gaze traveled on by as if there was nothing untoward about her appearance. She looked down, squinting. In the darkness, the coat that had been thrown over her blended into the color of her dress. From the firelight, looking into the shadows, she probably did just look a little lumpier. Still, she didn't take a breath until someone diverted Dempsey's attention with the flask.

"Bob isn't back."

"Neither is Billings."

"I don't trust that man," another bandit muttered.

"Hell, you don't trust anyone."

The unknown man behind her continued to rub her hands, bringing the life back to them. She didn't see the point. They were only going to get cold again. "You need to *untie* me and get out of here," she whispered, putting particular emphasis on the "untie" part. Untied she'd have a chance.

"Shhh." Warmth enfolded her hands in a smooth tug. Gloves, he'd put gloves, still warm from his skin, on her. His hand touched her shoulder in a warning. "Wait."

Billings came back into the ring of firelight.

"Where's Bob?" José called.

Billings jerked his thumb over his shoulder. "Out there with his throat torn out."

"*Madre!*"

"*Hijo de la—*"

Men glanced uneasily at the impenetrable dark, reaching for guns, God, whatever they could.

"Shut up!" José hissed. Rising to his feet, a flask in his hand, he motioned to the dark. "And we are to believe this?"

"You can believe whatever the hell you want."

"You do not bring proof?"

"You want to drag a bloody corpse in, be my guest."

Their fear transferred to her. She yanked her arms. Fingers grazed the length of her arm. "Be still."

"I'm not being still until I get free." She yanked her wrists. "Untie me."

"No. You'll run."

"*Yes!*"

He fiddled with the edge of the gloves. "It's not time yet."

"Time?" He wanted a specific time. As far as she was concerned, it was past time. He was as crazy as the others.

"Be ready when I call you." The whisper reached around her again. Solid. Strong. Something to believe in.

There was a tug at her wrist and then something warm and smooth dropped into her palm inside the too-big glove. She curled her fingers around it. Her worry stone. She'd recognize it anywhere. She glanced over at the men. No one was watching her. They were all facing the darkness and the demon they feared.

"Where'd you get this?"

There was no answer to her question. No response. She was alone again, protected from the cold by *his* jacket, *his* gloves, her hope restored through the strength of his presence and the stone in her hand.

The stone *he'd* returned to her. The stone whose significance only a few understood.

"Who are you?"

The soft whisper drifted on the wind, unanswered. A howl reverberated out of the night. Chills raced down her spine. The men jerked. Dempsey fired off a wild shot. Manuel crossed himself again.

"Told you kidnapping a woman was bad business," Billings growled.

"Shut the fuck up. The woman has nothing to do with wolves," José snapped. "Dempsey, holster that damn gun down before you kill one of us."

A howl came again. Sparks shot in the air as a log was hastily thrown on the fire. The flare of light reached her corner of hell. It was too much to hope that no one would notice her now-covered state. She rubbed her worry stone harder, praying for invisibility.

"What the hell is that?"

José grabbed a branch from the fire and came over. She shrank back against the tree as he bore down upon her, shadows from the torch flickering around him like snakes. She hated snakes, hated dirt, hated disorder, and she was surrounded by two of the three.

José leaned over, hate and suspicion pouring off him. His eyes were narrowed to slits of evil. His filthy hand reached for her. Behind him the other men loomed, dark menacing shadows. She kicked out, catching José on the knee. He grunted and swore before drawing his foot back. She closed her eyes.

"I wouldn't do that."

It was a simple bit of advice, delivered by Billings in no particular tone. A shadow came between her and the light, plunging her into an instant of darkness. A twig snapped. Reddish light burned once again against her inner eyelids. Adelaide opened her eyes. José was looking over his shoulder. A day's growth of beard darkened his face, giving it a more sinister profile. If that was possible.

"Why not?"

A sulphur flared. The small flame threw Billings's face into stark relief. He was younger than she'd thought. Maybe in his late twenties. Handsome in the hard-faced way so common to men out here in the Montana Territory.

"Because I'm thinking whoever wanted her warm would take exception to anyone touching her."

"If whoever wanted her was capable of doing anything, then he'd have taken her rather than leave her."

Billings shrugged and stepped away. "You go right on thinking that."

José leaned down and then stopped, his hand inches from her shoulder. "Do you know something we should?"

"Just a bad sign when I see it."

"And you think this is a bad sign?"

"I think you bought a whole lot of bad signs when you went from bank robbing to woman snatching."

Around him, men murmured in agreement.

"So you already said."

Billings took a pull of his smoke. "So I did."

José snatched the coat off her. For a split second Adelaide was between warm and cold, an impenetrable place where nothing seemed able to touch her, then the wind blew. The men murmured. The coat fell to the ground. And the wolf howled again.

A chill swept over her. If her hands had been free, she would have grabbed for the coat, pulled it up over her shoulders. Her head. She rubbed the stone harder.

"Whoever is out there can do nothing."

"Maybe."

"Do you challenge my leadership?"

"Nah, just your assumptions."

José motioned two men forward. "Untie her."

"That's a mistake."

"No one asked you."

Billings stepped back and away. "Nope. That is the truth."

Another drag on the cigarette. The glow on the tip was very orange. She focused on it, sensing her situation had just gone from bad to worse.

Two men stepped forward immediately. She didn't have names for them. They hadn't done anything to stand out. Until now. Now, based on the grins on their faces, she was going to name them Lech and Lecherous. She kicked out. They avoided her feet with disheartening ease. She clenched her fingers over the worry stone as they cut the bonds between her hands. The gloves fell to the ground. They yanked her to her feet. Her arms howled in misery. Tears burned her eyes. She didn't let a sound pass her lips. She had the ridiculous thought, as they dragged her closer to the fire, that her would-be rescuer would be proud of her.

As soon as she got within five steps of José, the men shoved her forward. Her headlong stumble was stopped by José's hand under her chin. He lifted her face to his as he took a drink from his flask.

"Not so composed now, eh?"

She blinked the tears away. Her mouth felt stiff. The words sounded disjointed. "Everyone's composure slips now and then."

He took another drink, his gaze on the night behind her. "Like maybe the man who gave you the coat is about to?"

"Excuse me?"

Try as she might, she couldn't get her arms to move. All she could do was stand there as far away as his grip allowed. She couldn't even get a glare going for the agony shooting down her arms. She hoped she still had the worry stone in her hand. She pretended she did. Working it between her fingers. Two rubs on one side, and then rotate it to the other side, where she did three circles. Making five in all. The magic five. And then she started all over.

José made a tiny motion with his pinky. Just a couple twitches but it snapped every man present to full attention. Even Manuel stopped crossing himself to stare.

"Strip her."

Oh, Lord in Heaven! The next ten seconds passed in a horror of slowness. The footsteps coming up behind her. The harshness of men breathing in her ear as their hands grabbed the front of her sturdy wool dress. The disgusting anticipation in José's face as they took a step back and pulled. The tension that spread down her spine as the wooden buttons strained under the pressure. A splatter of brilliant red shot past her shoulder and splashed over José's face as his hands fell away. Wetness hit her cheeks. She listed to the side and then the other hands released her, sending her reeling back the other way. She heard two soft thumps and then two loud explosions. Rifle shots, she realized. And those thunks were her attackers falling to the ground. Which meant the wet stuff on her face was . . . blood. Human blood. Horror spread through her. Around her, men shouted and dived for cover.

She stood there, staring at the fallen men, her skin crawling, memories screaming. War cries. A woman's screams. Her mother's shout to run. But she couldn't run. She couldn't move. She could only stand there and watch them come for her.

No, she thought, holding her memories at bay with sheer determination. *No. This is now. Not the same.* And the blood was that of the enemy, not her mother's. The explosions were gunfire. And someone had just saved her from being raped. This time things were going to end differently.

Adelaide spun around, her arms swinging uselessly as she stared into the darkness toward where she thought the reports had originated. Her lips shaped around the words "Thank you."

Dear God, thank you.

⇥ 3 ⇤

THANK YOU.

Isaiah stared down the scope and blinked as he read the woman's lips. She was thanking him. The men around her were diving for cover like squirrels surprised at a party, firing random shots into the dark, and she stood there like a symbol of calm amid the chaos, looking directly toward where he hid. Proud. Beautiful. Not looking through him but at him. And thanking him. Son of a bitch.

He lowered the rifle, feeling the shock of that look down to his gut. She'd been as brave as all get-out when those sons of bitches had come up behind her and put their hands on her, that chin coming up in an unconscious challenge as they got ready to strip her bare, to shame her in an effort to shame him. As if all the shame hadn't been beaten out of him years ago. Assuming he'd ever had any.

She'd stood there and dared them, her arms hanging uselessly from the too-tight bonds to make it happen. He'd been as unable to let it happen as she had been to cower. The leader came up behind her, grabbing her by the hair and yanking her around. Her cry raked down Isaiah's spine, raising the beast. A drop of blood spread over his tongue as his fangs cut through his gums.

He sighted down the rifle barrel, drawing a bead on the inch of flesh between the leader's eyebrows as the man yanked her up against him. With anyone else he might have taken the shot, risked it, but he couldn't bring himself to do it. Not with this angle. The unfamiliar hesitation was about as welcome as all of the feelings she brought out in him.

One step to the side, asshole. Just take one step to the side.

A bullet screamed off the rock to his left. He cut a glance at the source. Billings stood, rifle at his shoulder, drawing a bead of his own. Isaiah slid into the next shadow. Billings was the wild card in this mix. As skilled as Isaiah, he only had one weakness. He had a tendency to bring his conscience to the job. A conscience that had cost him plenty, but it didn't make him any less deadly. Propping his rifle along a log, Isaiah took aim at the other Reaper. It would make sense to take Billings out now, increase his odds. Billings was easily worth five of the other outlaws when it came to a fight. As if sensing his eyes on him, Billings smiled. Son of a bitch, the rumors were true. The Reaper had a death wish.

Isaiah tightened his finger on the trigger. The leader shouted, "Take her." A man with a large handlebar mustache raced forward. Choice time. Billings or the leader? The answer was obvious. Just before Isaiah took the shot, Billings stuck his foot out. The mustachioed man went face first into the rocks. Isaiah eased his finger off the trigger. Well . . . that was a first. Apparently, Billings was on his side. They'd never worked the same side of a war before. It could be interesting.

The leader took a step back, taking Adelaide with him, keeping her as his shield. Isaiah's lip curled with disgust as the man yanked her against his chest, leaving his head open and clear. He toyed again with the idea of taking him out but another shot would give away his position and there wasn't enough cover here to protect him from a return volley.

Billings's protection aside, Adelaide needed him alive. It was a calm, logical decision. His training had become second nature and almost overwhelmed the logic. Training demanded he take the shot no matter the threat to himself or others. Training demanded he complete the kill. He brought Adelaide into the gun sight. Training didn't take into account the human factor. He was more than his training. He moved the sight back to the leader.

Sweating, Isaiah fought the compulsion and forced himself to take his finger off the trigger. This time his snarl was for the woman. She'd been doing this to him for months, disturbing the calm he'd worked so hard to resurrect, dragging forth his demons, his night-mares. She made him feel and that was unacceptable. As unaccept-able as the terror he could see on her face as José shouted to his men and threw her into the middle of the chaos.

Isaiah moved down the hill to the next position, keeping his eye on the camp.

Panic reigned around the fire. Men shouted and fired wildly into the darkness. Any control the leader had was gone. There was noth-ing left of his command but chaos. Isaiah smiled. He could work with that.

Run.

Isaiah sent the thought toward the woman. As if she heard, she broke free, spun around, and took two steps before José grabbed her by the hair again. She rounded on him, all spit and fire, the hold she had on her temper released in a scream that was absolute rage and frustration, striking Isaiah with the force of her fist to José's gut, ex-cept it wasn't José who gasped, who had the air knocked from his lungs. It was Isaiah. All because of that scream. It skated down his spine, joining the memories of other screams, other times. Faces of men, faces of women, faces of children, all grotesquely contorted, all dead, blurred within the circle of light thrown by the campfire. Spinning slowly when everything else was racing, giving him time to recognize the words tumbling from their lips in a senseless buzz. He stilled, counted slowly as he blew out a soundless breath. He blinked and the scene righted.

Adelaide was on the ground, holding her face. José stood over her, hands on hips, searching the dark nervously, his human eyes too weak to penetrate the darkness, but Isaiah's weren't. He could see easily. The shock on Adelaide's face. The blood forming on her lip. The outlaw was right to worry. There would be revenge for that blow. Not the impersonal impact of a bullet. No. His hand dropped to his knife. This revenge would be personal. Isaiah might have failed to protect the woman from that strike, but his moments of insanity were mostly short lived and controllable. The stretches between were what the leader should fear. Reapers had been created for one purpose. To exact the revenge their handlers deemed necessary, though they no longer had handlers. But they were still damn good at revenge.

Thank you.

But not so good at protection. His gut wrenched. Adelaide had thanked him for one thing and he'd turned around and failed her on another. He'd never been worth a damn when it came to constancy. And sure as shit she wouldn't be thanking him if she knew his history. About the only thing he'd ever managed to be good at was killing. Once someone made his list, they never got off. His grip tightened on his knife, his fingers tingling. And he was very good at killing, as the leader would find out before this was over.

Isaiah narrowed his eyes and focused on the other man's lips, reading the words he shaped enough to know what he was saying was filth. The knife slipped free of its sheath. There were all kinds of ways to kill a man, some clean, some not so clean, and some flat-out hellish. Isaiah knew them all. It was his only skill. His only dependable talent and one with which José would soon become acquainted. Normally, kills were a dispassionate necessity, but he was going to enjoy killing the leader. The rage simmered and built. He was going to enjoy making him pay for *her* fear, *her* pain, *her* humiliation.

He swept the area with an all-encompassing gaze. The men who huddled nervously by the fire watched the darkness with more fear than their leader, followers who scented death approaching, doubting the strength of their leader, reconsidering their loyalty.

With a small smile Isaiah let loose a howl, feeling the beast rise as he glided effortlessly along the edge of light, using the trees and rocks as a barrier to the volley of shots that converged where he'd once been, heading toward his targets.

"What do we do, José?"

"Shoot *el bastardo loco!*"

The leader's name was José. Isaiah tucked the information away.

José called for his sentries. Billings rose to his feet, his discarded smoke glowing faintly at his feet as he smiled grimly into the darkness when José shouted again.

There wasn't going to be a response. Isaiah stepped over the body of one of the sentries. There would never be one. The price for invading his territory was high. He'd exacted it with ruthless efficiency. He'd even enjoyed it. They should not have touched her.

Adelaide scrambled to her feet, brushing at her skirt with awkward movements of her hands. Good, she was getting the feeling back. He'd worried that the bonds might have numbed her arms to the point of uselessness. Billings grabbed her arm and pulled her against his side. Around the camp, men faced the darkness, guns drawn. The firelight gave him a clear shot at anyone he wanted to take out. Isaiah growled. They always made it so easy to pick and choose.

Except Billings. He was the only one standing away from the light, back against the tree. He'd taken the woman with him.

Isaiah would have done the same. Reapers were highly trained in only two things: survival and killing. Of the two skills, only the latter mattered to those who had created them from hell. The lesson had been drilled into the Reapers' heads until they contained nothing else, and then they'd been recruited to tip the scales in civil wars within countries that had no winners. But that hadn't concerned their creators. Their focus had been much more individual. Until the day the creators found they hadn't been able to call back what they'd unleashed. That the monsters they'd created couldn't be controlled. That day hell had come to earth.

After another unanswered call, José stepped back to the fire. Isaiah shook his head. Men always went to the light when in search of salvation. He drew his knife and crept up behind the bandit at the edge of the ring with his back to the rock. Redemption wasn't coming tonight.

He dispatched the man with a single slice of the knife, disappearing back into the shadows as the bandit's death gurgle alerted the men around him that a Reaper was in their midst.

Manuel jumped back from the spray of blood, crossing himself. *"Madre de Dios!"*

"Holy shit!"

The curses floated on the cold air, sharp pinpoints of terror. Satisfaction filled Isaiah as they scrambled about. No one caught the man as he fell, as if touching him would seal their fate. As if that fate hadn't already been determined the moment they'd taken *her*.

Isaiah took stock of the situation. Nine men left and eight hours until daylight. He pulled his throwing knife, took aim across the camp, and let fly, ducking behind a tree as men spun and fired and then thought to cover their own asses. Too little, too late. They were scared, scattered in loyalties, every man focused on his own survival. Easy pickings.

He glanced to where he'd last seen *her*. The area was empty. Even the glow from the discarded smoke was gone. Only a Reaper could do that. Billings had taken her. Isaiah palmed another throwing knife and glided back along the edge of the camp, moving soundlessly through the gloom toward where Billings and Adelaide had stood, knowing there'd be sign. Maybe not enough for human eyes, but enough for his. Dragging the woman would make a seamless escape into the environment impossible. Isaiah got to the spot where Billings had slipped through the brush with Adelaide. A broken branch at eye level screamed a message. *Follow me.*

He glanced back over his shoulder. The men were regrouping. Leaving them now meant losing the advantage. Leaving them alive went against everything inside that screamed for retribution, but *she* wasn't there anymore. She was with someone as deadly as he, someone as unstable as he, her fate left to an unreliable force that could be either threat or salvation, depending on his mood. And moods in Reapers were notoriously unstable things.

The moon crested the trees. A howl echoed across the valley. A challenge and a dare.

With a lift of his lip and a flex of muscle, Isaiah tilted his head back and answered.

THE howl came out of the darkness, sending shivers down Adelaide's spine. Dark and compelling, it connected with something primitive inside her. She turned back toward the sound. Goose bumps raced down her arms.

"Come on." Billings tugged her forward. She stumbled. "Move."

She tripped over a branch as he dragged her forward, her feet tangling in her skirt. "I would if you'd let me get my feet before haul-ing me around."

There was a grunt, another yank. "I don't have time for hysterics."

"Who's being hysterical?" She yanked at her skirt with her free hand. A bridle jangled. A horse snorted. They were near the horses? "I'm just pointing out the illogic of expecting me to see in pitch blackness."

"I'll do the seeing."

The "trust me" was implied. She wasn't trusting anyone. "As if you can see any better."

"I can." From the way he hauled her the next ten feet, maneuver-ing them around obstacles, maybe he could.

"How is that possible?"

"I'm special."

He was something, but she wasn't sure "special" was it. She ran into his back, bumping her nose, as he came to a dead stop.

"Ow."

"Quiet."

Rubbing her nose, she glared at his back. "Then stop hauling me around." Billings put his arm around her waist. She pushed at his arm. "Hey! Let me go."

"In a minute."

"But—" She reached out and bumped something warm, alive. The horse. Bracing herself against his side, she pushed backward.

Billings didn't even acknowledge her protest with a grunt. "No buts. He'll catch up to us later."

He would?

With a simple shift, Billings foiled her defiance. She would have fallen if he hadn't been holding her so tightly. Darn it. Falling would have at least broken his hold. While she was fussing, he lifted her. She let her legs dangle. They bumped against the horse. He couldn't make her sit.

"Who are you?" she asked over her shoulder.

"The only friend you've got right now, and if you want to live long enough for him to catch up, you'll stop being a fool and put your leg over that horse's back."

"Why would I want that?"

"Because your kidnappers will regroup quickly. And because he's the best protection you'll ever have."

That was something to consider. She let him seat her in the saddle. She grabbed the saddle horn as the horse stomped his foot. Her skirt was uncomfortably twisted. She yanked at it. "Better than you?"

"Yeah."

The lump under her butt came free. "How so?"

"Because I don't give a shit."

The man certainly believed in blunt speaking. The horse shifted sideways as Billings took the reins. The howl came again. Just as dark, just as compelling. Just as irresistible. There was a sadness to it that made her want to reach out and touch, a determination that gave her confidence, and a feral edge that sent goose bumps chasing over her skin. Billings swung up behind her. His arms came around her. A shiver slid over her skin, and not the good kind. He didn't give a hoot, which only left one question. "So why are you helping me now?"

"Because I owe him."

Him. The one who howled rather than shouted. She didn't know whether to kick the horse in the direction of that howl or to turn around and run. Billings took the decision out of her hands. Kneeing the horse forward, he rode into the veil of darkness before them. She clutched the saddle horn, praying that if the horse couldn't see, it would at least follow Billings's directions and they wouldn't end up sprawled at the bottom of a ravine with their necks broken. She prayed for that with every breath. And with every prayer, she fought the need to turn back toward that mournful howl. She pushed the hair off her face and grimaced as her finger snagged in a snarl. She hated snarls. Hated untidiness. She started finger combing the snarl out, blowing out a breath as she accepted that her hair was the least of her problems. Her neat and orderly life was a rat's nest of chaos, from the kidnappers on her trail to the strange men who'd rescued her. And there wasn't a thing she could do about either.

Could her life get any crazier?

HOURS later she had her answer. Maybe it couldn't get crazier, but it could get worse. She sat on that horse with nothing to do but feel her thighs rub raw against the leather of the saddle, and let her mind race over all the possibilities of what could happen. Hours in which her mental and physical misery multiplied until she wanted to jump out of her skin. And then, as a final insult, the clouds opened up. Cold rain poured over her, plastering her hair to her head, chilling her to the bone. The man behind her on the horse didn't seem affected at all by the elements. Didn't seem affected at all by her shivers. Didn't seem affected by anything. He just kept the horse pointed the way he wanted to go and rode in miserable, irritating silence.

She groaned as a cramp seized the muscle in her calf. Taking her foot from the stirrup, she tried to ease the ache. It didn't help. The cramp grew right along with her misery. Another shiver went down her spine. She clenched her teeth against the chill. When was this going to end? Another chill shook her from head to toe, leaving her exhausted. Oh God, she didn't even care anymore how this ended. She was just so miserable she only needed to know when.

Gray light pierced the horizon and a few birds chirped. Morning was coming. Did that mean the nightmare was going to end? A glance over her shoulder revealed the truth. Not if she left it to her rescuer. His gaze was set straight ahead and the expression on his lean face said he was prepared to go for hours. She rubbed her thumb over her worry stone in her pocket, searching for courage. She found it in the next hope-killing shiver.

"We need to stop."

"No."

At least he was predictable. She grabbed the reins and hauled back. "Yes."

The horse snorted and sidestepped. "Son of a bitch." With a soft whisper, Billings quieted the animal. "Don't do that again."

She ignored her instinctive flinch of fear. Misery loved company and he was too complacent for her peace of mind. "Then listen to me."

"You don't want to stop now."

"Yes, I do."

"It's too soon."

"For what?"

"Reapers are unstable after a battle."

So they were Reapers. Those legendary shadowy figures that haunted the hills surrounding the town. She didn't know whether to be comforted or panicked. All she knew of Reapers were the whispers that floated out of the saloons. Some said they were demons sent to earth. Other's said they were God's avenging angels. No one said they were safe. And she was riding with one. Dear heavens, her luck was nothing but bad. "Rumor is, Reapers aren't that stable *before* a battle, either. Or any time in between."

That twitch of his mouth might be a smile. "That's true."

"But what does that matter to me?"

"Beyond the fact that you're riding with one?"

"Yes." Beyond his physical stoicism, she didn't see much difference between him and anyone else. He looked neither demon nor angel. He was certainly less expressive than her cousin. Cole wasn't one for holding back when he thought someone was playing the fool.

"He'll make his move when we stop."

That sounded ominous. "He will?"

"He'll take it as a sign."

That sounded worse. She kicked the horse. Maybe she should heed the saying "Stick with the devil you know." She knew Billings. "Let's go then."

Billings looked over his shoulder and stiffened. "Too late."

"No, it's not."

Her nerves went taut in a flare of alarm that wasn't the least soothed by his "You made the decision."

"You didn't give me all the information I needed." A glance over her shoulder showed the guy's jaw was set and his eyebrow cocked.

"Yet you made the decision anyway and now trouble's come calling."

Trouble? She didn't need any more trouble. She said so.

He shrugged. "No one really cares."

She cared.

He turned the horse around so it faced the way they'd come.

She looked back over her shoulder. "What are you doing?"

"He'd only run us down."

A man who could run down a horse? She swallowed. "Who is *he*?"

Billings's hand on the top of her head turned hers. In front of them, at the edge of the woods, stood something—someone—tall, big, and bulky. Menacing. Every horrible tale she'd been told of the demons and monsters that lived in the hills flooded her mind.

⫷ 4 ⫸

"HELLO, ISAIAH," BILLINGS SAID.

At least this demon had a name.

The only response was a grunt that didn't cross the line from beast to man. Adelaide rubbed her thumb over her worry stone, taking comfort from the smooth, rhythmic motion. Closing her eyes, she imagined she was home in her bed with its crisp white sheets, white-and-yellow-checked quilt, and fluffy pillows. She imagined she was warm and cozy under the covers. Safe.

"You've come looking for this, I suppose?" Billings's hand in her hair snapped her eyes open. With a tug, he tipped her head back.

A growl rumbled out of the gloom and the figure took a step forward.

It was a man, she could see that now. Tall, broad shouldered, and unkempt. His hair was long and wavy, brown touched by sun at the ends swept back over his shoulders and anchored there by his dark Stetson. His beard was thick. Dark clothes covered his body down to his black boots, but nothing could hide the power beneath. Something gleamed dully in his hand. A knife? A gun? Whatever it was didn't matter. It was always the man holding the weapon who radiated the threat.

As she studied Isaiah, Adelaide had the absurd thought that everything about him was a shadow. But then he took another step forward, and she took back the thought. He was substantial and she knew him. She'd seen him flitting away from her back door a time or two. A shiver that had nothing to do with cold went down her spine.

Reaper. An icy rivulet of rain slid down under Adelaide's hair, following her spine. It was bad. It was cold but no colder than the chill that shook her at the term. They were both Reapers. Isaiah was one of those strange men who had moved into the area last year after the end of the War. No, last year right before the War had been declared over. Shadowy figures whom the townsfolk feared and to whom they attributed all wrongs since they'd first noticed their arrival. She had, too, at first, but her own past had made her conscious of how rumor could distort fact. As time went on, she'd noticed that the number of wrongs had gone down since the Reapers had taken up residence in the hills. So when she'd seen the man hanging around outside her door, she'd started leaving out baked goods for him, the ones that hadn't sold. It seemed such a paltry thing to do, she'd do the same for a stray dog, but she'd been compelled to do it.

The War Between the States had been horrible to read about, but until the men had started to come home at its end, she'd never been able to appreciate the depth of the horror. So many of the men who'd come back to Montana after the War were broken, shadows of what they'd been. Some were missing limbs. Some missing their minds. Some both. Some had been heroes for the South. Some for the North. But when they rode home, it was hard to see beyond the shattered looks to the heroism.

Then the Reapers had come. Men the townspeople rarely saw but who patrolled the perimeter of their valley. Silent guardians who had yet to ask for anything in return except to be left alone. Who was to say the Reapers were anything but war heroes lost to who they used to be?

She glanced to his right hand, where that "something" still gleamed. She licked her lips and reconsidered. They could also be exactly what rumor said they were. Lethal monsters of the night who only allowed the townspeople to live for reasons yet to be explained. She'd been comfortable, caught between the two beliefs, making her own compromise by putting the food out and darting back into the house and immediately locking her doors.

In all honesty, she'd never expected to come face-to-face with a Reaper. Yet she was riding with one and here in front of her stood another, the man who'd lurked around her home. His name was Isaiah. Her rescuer. He needed a bath and a shave and he wasn't the most talkative, but he'd still come for her. Risked his life for her. She owed him for that.

She forced a tentative smile to her stiff lips. His response was another growl. She leaned back against the man behind her. She didn't owe him that much.

"I think I'll stick with you." *Like a burr.* Isaiah was one scary man.

"Oh no, you don't." Billings pushed her forward and to the side.

She grabbed for the saddle horn before she could slide off. He pushed harder. She held tighter, aware that at any moment he could get serious and toss her to the ground. Just the thought of rolling in the dirt turned her stomach. The thought of being that close to the compelling, terrifying Isaiah upset it more.

"I'm not getting killed over a bit of fluff," Billings bit out, keeping the pressure on.

Never in her life had she been called fluff, and if she wasn't hanging on for dear life to the saddle horn, she would have slapped him.

There was another snarl and then hands were at her waist, taking the choice from her. She screamed, let go of the horn, and jabbed back with her elbow. Pain ricocheted up her arm. It felt like she'd hit a rock. This time she screamed because it hurt. Jerking her other hand free of her pocket, she lashed out again. Her worry stone bounced off her toe. Twisting, she grabbed for it, catching a glimpse of her captor from the corner of her eye. She blinked when she realized it was Isaiah who had her. How had he gotten to her so fast?

She stopped struggling, her gaze locked to where her stone had most likely fallen. "Let me go, damn you."

She couldn't see her stone in the gloom. She needed the stone—it was the only thing left of her former life.

Another growl, this time in her ear. It should have scared her but it sounded too familiar. Too right. Goose bumps skittered down her arm.

"Take it easy, Jones," Billings said. "All I did was keep her safe until you calmed down."

From Isaiah's snarl, he had no interest in being peaceable about anything. Yet strangely, Adelaide wasn't afraid. No matter how she tried, she couldn't detect any threat in the hands holding her so tightly that it was hard to breathe. Just a certain possessive determination. Cole had held her the same way when he'd found her living in that Indian camp after two years of searching. People only held people that way when they mattered to them.

"Maybe we should have kept riding," she gasped, trying to see Billings's eyes beneath his hat as Isaiah backed slowly away.

"I told you to trust me."

She had to try. Of the two, Billings seemed the more stable. "I trust you now."

"Too late." Billings backed the horse up.

Traitor.

"He's all yours."

"What am I supposed to do with him?" She wasn't even sure he was sane.

"My suggestion would be to do whatever you're told."

"Of course," she huffed. She had yet to meet a male who didn't think following a man's lead wasn't the best course of action.

"I'm serious."

"You do what you want."

She blinked. The voice was low and gravelly, as if from lack of use.

Isaiah's hands were like vises on her ribs, squeezing the breath from her. At least he was not holding the weapon now. But she knew he still had it. She dug her nails into the backs of his hands. He didn't even flinch, just kept backing up into the gloom. She kept her eyes glued to the spot where she thought the stone had landed. She couldn't lose her stone again, couldn't go through this again. She struggled and kicked. "Let me go."

She might as well have been talking to the wind for all the attention the men paid her. Their gazes were locked in a silent duel. Beneath their shirts, she could see the bulges of muscle. The tension in the air was so thick she could cut it with a knife. They stared at each other like dogs competing over a choice bone.

"It's not like I was planning on keeping her," Billings said, that smile that just made her want to smack him on his lips. "The woman never shuts up."

She felt Isaiah's nod. "I know."

"She's not much for quiet."

Isaiah nodded again. "I know that, too."

The heck he did. "I do not talk too much."

She might do a lot of things, but she didn't do that. She was known for her silence. Her discretion. Her common sense.

Billings chuckled. "She's also got a temper."

Isaiah took another step back, dragging her with him. "She hides it."

"Not too well." This time, Billings didn't take a step back.

Isaiah stiffened and shoved her behind him. Despite the congenial exchange, she'd only give it another minute before they came to blows.

Isaiah took a step forward, and suddenly, she'd just had enough. They wanted to think she had a temper, then they could just have a taste of it. Grabbing Isaiah by the arm, she spun him around, part of her horrified by the action, another part of her thrilled at the illusion of control. His eyes narrowed as his gaze snapped between her hand on his arm and her expression.

"I'm not a bone to be fought over," she spat, letting go of Isaiah's arm. She shoved her hair out of her face, wrenching her fingers through the snarls. She was dirty, she was wet, she was cold, she was unkempt, and it was their fault. All their fault.

She fed the anger, driving back the fear. She didn't want to belong to these men, and it would be a cold day in hell before she belonged to either of them. Nobody but she would ever dictate her future again.

"You're what I say you are for now." Isaiah caught her hands, pulling them gently away from her hair but keeping her there.

"No."

She didn't have any choice. He had her hands. He had the muscle. He wouldn't let her go. She bit him hard on his forearm. He didn't even flinch, just let her do her worst while he kept himself between her and Billings. Protecting her, she realized when she looked up at his face to gauge his reaction. He thought Billings was a threat. She let go. Isaiah pushed her behind him. She let him, because when all was said and done, he was the man who had come after her while Billings was the man who'd been riding with the bandits.

"Move on, Blade."

She blinked. Blade? The man she thought was her savior was called Blade? This time she was the one who took a step back.

"Was planning on doing that in a minute."

Isaiah didn't relax. Neither did Blade.

"Do it now."

Was the tension between them a result of something that had happened during the War? Something they hadn't let go? "The War is over, gentlemen."

Isaiah unceremoniously pushed her back. "Not for us."

"She's right," Blade said. "War's over, Isaiah."

"You know that's not true. It's never going to be over for us."

"Yeah." Blade jerked his chin in her direction. "You know what you're doing?"

Isaiah didn't hesitate. "Yes."

Should she be grateful or worried?

"Not sure she's worth the risk."

Isaiah caught her before she could take another step aside and hauled her up against him so tightly she had trouble getting a breath. Again. "There's no risk."

"I'd find it easier to believe if you didn't have her pinned so tightly to you."

Abruptly the grip on her ribs loosened and Adelaide could take a deep breath. Another one of those grunts from Isaiah that could have meant anything interrupted the silence.

She stopped struggling. There didn't seem much point since she wasn't having any effect. But she could listen and learn. Her cousins would approve of that. And no matter how terrified she was, there was something fascinating about both men. Something that had nothing to do with their handsome faces, muscled physiques, or confidence. Something intangible that came from within. Something stronger in Isaiah. She looked over her shoulder, trying to figure out what "it" was.

"Shit."

Blade's exclamation brought her gaze snapping back to his face. He sat on his horse as if he had a God-given right to judge, his mouth set in a firm line. He looked at her. He looked at Isaiah. And then he shook his head the way men did when they saw a certainty that couldn't be helped.

"I hope the hell you know what you're doing, Isaiah."

"I know."

"This won't go well."

Isaiah moved her behind him, not letting go of her hand so she couldn't run as she wanted to do. "Everything will be fine as long as they don't find out."

Blade snorted. "You putting a lot of hope in that happening?"

"Not a lot."

Blade's horse snorted and tossed its head as he pulled back on the reins. "Well, if you have a need . . ."

Isaiah tipped his hat. "I owe you."

Blade's grin flashed white in the gloom. "Yeah. Big, the way I figure it. Don't worry, I'll be collecting."

"So I've heard."

Blade's grin faded. "You're still the same ungrateful son of a bitch you always were."

Blade turned his horse and blended into the shadows that retreated before the dawn. How did he and Isaiah do that?

In the last moment before Blade completely disappeared, Adelaide stated, "That was rude."

"You don't know what you're talking about."

"I know rude when I hear it."

"And I know foolish when I see it."

She was suddenly conscious of how alone they were. "I think I preferred it when you growled."

"Trust me, lady, no one prefers it when I growl."

Backing down would be a mistake. Her experience with her cousins had taught her that, so she raised her chin and took a stab at bravado. "I didn't give you permission to call me 'lady.'"

"I didn't give you permission to speak at all."

She jerked her arm. "We just fought a war to free the slaves."

He didn't let her go. "It's not going to make a difference to you."

He was obviously the type of man who had to have the last word. That being the case, she changed the subject.

"Let me go."

"Why?"

She pried at his fingers. He had beautiful hands with long square-tipped fingers. And unfortunately, very strong.

"I'll take you wherever you need to go."

She wasn't going anywhere with him. "I can get there myself."

"You'll get lost."

Her next tug got one finger loose. She took it as a positive sign. "I'll take my chances."

"No."

Digging her elbow into his chest, she turned around until she could see his face. There was little more than an impression of full lips tucked inside a beard, and eyes full of pain. And intelligence? Yes, it stood to reason he was intelligent. Only an intelligent man could have defeated so many bandits in so short a time.

"It's my life. I'll do with it as I want."

"I saved you."

"So?"

"That makes it mine now."

Damn. He meant it. She closed her eyes, trying to find the

strength to deal with yet another determined male. Before she could find it, he was dragging her toward the woods. *Oh no!*

"My worry stone!"

He stopped dead. He couldn't really understand what that bit of rock meant to her, could he?

"Where?"

"I dropped it when you jerked me off the horse."

She expected him to ask her why she needed it or berate her for the delay, but instead his fingers tightened viselike around her wrist and he dragged her to where the horse had stood. As he bent to retrieve something she couldn't see—her stone, she assumed—she realized it made sense he wouldn't ask.

Someone had brought her worry stone to her at great risk to himself. That same someone who had wrapped her in a coat when she'd been chilled. That someone had to have been Isaiah. Rubbing her hands up and down her arms, she wished she had that coat now.

"Did you find it?"

A grunt was her answer. As he stood, she held out her hand. Without hesitation he put it on her palm.

She closed her fingers around it. "Thank you."

He didn't say anything. Maybe she heard an expulsion of breath that could have been another grunt and an answer. She wasn't sure.

Just as abruptly as he'd dragged her to where the horse stood, he dragged her into the woods. She stumbled along behind him, tripping over every stick, expecting to eat the dirt. But every time she tripped, he was there, as if anticipating her moves, knowing ahead of time what was going to happen. It had to be that, because nobody could move that fast that consistently.

They kept walking long past the time she had expected them to stop. Long past when she expected him to reveal a horse hidden away for the getaway. He had to have a horse somewhere. How else had he kept up with Billings? Fifteen minutes passed before she realized no horse was lurking in the next clearing.

"Where are we going?"

No answer, just that steady pull on her hand. Beyond the trees it was getting lighter, but where they were going it was darker and eerie. He was taking her into the forest instead of out.

The terrain changed, turning from level to steep. They were going up. She looked for their destination, but all she could see was trees. Nothing but trees. After a half hour her muscles were screaming, her lungs were laboring, and she'd had enough.

"Stop."

A tug on her arm was the only response.

"How much farther?"

Isaiah looked up at the trees. Very little sunlight filtered through. "Half a day."

Any notion she could hold out collapsed under the weight of that reality. Adelaide stopped arguing and simply sat down.

That at least brought him to an immediate stop.

And that just might have been a growl that escaped his lips. And that growl just might have been directed at her. She was too damn tired to care.

"Get up." The order was accompanied by a tug.

"No."

She could see the whiteness of his teeth. If that had been a growl before, he was working up to a snarl now. She wished she had the energy to worry about it.

"If you want me to go any farther, you're going to have to drag me." To her horror, Isaiah appeared to be contemplating it.

He let go of her hand. Apparently, a woman who had to be dragged up a mountain was too much of an escape risk.

"You really can't walk?"

He didn't have to sound so shocked. A woman didn't have the stamina of a man. "You'll be lucky if I don't die right here on the spot."

He looked alarmed. At least she thought that flicker in his eyes was alarm.

She waved her hand and lay back among the weeds, not even caring what might be crawling in them, getting in her hair. "Feel free to go on without me."

She took her worry stone out of her pocket.

He looked at her hand, at her position. "You're lying in the dirt."

"I'm dying in the dirt." He could at least get it right.

"You don't like to be dirty."

"I'm not enjoying the death, either."

"You're not dying."

"Fine. I'm not dying. Just wishing I were. Now go away and leave me in peace."

"You don't know where you are."

Did the man not have any sense of humor? "I'm not with those outlaws. So the way I figure it, anywhere I am has got to be better."

He cocked his eyebrow at her and there was that hint of a smile again. Or maybe he was growling. The man was very hard to read. "You would think."

"I know I am supposed to be scared by whatever it is you're implying." She put her hand to her chest, as if to keep her heart from pounding out through sheer force of will. A little theatrics never hurt a woman's cause. "Well, I'm too tired to care what it is, so if you're trying to threaten me, you're going to have to be more direct."

He paused.

Dear God, she thought he was actually considering it. She held up her hands, staving off whatever truth he felt she had to know that was worse than being with the outlaws. "Never mind. I'm not ready to hear anything."

He squatted beside her, before reaching out slowly, as if he expected her to flinch away.

She met his gaze. Again there was that sense of sadness, torment, and intelligence.

His fingers reached their destination. Hair strands shifted, as did the energy between them. It seemed to fill the air like the approach of a summer storm. She pulled her hair away. He left his hand where it was, staring at his fingers and then back at her before closing them slowly.

"Blade's right. You're trouble."

"Now, I like that." She pushed herself up on her elbows. "I get stolen from my house in the middle of my evening tea, get dragged halfway across the territory, get beaten, abused, freeze my butt off—"

"I gave you my coat."

"Yes, well, do you see it with me now?"

He looked oddly guilty. "We were in a hurry."

Oh, for God's sake. She understood that. Couldn't the man just let her rant in peace? "And now I am in the middle of God knows where, surrounded by God knows what, with a man whose grasp of conversation seems to be limited to grunts, snarls, and five-word sentences. Excuse me if I'm not feeling charitable."

❧ 5 ❧

ASK ME IF I CARE.

Ten minutes later, some suicidal part of him wanted to ask that very thing. Some residual fragment of humanity also wanted to ask her why she trusted him to the point she obviously did. The trust was in the way she sparred with him. It was in the way she took his hand when he offered to help her to her feet. He wanted to ask her why. And when she finished explaining why, he wanted to ask her how. After all the things that had happened to her in her short life, how could she still trust a stranger? How could she trust him? How, when she truly hadn't been able to get up and he'd offered to carry her, she could quip a sarcastic comment but then hold up her arms and let him?

He wanted the answer to that as much as he wanted to understand why carrying her offered him such pleasure. He was tired, she wasn't a lightweight, but he found carrying her provided him with a sense of connection he couldn't ever remember feeling before. He'd been alone before he'd been taken to the darkness at the age of thirteen. He knew that. He didn't know how he remembered that, but he knew it. He'd been alone for every second afterward. He ducked under a tree limb and glanced down at the woman in his arms. But now, he wasn't alone. Now he was responsible for another life. At least for as long as it took for him to get her home. Shit, if he had any sense at all, he'd drop her straight in the dirt.

Since the first time he'd seen Adelaide, Isaiah had been drawn to her like a moth to a flame. He'd felt connected. Connecting with anything was bad. It created a weakness that could be exploited. That's what he'd been told. That's what he'd seen. It was one of the hard-core lessons he'd learned from the time *They*'d imprisoned him that carried over into his actual life. Or at least the life he was trying to build.

The qualification put a hesitation in his conviction. He was trying to build a life. One that contained more than cold detachment and ruthless pursuit of a goal. He experimented with that connection again. And again he experienced that flicker of light through the darkness. The faint seep of warmth into the frigid ice of his soul. He shook his head. If that wasn't the craziest notion he'd ever heard. Whatever soul a Reaper might have once had had long since been sacrificed to the life he'd been forced into.

The rage rose as it always did when he thought of *Them*. Faceless entities that had haunted his life in the form of voices. Voices that ordered torture, killed hope. Voices that demanded the murder of men, women, children with no more concern than they ordered delivery of breakfast. Voices that had finally had faces on the day the Reapers had risen up and extracted justice. He'd thought *They* were demons, but when he'd looked upon *Them, They* had just been men. Nothing more. Nothing less. And *They*'d controlled him. His beast snarled and gnashed its teeth. Never again.

Shit, had he growled aloud? A quick check revealed Adelaide slept on. He shook his head again. She was a fool to trust him the way she did, exhausted or not. The beast wanted her. The beast craved her, and the beast always got what it wanted. All that stood between her and the beast was the man in him that needed her. There was no winning that kind of war, but if he could keep it to small manageable battles, they'd be fine. At least that was the hope.

Adelaide turned her cheek into his chest. He imagined he could feel the heat of her breath against his skin through his shirt. It fed his sense of humanity. No. He shifted her up in his arms. He wouldn't be smart and drop her into the dirt. He wouldn't abandon her. He'd protect her. The way any man protected what was good. It was a step toward the future he wanted. One with a purpose.

Isaiah carried Adelaide the last two miles up the mountain toward the lean-to that served as his home. He'd built it under the ledge overhanging the narrow path ringing the cliff. The sun crested the adjacent mountain range, sending stray beams of light to play across Adelaide's face. His glance trailed the flow of light over her features, following the curve of her cheekbone, tracing the straight small jut of her nose, lingering on the dusting of gold on her lashes. Her skin was a fine, pale cream. Her mouth petal pink. The next step brought him farther into a beam of light. It blended into her hair before exploding outward in a brilliant, shining, multicolored halo.

He couldn't look away. The shine blended with the visions in his mind, expanding faster than he could control. He stopped moving, seeing nothing but that light, not daring to move until reality returned. Light and dark battled for supremacy in his mind. Voices behind the light surged forward. Old, new, he couldn't tell.

There's no point in fighting.

They had said that. The echo of his own "no" rang in his ears. It had still had power then. There'd been a lot of fight in him then. But then he hadn't understood *Their* power. The weapons *They* would use.

The changes *They* would create within him. Changes he still didn't understand, but they ruled his life with feral intensity.

We will win. Their promise echoed in his head.

No. His response echoed louder.

The anger rose along with the beast. The battle still waged. After five years, a winner had yet to be determined. The beast, always stronger than *Them*, than him, battled the light, pushing it back, leaving Isaiah with only the weight of the darkness to carry. He could manage that as long as he stayed in the present.

Reality came back in a blink. Ahead of him there was nothing but blue skies, clouds, and mountain peaks. Beneath his feet there was a portion of ledge, and then . . . nothing for a mile down. He took a breath. And then another. Waiting to see if perception would distort before attempting to move. The weight of the woman in his arms increased tenfold as he realized how close he'd come to killing them both. He'd have to be more careful. It wouldn't matter if his life came to an end, but she was good, and the vow his kind had made when they had left their creators and struck out on their own was that they would preserve good. He didn't have much to hold on to in this world. But he had that vow. And now he had her. Two things to fight for, rather than one. His life was picking up. If he could just keep the distortions at bay.

It would be easer if being near Adelaide didn't create the turmoil. And if he could have stayed away from her, he would have started long ago. He didn't like the distortions. He didn't like to be thrown into the past. He didn't like the weakness she created within him, the need. But despite all the negatives, he couldn't keep away any more than he could keep from sliding his finger along her arm. Couldn't keep from leaning down that scant inch necessary to breathe her scent. To breathe her.

She was like the drug they'd forced into his veins to keep him in line. Horribly addictive in the peace it offered. And like that drug, Adelaide had the power to change everything he knew. His claws extended in response to the threat of that. He looked at their ivory length, resting against her dress, and pulled them back.

She was right. She had to go home.

Isaiah rounded the corner, shifting Adelaide in his arms so he could make his way across a fragment of ledge that served as a path to his home. Made of sticks and dirt and leaves, the lean-to was more lair than home. He ducked under the ledge. Sprinkles of dust and leaves greeted his entrance. He laid Adelaide down on the pelts that served as his bed, wincing as he did. They were none too clean, and none too soft. He didn't waste a lot of time on creature comforts. But Adelaide did. He was willing to bet her bedroom at home was full of crisp cotton sheets, meticulously sewn quilts, and maybe some touches of lace. He liked the thought of her sleeping amid lace. All the houses he'd seen in his dealings had had at least a touch of lace. The wealthy ones had a lot.

He brushed Adelaide's hair back from her cheek, being careful not to wake her. A leaf clung to the tendrils of hair at her temple. He removed it. She turned on her side, a slight snore punctuating the move. He envied the innocence that allowed her to sleep fearlessly in his company.

Addy.

He remembered the name Cole had called her, during a visit when he'd been watching her. Less formal than Adelaide. More inviting. It suited the way he thought of her.

His claws lingered against her skin. He trailed them over the flesh of her cheek, over the soft curve of her jaw, down the creamy expanse of her neck. Goose bumps chased over her skin, but she didn't wake.

He would've woken. The beast within him would not have tolerated a touch when he was so vulnerable. Addy shifted again. Her cheek found the curve of his palm. He moved his claw away from her eyes as she let her breath out on a weary sigh. The trust in the gesture stunned him. He jerked his hand away as she started to wake. Closing his eyes, he willed the beast back into submission. Her eyelashes flickered and tension entered her previously supple muscles. He was what he was, and while he didn't entirely understand what that meant, to her, he wanted to appear human.

Addy came awake with another sigh. Her lashes fluttered. Her breath caught. Isaiah watched as awareness stole the comfort of sleep. Slipping his hand off her shoulder, he tucked his claws into his palms. Her lids lifted, revealing the blue of her eyes. And the fear within.

It was dark in the lean-to. He knew she couldn't see him, but that didn't change the lash of guilt when he saw the fear drain the color from her cheeks. He didn't like the guilt. Even more than that, he didn't like not liking it. He wanted to remain in that place where he felt nothing, cared about nothing. Shit, he didn't want to care about her.

Addy smiled uncertainly up at him. He couldn't smile back. She made him vulnerable, made him aware of things that he didn't want to know. Mostly emotions. The beast preyed on emotions. Took advantage of the distraction to seize control.

Isaiah had battled long and hard to gain that measure of control within himself during the time *They* had had control of everything else. He'd figured if he could control the beast, *They* couldn't control him. The best he'd managed was a compromise. He hadn't managed to control the beast, but he had managed to learn to rein in his emotions under most circumstances. He'd gone from fighting at the drop of a hat to the cool customer in the corner that no one could read. *They* had not been happy with the transformation. That had just made him more determined to broaden that void inside. To control more and more of his anger, to keep it away from *Their* manipulation. To piss *Them* off.

He smiled at the memory. *They* had not been happy. *They* couldn't have their wild card back. He touched the faint thread of scars on his neck. All that was left of the slicing *They*'d done to change his mind. The beast couldn't heal all the damage, but he'd healed most. Isaiah hadn't cared because, by learning to control his emotions, he'd learned that control could go both ways.

Addy misinterpreted that smile. "Hi."

The softness that replaced the fear in her eyes found an answering softness within him. He squashed it immediately. He couldn't afford weakness.

After the War was over for him, it had been even easier to keep his emotions locked up tight. For a blessed year he'd felt nothing, roaming the country, looking for a place he could make his home. For a year he'd known peace. For another year he'd protected it. And then he'd met Addy. A woman whose scent haunted his dreams. A woman who drew him back to civilization time and time again. A woman who stole his peace. A woman who didn't belong here in the wilds of his mountain. A woman he couldn't resist.

He pulled his hand away from Addy's cheek, straightened, and looked around.

He'd found peace up here on his mountain so high above the valley. Humans rarely intruded. It was a good place. Maybe too high for most. But there were some advantages to what had been done to him, for someone who had been given a beast. He had more stamina, more speed, more strength. The mile trip down the mountainside to where the game fed was accomplished in the blink of an eye. The cold nights didn't affect him and the loneliness was a blessing. There was no one here he could hurt.

He looked at Addy lying on his bed, eyeing him so warily. And reconsidered. There hadn't been anyone he could hurt before, but now she was here. The one who kept the madness at bay. The one who reminded him of a time he couldn't remember. The one who provoked that vague sense of "should know." The one who reminded him of what he'd dreamed of for all those years *They* had held him against his will. The one who made him feel human.

They had stolen a lot from him in the dark place, and what *They'd* given hadn't replaced it, but he was going to get it back. He was determined to get it back. He might not ever be normal again, but he would know his past and he would own his future. And he would make a place for himself in the world that had never been kind but had once been his. The human world.

Adelaide licked her lips and propped herself up on her elbows. Her hand furtively snuck into her pocket, reaching for her worry stone, no doubt, a sure sign she wasn't as calm as she would like him to believe as she asked, "Where am I?"

"My home."

Her body didn't move but her eyes looked left and then right. Her lashes fluttered as she absorbed the interior. Just twigs and mud and leaves mashed together to provide shelter of a sort. His kind didn't need much in the way of shelter, but she did. He was going to have to take her home.

Inside the beast howled, *No*. The beast was lonely. The beast wanted her here. He ignored the protest. The beast could just waste away. Adelaide wasn't built to survive up here, and her clothes wouldn't keep out the bitter cold. Damn, he should have shifted one of the pelts aside to cover her.

"You live here?"

He couldn't blame her for the skepticism. She thought of him as human.

"Yes."

"Why?"

The unfamiliar urge to smile twitched his lips. It was just like her to ask why. "It suits me."

She shifted and looked around again.

"This doesn't suit anybody."

He shrugged. "I think it does."

He could tell she wanted to say more, but a belated sense of discretion kept her mouth shut. At least he hoped it was discretion. He was too tired to deal with more scheming.

Through the material of her skirt, he could see her working the worry stone. He was tired. He was hungry and her being around kept his beast on edge. If he hoped to keep her in the dark about what he was, he needed balance.

"Are you hungry?"

She looked around again. He could see the "no" on her lips. She was a fastidious woman. No doubt she thought anything cooked here wouldn't be safe to eat, but she was also a sensible woman and that common sense showed in the next second when she nodded her head.

"Yes."

"Good answer."

She raised her brows at him.

"You can't escape without your strength."

She blinked. His admiration for her grew as she met his challenge head on.

"I *will* escape, you know."

"I bet you will." And it couldn't happen soon enough for him. He stood and brushed the dirt from the knees of his torn, filthy pants. Her eyes followed the movement. He saw her flinch. She really did have a thing against dirt, even when dirt was the normal result of activity. He would like to know why. He wanted to know everything about her. He knew precious little, but there had been rumors about something in her childhood. A bad time that no one spoke of, just hinted at. She would tell him about it before he let her go.

"I'll get you something to eat."

She sat up. "Thank you."

He headed for the opening.

"I'll start a fire if you've got a sulfur."

That pulled him up short as he realized how far he'd slipped from civilized. He didn't have a sulfur. He didn't have many of the normal conveniences that made life comfortable. He could present her with a dead carcass but he couldn't provide her with the heat to cook it. Shit. A foreign feeling tightened his muscles.

"I'll take care of it when I get back."

She glared at him, clearly offended. She always got offended when she thought someone thought her incapable.

"I can build a fire without burning your house down."

He was sure she could if she had the proper tools. "I'll handle it."

It took a while to recognize the emotion that flowed over him. Shame. He was ashamed.

"I'm cold."

He turned around and stared at her, the humiliation lashing at him. He was sure there was a time when he would have carried sulfurs, would have lived in a house. Would have had something to put around her. But that was gone, stolen from him. He closed his fingers into a fist.

"Use a pelt."

She flinched at the anger in his voice and his shame grew. He hadn't meant to snap, but the truth was, he didn't have anything to offer her. A blanket, a coat. Nothing.

"I'll take care of it."

"How?"

"I said I'll take care of it." His claws extended. The beast unfurled, sensing her discomfort, demanding he alleviate it. As if he needed anything else pointing out his shortcomings.

"When you get back," she finished for him, her chin coming up.

"Yes." Somehow.

She stood, then bent, grabbed up a pelt, giving it a firm shake before holding it out in front of her for inspection. "Then be sure you come back."

The pelt was old and none too clean. He wanted to snatch the pelt out of her hands. She deserved better. He refrained. Sometimes a man had to bow to common sense and the woman needed the pelt to survive. "I'll be back."

She stood there, hair tangled around her face, a smudge on her cheek, her clothes torn and filthy, yet still looking regal and composed. He admired that.

"When?" she asked.

When I get here, he wanted to snap, but he didn't. She was alone and scared and even he could recognize she needed the reassurance. He looked up and pointed. "See that big pine by that boulder?"

She followed his gaze. "Yes."

"When the sun gets straight above that, start looking for me."

She frowned. "Start?"

Keeping his lips tight over his teeth to hide the canines that always appeared when he was upset, he answered, "Yes."

He made it ten feet down the ledge before he heard his name called, a note of uncertainty coloring the syllables.

He turned, his beast growling. She was standing with the pelt around her shoulders. "What?"

"You'll come back?"

"I already promised I would."

She shifted. He bet she was rubbing the shine off that worry stone. "Are your promises worth anything?"

She must be really agitated to lower her pride to ask again. And scared. Isaiah put his hand on his knife hilt. It fit solidly in his palm. At least he had this answer.

"The ones I make to you are."

Her head tilted to the side. No doubt she was tucking the information away in that active brain of hers like a squirrel hoarding nuts for a winter's day.

"Why?"

He turned on his heel. He wasn't going there. "Because I said so."

⪧ 6 ⪦

SHE WATCHED HIM GO WITH A SENSE OF ANGER GROWING
inside. Who was he to judge her? She looked around at the crude
shelter set amid the rock and dirt above the tree line. He didn't even
live in a house. As if chastising her lack of gratitude for her rescue,
the wind blew up, biting into her skin. Oh God, what she wouldn't
give for the coat she'd lost earlier. As dirty as it was, it was cleaner
than this.

She wrapped the pelt around her shoulders, moaning under her
breath as her muscles cramped even tighter, pulling her into the
hunch of an old woman. The pelt smelled. She wrinkled her nose and
loosened her grip. The wind gusted again. She tightened her grip
again, despite her disgust, realizing as she did that she was getting
better. A few years ago she would have chosen to freeze rather than
have the dirt touch her. The little victory bolstered her faltering confidence. She was winning the war.

She looked around again. The only twigs in sight were the ones woven together to form the top of the lean-to. Considering the lean-to was likely to be her shelter for the night, she needed another option. Which meant climbing down the mountain or else. She eyed the lean-to again. She'd had a bit of education during her captivity with the Indians. She knew how to build a lean-to efficiently. This one was not efficiently built. Almost as if the builder didn't fear the elements. Which was absurd. Everyone knew how bad mountain weather could get.

She tried to straighten. Pain shot down her back and through her thighs. She took a breath and then another, controlling the reaction as she clenched the pelt in her hands. It took her a minute, but she succeeded. By the time Mr. High-and-Mighty Isaiah came back, she'd have a fire started. Some of her education might be controversial, but what her cousins had taught her was good. They'd taught her how to be prepared.

Looking around cautiously to make sure Isaiah hadn't returned, she lifted her dress. The last thing she needed was Isaiah getting ideas about her as a bed partner. She'd never been anyone's bed partner and had no intention of starting now. She's seen how the Indians treated the women captives as conveniences to be used. Even when those women developed feelings for the men, the men never saw them as anything more than vessels for their sexual release. When she'd come back to the white world, her eyes opened, she'd realized that white men didn't treat women any better. Even her own cousins had women in town they visited but to whom they'd never introduced her. And those women were replaced often. Her cousins never talked of them and never, in her presence, referred to them with disrespect, but it didn't change the reality that they viewed them as disposable. Disposable was almost as bad as invisible. She had no intention of being either ever again.

Anchoring the folds of her dress over her wrist, she slipped her fingers through the slit in the side of her pantaloons and found the small, thin bag of emergency supplies her cousins had said she'd always need. For years she'd never needed them. For years she'd told them it was an unnecessary precaution. They were going to gloat annoyingly when she confessed she'd found them useful.

She felt between the spirals of twine for snares, pushed aside the fish hooks wrapped in leather, until she felt the flint and stone. She shook her head as she pulled them out. Cole would be the worst with the I-told-you-so's. He was annoying when proven right. Not that he said much. He didn't have to. He had a way of smiling slightly that made his point so much stronger than words. She hated that smile as much as she loved him. Right now she'd kill to see that smile again. Rubbing her fingers over the two objects, she closed her eyes and focused on what she'd been taught about starting a fire.

Starting a fire with flint was tedious, but as her cousins had pointed out, sulphurs were unpredictable, and if you were alone in the woods and needed fire to keep warm, to cook food, or make a signal, you needed something that could withstand the elements. Flint fit that bill.

She carried it with her always. Along with her worry stone, her emergency pack was her constant companion. As always, being prepared left her feeling stronger, more confident. There might be a lot of things that she couldn't do, but she could light a fire, set a snare, and fish for dinner. She smiled. She could survive. She just needed to remain calm and think. She opened her eyes, her focus restored.

It was wet outside. There was no dry grass to be found, but inside the lean-to were a few pine needles, some leaves and twigs kept dry by the meager shelter. It could be enough. Keeping the pelt around her shoulders with one hand, she gathered her supplies before fluffing the pine needles into a pile and adding a few stray bits of dry grass she could scrounge out of the ground. Sitting on her heels, she surveyed the dismal results. She only had enough for one attempt. Maybe Isaiah was a drinking man. Alcohol would ensure the fire lit and burned hot.

There wasn't any sign of a bottle in the interior. There wasn't actually much of anything, but as she glanced around, she realized as sparse as the interior was, there was a certain order to it. The entrance was open and unobstructed. The bed was perpendicular to the back wall on the left side. The furs were evenly layered. Even now, they were only slightly disturbed from her lying on them. There was a small box wrapped in oilcloth to the left and center. It was too small to hold a bottle. Anything placed in it was of a nature that needed to be kept dry. The location would help ensure it. Isaiah was clearly a man who planned and liked order. It was a comforting thing to realize about her rescuer.

Bracing herself for the chill, Adelaide let the pelt slide off her shoulders. She struck the flint against the tinder. Nothing happened. She tried again. This time she got a small spark but nothing caught. She needed something better. The box wrapped in the oilcloth called to her, drew her like a magnet. Gunpowder was flammable but it had to be kept dry. She couldn't think of anything else a man like Isaiah would have wrapped in oilcloth, as if he valued it.

She inched over to the box, reaching for it, feeling as if she was violating a trust, which was stupid because there was no trust between her and Isaiah. He'd saved her, but he'd also kidnapped her for his own reasons, which negated the saving part—to a point, her sense of fairness insisted on adding. He wasn't brutal like her first kidnappers. He was actually nice in an unsocial, awkward sort of way.

She caught herself before she could make another excuse for the man. The absurdity of it made her shake her head. Isaiah's kidnapping of her made him an enemy. As soon as Cole found her, and she had no doubt her cousin would find her, Isaiah would be dead so there was no sense getting attached to him. There was no one meaner that Cole when it came to a fight. He was good with his fists, better with a knife, and excellent with a gun.

An image of Bob lying on the ground with his throat ripped out flashed through her mind. She closed her eyes against the gory imaging. She knew Isaiah had been the one to do the ripping. She had no doubt that Blade was capable of doing the same thing.

She didn't know who these men were, but she believed them when they said they were Reapers who had declared themselves protectors of the valley. Some said it was because there was an old debt that needed to be repaid. Some said it was because they were spirits come back to haunt those who'd done wrong, but Isaiah wasn't a spirit and neither was Blade. They were men with haunted eyes, lethal ways, and traditions she didn't understand. And they might just be a threat to her cousin should he decide to take revenge. Another thing to consider.

She picked up the box. It was lighter than she'd expected. Keeping an eye out for Isaiah, she unwrapped it. She didn't know what to expect when she took the covering off. Maybe she'd been secretly hoping for some revelation of his past. A diary. A book. Information about the Reapers. But nothing that exciting jumped out at her when she lifted the lid. Inside was an oilcloth package. She picked it up and unwrapped it. It was the gunpowder she was expecting. When she started to close the box lid, she noticed another package on the bottom. She'd missed it because it was wrapped in the same oilcloth. She put the gunpowder to the side and picked up the package. This one was flat. Not a box. She hesitated a moment, holding it in her hand, considering whether she had a right to look at it. She needed the gunpowder. She could justify opening the box for that, but going further? That was an invasion of Isaiah's privacy.

She rubbed her fingers together as her conscience stepped up, front and center. A conscience could be an unwieldy thing. Digging into her pocket, she touched her worry stone. As always, the initial coolness focused her attention. As the heat from her skin seeped into the stone, so did her unease. There was no reason for her to hesitate. Cole would want to know everything he could about Isaiah. It was her duty to find out. Decision made, she quickly unwrapped the package. It was a tintype of a woman. She was young, attractive in the austere way people always were in pictures. Adelaide doubted that she'd remember her if she passed the woman on the street. But she was important to Isaiah. That made her intriguing. Was it his mother? She looked too young to be his mother, but then it was hard to tell in tintypes. Maybe a sister. Adelaide rubbed her worry stone again, guilt coming stronger. Whoever she was, she mattered.

She rewrapped the tintype and put it back exactly as she'd found it. Picking up the powder, she put a little bit in a piece of paper, folded it up, and took it back outside under the edge of the lean-to, in far enough that it wouldn't get wet but far enough out to catch a draft. There was nothing worse than being in a smoke-filled hole.

Unwanted images flashed in her mind. Tepees set up on the plains, bitter cold, smoke-filled. The screams because she'd done it wrong, the laughter afterward. Life had been a disaster during her captivity. She had never felt more incompetent than she had as a prisoner, more helpless. Everything had been lost. Nothing had been right. There'd been no order. No direction. No matter how she'd tried, she could never do anything right. She'd been the butt of every joke.

When her cousins had rescued her, the first thing she'd done was cry. The second was to vow that her life would never be chaos again. When she'd gotten home, she'd set that vow into action. Piece by piece she'd rebuilt her life with one rule holding it all together— everything would be in order. And nothing would ever take her by surprise again.

Looking around her current situation, she sighed. Until two nights ago she'd kept that vow. She tugged the pelt up over her shoulders again, the musty smell a mockery of all her brave plans. She smothered the echoes of long-gone laughter. But just because her plan had faltered once didn't mean it had to continue to falter. She could take command of this situation the same way she'd taken charge of her life when she was fourteen. One detail at a time. One step at a time. And the first item on the agenda was still getting the fire started.

She briskly set about building the fire, sprinkling the gunpowder on a pile of leaves before arranging twigs on top. The days when she was a victim were long gone. She struck the flint on the sulphur. It took two tries before she got the angle and the pressure right but then, with a flash, the gunpowder caught and the leaves started to smoke. She leaned forward and blew very gently, encouraging the flame. Her patience was rewarded as it always was. Leaning back, she fed a small twig to the hungry flame, watching it grow, adding more and more until she had a good base. A sense of satisfaction grew right along with the flames.

She'd learned the benefit of order and control. She glanced around the campsite again. What little was there was in its place. Maybe Isaiah had learned some lessons from life, too. She tucked that information away along with the details about the mystery woman. When it came to Isaiah, she was going to need all the weapons she could get because he was tenacious and smart, and for whatever reason, he'd decided he wasn't going to let her go.

Her fire sputtered and hissed. She needed more wood. Sighing, she pulled her skirt up and knotted it at her hip. Which meant she was going to have to hike down to the tree line and get some if she wanted to prove anything to anyone. Pulling some smaller sticks from the roof, she placed them on the fire to hold it until she got back. And then headed down the mountain.

* * *

HE wasn't going to let her go. Isaiah chased down the rabbit, caught it by its ears, and mercifully killed it before draining the blood and tying it to the string along with the other two he'd caught. It would be enough.

As he searched for sticks that would serve as suitable spits, he told himself it wasn't a matter of wanting so much as it was a matter of couldn't. He'd vowed to protect her. He'd failed in that vow once. He wouldn't again. Until this threat against her was as dead as the rabbits, he was going to stick to her side like glue.

To the right were some saplings that would do as spits. He cut them off and stripped them quickly. At least he could offer her food. A glance at the sky confirmed what he'd estimated. He'd been gone about an hour. Not that long, but long enough that an impatient woman could get twitchy. For all she feigned differently, Adelaide did not have that much patience. He sprinted up the hill, smelling the wood smoke before he reached the home site. He slowed and circled the area, taking stock of the surroundings. There were no other scents except wood smoke and Adelaide. The wood scent was strong. Adelaide's scent was not. How the hell had she built a fire? And where the hell was she that her scent was so weak? He checked the lean-to, noted the disturbance of the box, the bed, a couple areas on the roof where she'd rearranged the sticks. At least he knew where she got the wood for the fire. He probably should be grateful she hadn't dismantled the whole thing while looking for fuel.

He braced the spits by the fire and looked around. More than likely, Adelaide had just gone to relieve herself. He took the carcasses down by the stream and skinned and dressed them, burying the pelts and entrails. When he got back to the site, Adelaide still wasn't there. And her scent was fading. Shit.

It only took a couple seconds to spit the rabbits and brace them over the hot coals of the fire. It was two seconds more than he wanted to spare, but he couldn't forget the rumble of her stomach. She would be hungrier still when he got her back. He didn't want to sit there again in that small space and know he had nothing to offer. He adjusted the spits a bit higher, buying himself a little time.

It wasn't hard to track her scent. She'd headed down, which wasn't a surprise. His beast snarled as the trail led him farther away from the camp. Her path was a zigzag from wooded area to wooded area. She'd been looking for wood to add to the fire. His beast's snarl subsided to a growl. She shouldn't have left from where he'd put her, and they'd be talking about that later, but she wasn't running away.

He found the point where she'd decided to head back, noted from the rotation of the footprints when she realized she was lost, and followed her determined steps as she headed back up the mountain, about thirty degrees to the right of the direction she needed to go.

He shook his head. He'd have to train her in how to use landmarks to find her way back to her point of origin. Otherwise she'd be lost half her life. Sprinting, he soon caught up with her. She was sitting in the middle of a clearing, hands in her lap, staring directly at him. He paused. Had she heard him? He slowed his approach. Impossible. Yet there she sat, a pile of wood at her side, looking for all the world as if she'd been expecting him.

"I've been waiting for you." Her voice was thready. He narrowed his eyes and studied her. She was out of breath.

"If you'd stayed at the campsite, the wait would have been short."

"I needed wood."

"The wood could have waited."

"No."

"Why not?"

She didn't give him an answer. Probably because all she'd managed to achieve with her efforts was to exhaust herself while getting lost.

He came closer. "Next time, stay where I put you."

Her eyes narrowed. "There's not going to be a next time."

If she continued her stubborn ways, he could see a lot of next times unless he took control. "I agree."

Isaiah's arrogance grated Adelaide's already raw nerves. She counted to four while rubbing her worry stone. When she got to five, she just kept going. By the time she hit twenty, she had a semblance of control. She opened her eyes. Isaiah was still standing there staring at her with that calculated patience that reminded her of a predator. She had the impulse to check her buttons to make sure they were all aligned. But what was the point? After the night she'd just had, she was no doubt a mess, and ascertaining it would just send her into an episode. She couldn't afford an episode.

Isaiah held out his hand. "Got your breath back?"

She didn't know about back, but she wasn't breathing like a winded bronc.

"Are you taking me home?"

He wiggled his fingers. "I'm taking you back to the campsite."

She sighed. Not what she wanted, but the campsite was still better than here. She placed her hand in his. Hers was hot and sweaty. His was cool to the touch. He pulled her to her feet. Her knees buckled. She expected him to laugh. He didn't.

"Do you need me to carry you the rest of the way?"

She ran her free hand through her hair. She was so tired of this. "I need you to take me home."

"Not yet."

Her hope latched on to that "yet" like a chicken on a June bug. "But you will?"

"We'll see. Can you walk?"

She didn't think she could do anything but collapse. Pride—either her savior or her downfall—stiffened her spine. "Of course."

The corner of his mouth twitched. "Let's go then. Supper's waiting."

"Supper?"

"Uh-huh."

She let go of his hand to retie her skirt. The memory of his touch lingered on her skin. Adelaide curled her fingers into a fist, rubbing her thumb across her knuckles. What was it about the man that stayed like a sweet memory tugging her toward him? He started forward up the path. She groaned. Up. He was still going up?

She got to her feet and shook out her skirt. "There are other directions, you know."

"This is the one I want."

He didn't even look over his shoulder as he said that, just kept walking as if he expected her to follow. And why wouldn't he? What other choice did she have? Turn around and go back to the men who'd kidnapped her? Go right or left and get lost in the denseness of the forest? Up was all she had. And so was he.

She sighed and took a step. A stick snapped. He turned around, his hair fanning out slightly, catching the morning sun. The clean lines of his profile struck her anew. She hadn't thought of him as handsome before, but she bet if he cut off that beard, he would be.

"How much farther is it?"

He looked up the path. She didn't like the angle of his chin, which implied a long way up. She'd thought she was almost there by the time she'd had to sit.

"We should be there in time for lunch."

Her stomach growled at the mention of lunch. It'd been hours since she'd eaten. Almost a day. She was hungry. She couldn't be sure, but she thought Isaiah paused. There was no way he could have heard her stomach growl. Could he?

He started walking again. She followed, but with every step, he got farther and farther away. She couldn't keep up that pace, so she just kept walking in his wake, and when he disappeared from sight, she followed what she thought were the slight breaks in the underbrush marking the trail he'd taken. She was done yelling at the man. Sooner or later he'd find out he'd outpaced her.

Step after step, she kept going, wanting to cry at the agony in her legs and the burn in her lungs. In fifteen minutes, she had no idea where she was, where he was, and the bandits in her memory became a lot cleaner, a lot nicer, and a lot more viable as an option to run back to. Which was ridiculous and just proved how tired she was.

A hand closed over her arm. She screamed. Another clapped over her mouth. She recognized the scent immediately. Isaiah.

"You can't escape me."

She wanted to scream. She wanted to do a lot of things. Violent, out-of-control emotions washed over her. Unwelcome companions from her past. She stood there while they battered her control. Anger, pain, frustration . . . They all flowed together into an ugly mess inside. She hated messes. She yanked at Isaiah's hand. Not surprisingly, he didn't let go. Just one more frustration to toss into the mess.

She bided her time until he eased his hand from her mouth.

"I wasn't trying to escape. I was following you."

"You left my trail ten minutes back."

"Well, why the heck didn't you say something?"

He blinked. "I wanted to see what you would do."

"Well, now you know. I got lost." She was sure her feet would never be the same. Her boots had rubbed them raw. Just standing there was agony. Isaiah's nostrils flared. His brows came down.

He knelt. "Sit down."

"Stop giving me orders."

"Stop being foolish. Your feet are bleeding."

How could he possibly know that? "So?"

This time his eyebrows rose. And he waited in that way that said he knew he was going to win in the end so why was she bothering with her token fight. Well, she needed this token fight. She needed something. Some control, somewhere. She reached for her worry stone. It wasn't in her pocket. Damn. Damn. Damn. Tears burned her eyes. She'd lost it. A tear rolled down her cheek.

The big brute just stood there and watched as a second joined the first. She could feel more trembling on her lashes. Soon she'd dissolve into full-out bawling.

She sniffed and wiped at her cheeks. "Don't look at me."

"There's nothing else to look at."

She hated logical men.

"Find a bird." She didn't want him to see her cry. No one had seen her cry since she was eleven years old. She fumbled in her pocket again. Her worry stone had to be there. There was no way it had fallen out. She'd taken a few tumbles looking for more wood, but her pocket was deep. She sighed as she found nothing but a few loose threads. It was possible, if the skirt bunched at the right angle, it could have fallen out. Tired, she'd tripped over a fair amount on logs and stones and her own two feet. It was possible.

She sat before she crumpled. "It's all your fault."

"No doubt."

It irritated her that he didn't even argue with her.

"Mind telling me what it is I'm guilty of?"

She hated that she liked that gravelly edge to his voice.

"I lost something."

"What?"

"My rock, all right? I lost my rock."

Isaiah reached into his pocket and pulled something out. She swore to God if he handed her the worry stone, she would scream. It was just the ultimate unfairness that the cause of her misery could so easily provide the solution to her problem.

He opened his hand.

She grabbed the stone and screamed as loud and as hard as she could. It felt good, so good. She had a lungful of air and she planned on expending it all on a screech loud enough to wake the dead, but all she got were a couple seconds before he tackled her, knocking her to the ground, taking her weight on his chest as he rolled, tucking her against the shelter of a log, before leaping to his feet so fast she wasn't sure he actually moved. But there he was in front of her, legs splayed in a half crouch, hands open at his sides, ready to attack, facing the direction she'd been looking. Protecting her.

"What is it?"

She closed her fingers around her worry stone and quickly tucked it in her bodice. Isaiah was going to be ticked when he realized she'd screamed out of pure frustration. He looked the type who might take the stone back. She licked her lips and glanced around. The answer to her dilemma shone with the morning dew. A spider web.

"I saw a spider."

He didn't move for two seconds. Then he slowly turned back to her and just . . . stared.

"A spider?"

She nodded. "Horrible things, spiders. I hate them."

"You screamed."

"Yes. It surprised me."

Good grief, she hoped he didn't keep asking questions. She didn't have a lot of lies stocked up. The worry stone was a heavy weight between her breasts. An inappropriate place to rub, but she wanted it safe with her because she was pretty sure a man that big, who carried that much aggression in his shoulders, wouldn't be fun to see angry. She feigned innocence.

"Don't tell me you like spiders?"

He didn't even blink. "I don't like bugs at all."

"Then you understand."

He leaned down. She scrambled back.

Hooking his arm around her waist, he lifted her. He didn't put her down until there were ten feet between her and the spider. It was actually kind of sweet. For a kidnapper, he had some chivalrous impulses.

"Worried about seeing another one?" she asked as he looked around.

His mouth tightened. It felt perversely good to irritate him. "Yes." He motioned to the ground. "Sit."

"I'm not a dog."

"It'd be easier if you were."

His right hand clenched into a fist. She reminded herself she didn't know him that well. He might have brought her worry stone, he might have saved her from the bad guys, but she really didn't know him that well nor what he'd do when his patience snapped. She sat.

"That's good to know."

"What's good to know?" she asked.

"That you can take an order."

"I don't take orders."

That irritating smile sat on his lips. "You're sitting."

"That's because my feet hurt." She hitched the pelt up around her shoulders. "It makes sense to sit."

A cock of his eyebrow accompanied the motion of his hand toward her foot. "You're bleeding."

She was pretty sure she had a blister, but bleeding? She put her foot in his hand. He unlaced her shoe with deft movements.

"I don't think so."

His "I know so" was a simple statement of fact.

He gently slid the boot off her foot. When he slid the stocking down, it stuck. He might just be right. She forgot all about asking how he had been right when air hit her foot.

"Ow!"

His thumb rubbed her ankle. "You can't walk on that tonight."

It burned like heck. "Maybe not ever again."

"I'll take care of it."

He slid the stocking back on. And then the boot. "Don't you want to see the other one?"

"Nope."

She did. "Why not?"

He stopped her before she could reach for the laces. "No need to waste time. We can't do anything about it until we get back to the lean-to."

"And what will we do with them there?"

"Soak them while I cook the rabbits I caught."

Her stomach rumbled at the prospect of food.

"How many rabbits?" Rabbits were notoriously short on meat.

He smiled and slid his arm around her back. His scent enveloped her along with his arm. How could he always smell so good? His other arm slid under her knees.

"Enough to quiet your stomach."

He lifted her. She resisted the urge to slide her arm around his neck and turn her face into his chest. She was so tired. He started walking as if she weighed nothing. "How come you don't get winded up here?" she asked as he began climbing.

"I'm used to it."

Being used to it didn't begin to cover the exertion carrying her back up the steep slope required. But she was tired, and there was the foreign thrill of being carried. She'd thought that was a luxury reserved for small, vulnerable women. It was revealing to discover, in Isaiah's arms, she felt small and vulnerable. It was even more revealing to realize she liked feeling that way. The last twenty-four hours had revealed many flaws in her assumptions, and when she had more time, she'd have to examine them. But right now, she could use another nap.

Adelaide let herself drift as Isaiah carried her back above the tree line, marveling at the strength of his legs as he never faltered, wondering how they'd feel under her hands. She slid her fingertip over his chest. It was hard, with no give. She bet his thighs were harder. The space between the buttons beckoned. She'd never felt a man's chest, but that slight gap tempted her with the promise of the forbidden. Oh my God! She closed her eyes. She'd turned into a hussy.

"What's wrong?"

She wasn't answering that question. Honestly anyway. "I just feel so guilty that you have to carry me again."

"I don't mind."

He'd probably mind less if he knew the latent hussy who had just emerged. "Still I'm sorry."

"I said I didn't mind."

Well, she wasn't going to apologize again for that anyway. "I'm sorry I left the campsite to get wood."

His hair brushed her head. "You were cold."

"Yes."

"It was smart of you to start a fire."

The morning wasn't a total waste. At least he'd noticed her efforts. "Thank you."

"How did you start it?"

That was a question she didn't want to answer. She feigned sleep. "I used some stuff."

"Gunpowder?"

It was hard to keep faking it when she was burning with curiosity. "How did you know?"

"The smell."

What kind of nose did the man have? She'd ask but then she didn't want him discovering her emergency supplies and maybe taking them away. She settled for a simple "Oh."

Feigning sleep had the benefit of bringing on reality. It seemed like only seconds before he was setting her down. The drugged feel to her senses told her she'd drifted off. The smell of roasting rabbits replaced the scent of his skin. She couldn't decide what was more delicious. The rabbits were propped over the fire and drippings sizzled in the flames. Saliva flooded her mouth. The rabbits won for the moment.

"Where did you get the wood to rekindle the fire?"

"I had some behind the lean-to."

"There's a ledge behind the lean-to."

"There's a small cave. It stays dry there."

A place for everything. She smiled. "I'll remember."

He went behind the lean-to and pulled out a large, shallow wooden bowl. She admired the line from his broad shoulders to his lean hips as he poured water into it from a flask. Clearly she should have explored more. He bent over the bowl. Her eyes jerked up as he did . . . something.

"Did you just spit in that water?"

He turned, holding the bowl carefully. "Why would I do that?"

She didn't know. "I just thought—"

"Take off your shoes."

She eyed the water. "Why?"

"So we can soak your feet."

"What are those green things floating about?"

"Herbs for healing."

They didn't smell obnoxious. And now she knew what he'd been doing. She took off her shoes and gingerly placed her feet in the cold water. After the initial shock there was a strange tingling. The area around the blister felt warm. And then the burning pain eased.

"Better?" he asked, turning the spitted rabbits.

"Actually, yes." She twisted her foot into the bottom, enjoying the smooth wood against her soles. "What kind of herbs are these?"

"A concoction I picked up somewhere."

She wiggled her toes, admiring the utter symmetry of the bowl. Whoever had crafted it had an eye for detail. "Can I see the bag?"

A stillness took Isaiah, and for a second she didn't think he was going to answer, but then he shrugged and said, "That was the last of it."

"Oh." So much for learning the recipe. Which was a shame, because her feet felt miraculously better. Her stomach rumbled.

Isaiah looked over. "It will be a few minutes before the rabbits are ready."

She kept her expression neutral while she cursed the blush that heated her cheeks. What was it about the man that kept her so unsettled? A woman her age, with her experience, should be long past blushing.

She let the pelt slide off her shoulders. "Then, I'll set the . . ." Isaiah stared at her. Too late she remembered there wasn't a table. "I'll get the silverware."

His stare got harder.

"We do have silverware?"

"Does this look like a fancy hotel?"

"No." It looked like a hole in the side of the mountain, but that didn't mean the basics couldn't be observed. "You must at least have a fork."

He reached for his hip and pulled out a big knife. He handed it to her, hilt first. She didn't take it. "I don't think so."

"It's either this or your fingers."

Her fingers were as dirty as the knife. "Is there a place I can wash?"

"There's a stream to the left."

"Soap?"

Another stare. Eating with her fingers was distasteful. She looked at the knife. It at least was a utensil. She reached for it and then stopped. How many men had he killed with it? She caught herself before she could ask the question. "Then I guess I'll be eating with my hands."

He put the knife back in the sheath. "I thought so."

She bit her lip on a sharp retort and tugged the pelt up. If he continued to be this much of an ass, he was going to end up with one of those spitted rabbits up alongside his head, which was going to make dinner conversation extremely awkward.

❧ 7 ❧

IF THE MEAL WAS AWKWARD, THE AFTERMATH WAS WORSE.
Isaiah was sullen and quiet. Addy was exhausted and could barely
keep her eyes open. All she wanted to do was go to sleep, but there
was only one pallet on which to sleep, and quite frankly, Isaiah wasn't
a man with whom she felt comfortable just closing her eyes and letting down her guard. Quite the opposite, as a matter of fact.

She took the remnants of the carcasses, stripped bare of meat, and
set them aside. This wasn't her home so she didn't know what to do
with the refuse. There weren't any dogs. There was no clearly delin-
eated area for garbage. "What do you want to do with the carcasses?"

"Leave them."

Leaving them meant attracting all sorts of wild animals. Maybe
even a bear. She gathered up the bones and set them in the wooden
bowl. "I can take them and—"

"I said leave them."

"Bury them," she finished, muttering to herself before saying louder, "I'm not leaving them."

They were filthy clutter.

He stabbed the knife with which he'd been eating into the dirt and glared at her. "Did you ever think you'd live longer if you learned to do as you're told?"

Was that a threat? It didn't matter. Her muscles twitched with the need to dispose of the mess. "Yes, but there are just some things I can't abide."

Filth was one.

He snatched up the knife and stood quickly. She jerked back. He reached out. For the scraps, she realized. A blush burned her cheeks as he took them. "Thank you."

"You like things ordered. There's no fault in that."

Looking at him gave her all sorts of uncomfortable feelings. A couple she could identify. They were the usual—fear, apprehension. The others put that particular hitch in her breathing and unrest in her nerves, like maybe her skin had shrunk. She wanted to move and fidget, and she never fidgeted. "No, there isn't."

The grunt he gave her in response was not enlightening. She stood and, with the back of her hand, brushed the leaves off her skirt. A stain at the hem irritated her. This dress was fairly new. She'd spent a lot of hours making it and now it was ruined because people couldn't leave her alone.

"I'm going to wash up."

Another grunt. She eyed a pebble on the ground. She had the irrational urge to kick it at Isaiah. He was her rescuer—why wasn't he making this easy?

"Which way is the stream?"

He pointed to the right to the narrow ledge—the "path." Perfect. Just perfect. "Thank you."

"Be careful."

She was always careful. "Of course."

Once she was on it, the ledge was even narrower than it had looked. If that were possible. The bulk of her skirt prevented her from pressing her back as close to the wall as she'd have liked. How had Isaiah carried her here? Holding her breath, she crept along the ledge, her eyes glued to the drop-off to the left. She was sure having a house, if one would call that lean-to a house, perched so precariously was great for defense, but she wouldn't want to have to get up in the middle of the night and go relieve herself. With her luck she'd tumble off the edge and land at the bottom of the cliff. She leaned forward. And it was a long way down. She'd heard of people who'd just walked off ledges. She'd never quite understood the temptation, but now she did. There was something hypnotizing about that long tumble of space, something that encouraged a body to lean forward.

A hand caught her left arm and pushed. She screamed as she stumbled forward.

"Don't look down."

The hoarse order did nothing to calm her. She plastered herself back against the ledge as her heart thundered in her chest. "What are you doing?"

"Helping you."

She pressed her hand to her chest. "To what? An early grave?"

"You were looking down."

She lied through her teeth. "It's a nice view."

"You were getting close to the edge."

"I'm fine." At least she would be when her heart resumed a normal rhythm.

Another push. "I'll walk you."

Obviously, his definition of "walk" included force-marching her along the edge at a pace that far exceeded what she thought was safe.

She dug in her heels. "It's not necessary."

With a flex of muscle, he popped her forward. "Humor me."

He didn't leave her much choice as he propelled her onward. Dirt stuck to the grease on her fingers, irritating her almost as much as Isaiah's shoving. She wanted to shrug away but where would she go? She was already halfway across the ledge. So she stepped forward, nerves twitching, fingers clenched into fists, following the path until they got to the wider part, where it split. At least her feet didn't hurt anymore.

"Take a left at that tree lying across the boulder."

She took the left. Isaiah grunted again. If she listened carefully, she could hear the water tumbling down the mountainside. As soon as they were clear of the ledge, he stopped and let her go.

"What?"

"I thought you might like some privacy."

First he acted like a domineering ass and then he pulled out his manners.

"There is just no understanding you," she muttered as she rubbed her hands on her skirt, wishing she could give up on the notion of staying clean. What did it really matter? She was carrying half the Territory on her clothes. But unfortunately, it did matter, down inside her where there was no negotiating. She looked at the stream and was pleasantly surprised to find it was actually more than a trickle. Over time the bend in the stream had hollowed out a wide pool. The sound of water tumbling was created from the excess water spilling over the rock ledge on the downhill side. The water looked inviting. The sunlight dappling the surface, cheery. A definite bright spot in her day.

"Why did you keep this from me?"

Isaiah gave her a strange look. "I didn't."

She harrumphed, and slid down the embankment. After only a

slight hesitation, she knelt at the side of the stream, trying not to think of the fresh dirt embedding in the material, focusing instead on the opportunity to clean up. She stuck her hands in the cold water and let it slide over them, sighing as it worked its magic on her nerves. She'd be so glad when this was over. She couldn't wait to get home, to throw this dress away, to throw this memory away. To get back to her life.

Scooping some pebbles off the bottom, she rubbed them over her hand. Looking over her shoulder, she could see Isaiah. He stood at the top of the hill, arms folded across his chest, shoulders squared, feet braced slightly apart.

He looked as harsh and intimidating as the mountain peak behind him. Downright scary. Except she could still see his eyes from here, and they drew her with that same senseless tumble that she'd experienced when looking over the cliff. Suggesting that if she looked hard enough, she'd discover something wonderful. Which was pure foolishness.

She scrubbed her hands harder. A man like Isaiah was not for her. She had to remember that. She'd picked out a nice steady gentleman for her future husband. Isaiah was exciting in that dangerous sort of way that only a man who lived out here could be. In a lot of ways he was like her cousins. In a battle there was likely no one better to have at her side, but when it came to settling down and handling the day-to-day calm of town life, he'd crawl right out of his skin.

She scrubbed harder still, letting the burn drive her point home. She had to keep all of that in mind because worlds were not easy to build and they could be broken so quickly, just one wrong move, one wrong thing, one wrong choice . . . She closed her eyes. For God's sake, this whole mess had started with her drinking her evening tea. Something she did every night at the same time. Such an ordinary thing to have launched such a horrendous journey.

Isaiah hunkered down beside her to rinse his hands. She hadn't heard him come down the hill, but she was getting used to his silent ways. Without looking at him, she asked, "Do you know why they took me?"

He shook his head. "No."

That wasn't good. That meant they could come try to take her again at any time. That meant she wasn't safe at home. She looked around at the vastness of the wilderness. Then at Isaiah. For an instant she had a wild notion to set another lean-to up beside his and hide right alongside him. But only for an instant. She wasn't the type of woman who hid. If she were, she'd be at her cousins' ranch living a stilted life under their protective thumbs. "I can't stay here."

He nodded. "I know."

But where would she go? Her cousins' ranch, which sat in the middle of Indian territory, might be well guarded, but the location played havoc with her peace of mind. Living there brought back too many memories, and no matter how strict a routine she established, or how many new ones she initiated, she couldn't control the way she reacted. She was always a mess when visiting there.

"You don't have to worry," Isaiah said, shaking out his hands.

She followed suit though a lot less aggressively. No need to turn the dirt on her skirt to mud by applying water. "I think I've got a lot to worry about. Someone wants me to suffer."

Just the thought had her scrubbing her hands again.

"I won't let them take you again."

He couldn't stop it.

"Your hands are clean."

She gave them another scrub. "I just like to be sure."

"I know." His hand covered hers. "It's one of your rituals." With a gentle pull he removed her hands from the water. "But you don't need a ritual for this."

"I don't?"

"No. I promised to protect you."

He had? "When?"

"A year ago."

A year? "Where was I?"

He didn't even hesitate before he answered. "Drinking tea in your kitchen."

"You've been watching me?"

He didn't even have the grace to look uncomfortable, just gave her that brutal honesty. "Yes."

She didn't want to know, but she had to ask. "You've been watching me for a year?"

"Yes. When I'm in town."

A year. That was almost as disconcerting as being ripped out of her home by kidnappers. She took a careful breath and let it go. "Why?"

"The usual reasons."

"Elaborate. Your usual might not be mine."

He shrugged again. "You're interesting."

She, with all her strange rituals, was interesting? "You have got to be crazier than I am."

Again, no hesitation in answering. "In all likelihood."

Maybe she could use that. She needed to think. She waved her hands to dry them.

"I want to go home."

"I heard you the first time you said it."

"Oh."

He stood. She waited for him to offer her a hand up. After a few seconds she realized the offer wasn't forthcoming. It wasn't the first time she'd noticed Isaiah lacked the common manners basic to society. It just suddenly got more significant. She lifted her skirts and hauled herself up. Her leg muscles screamed at the exertion. She teetered. Immediately, he caught her arm.

She let him. "You're supposed to do that before I stand."

"Why?"

"So I don't fall."

His expression turned to concern. "You have a tendency to fall?"

She sighed and stepped away. "It's considered good manners."

His expression froze to that cold blankness she hated. "I see."

A man could hide a lot behind an expression like that. Including embarrassment. "Where did you grow up?" she asked him, heading up the hill.

"Here and there."

Judging from his face, he was about thirty. Thirty years ago Montana Territory had been a very wild place. "Your parents must have been adventurous."

His expression didn't change. "Maybe."

She tried another tack. "Did you fight in the War?"

His lips thinned. That was obviously a touchy subject. He waved her on. She sighed.

"Fighting for what you believe in is nothing to be ashamed of, no matter which side you fought on."

Another one of those grunts that irritated her was her only answer, but at least it was a response. "Did you come back home after the War?"

"I left when I was finished."

That was an odd way to put it. "I bet your family was glad to see you."

"No."

He took her arm when they reached the ledge. She didn't protest. From this angle the path looked even more treacherous. Isaiah kept her steady and away from the edge until they reached the campsite. His home, she corrected herself. What was surprising was that she was comfortable with him doing so. She actually trusted him to keep her safe. That was even somewhat amazing. She assessed the breadth of his shoulders, the muscles in his thighs, the strength in his hands. And very convenient. From the top of his head to his feet, this man was a warrior. And a warrior was exactly what she needed. Reaching into her pocket, she rubbed her worry stone between her fingers.

"You said I did you a favor?"

Isaiah nodded.

"One you don't feel is paid back yet."

His eyes narrowed. "No."

A shiver of unease went down her spine, loosening her knees before surging back up her torso and then down her arms. She ground it out with the next pass of her fingers over the stone. "No, you don't feel it's paid back yet, or no, I'm wrong?"

"No, the favor's not paid back yet." The words seemed to rumble out of him.

Another shiver chased the first. But this one left a trail of heat in places she'd never felt heat. She narrowed her eyes. He was more dangerous than she'd first imagined. This was not a man with whom to let down her guard. "Would you like it to be?"

His eyebrow went up. "What do you want?"

"The threat to me isn't over, is it?"

"No. But it will be."

She wished she had an ounce of his confidence. She had to fake hers. "Who or what do you think is behind it?"

"I think somebody is trying to get at your cousins through you."

So he knew about her cousins. That would make things easier. "Are you any good with a gun?"

"Yes."

She looked at his belt, at the knives he wore there. "And with knives?"

"Yes."

"And your fists?"

He opened and closed his fingers. "None better."

"Good."

"You got a reason for sizing me up like beef at the market?"

"You need money."

The corner of his mouth kicked up. He glanced around. "You think the place needs dressing up?"

The glimmer of humor was encouraging. She didn't want to offend him, but good God, he lived in a house made of twigs and debris with barely enough blankets to make a bedroll. "A coffeepot wouldn't come amiss."

"I don't drink coffee."

"Your company might."

"I don't get company."

"*I'm company.*"

"I'll make a note for your next visit."

"What makes you think I'm going to want to visit?"

With a deceptive simplicity, he pulled his knife, flipped it in the air, and caught it. "My skills."

She blinked. "Oh." She licked her lips and ground her worry stone between her fingers. "I want—"

"Just spit it out."

"I would if you wouldn't be so rude as to interrupt."

"Sorry."

He didn't sound sorry.

"I want to hire you."

"For what?"

As if he didn't know. She shook out her skirt and pressed a wrinkle against her thigh. "I need a bodyguard. Just until my cousins can sort this mess out."

"These cousins of yours can't provide you with protection?"

She couldn't meet his gaze. "No."

"I find it hard to believe they don't have men to spare for this."

Oh yes, they had men. Men loyal to them. Men who'd report every little thing she did. Men who were free to make judgments, come up with verdicts, rein her in. Men who would eat her out of house and home when it came to her bakery, but wouldn't respect her as a businesswoman, because to them, she would be the Camerons' delicate cousin who needed looking after. Addy. The damaged one. The broken one. The one whom everybody whispered about. Said she had lost her mind.

"I'm sure they do."

"But you don't want them." His head cocked to the side. The sun slipped beneath the brim of his hat, highlighting his eyes. They really were a pretty shade of slate blue. Crisp with a touch of gray like one saw in the winter sky when a storm was approaching.

Dear heavens, the man made her fanciful. "I want someone loyal to me."

"And you think I fit that bill?"

"I think you're the best chance I have of finding a man who won't run when Cole comes riding into town."

"You're afraid of Cole?"

"Only of what he'd do to my life with his good intentions." Her smile felt shaky as she shrugged. "My cousins are a bit overprotective."

Catching her hand in his, he looked at her broken nails, then he turned it over, revealing the scrape on the palm. "Seems to me they're not protective enough. If I hadn't come into town when I did, there would have been nothing left of you but an empty teacup."

She curled her fingers around his. Her thumb fit naturally into the inside of his knuckle. She left it there. "But you did. Now, you have a debt and I have a need. And what I want to know is, would you like a job?"

Would he like a job? Isaiah blinked as Addy stood there, blue eyes wide and anxious, white teeth biting into her lip, thumb rubbing the inside of his knuckle. That wasn't what he'd been expecting her to ask. He'd half expected her to ask him to kill someone. That was what most people asked him. Her fingers rubbed harder. As she did with her worry stone, he realized. Except it was him she was clinging to and it was him to whom she was looking for help. The beast growled with satisfaction. The man echoed the sound.

"I'm sorry. It's too much to ask."

"No."

He closed his fingers over hers. When the Reapers had left the darkness, they'd made a vow to stay apart from humans and to do their best to keep whatever part of the world sheltered them safe. The plan had been shortsighted in some ways. They'd assumed no humans would come into their areas. They'd assumed they'd be satisfied with living off the land. But the reality was, it was impossible to stay apart. People kept coming into their regions. Their homes kept getting discovered. And there were comforts that they enjoyed. Comforts that required funding. In short, they needed jobs.

"How much you willing to pay?" He'd do it for free. But if he was going to fake normal, he needed to do it right.

"I don't know. What's a fair price?"

For her life, the sky was the limit. "Two dollars a day."

She gasped and pulled her hand from his. He couldn't blame her—money was tight after the War and things were just beginning to pick up. But it'd look strange if he didn't put a decent value on his services. She was the type who'd be suspicious if he didn't.

"That's a steep price." Her hand went to her pocket, back to her worry stone. The beast growled. It wanted her hand back in his. So did he.

"Not from the way I see it. You're asking me to put my life on the line."

The fabric of her dress rustled as she dragged her fingers across the stone. "I guess I am." She looked up again. "Are you any good?"

"You're standing here unharmed, aren't you?"

"That is a point." Which she conceded reluctantly, he could tell. She was looking for a bargaining area. A bit of leverage to wield in their bargain. He had to admire her for that. "Of course, there is the fact that you owe me. That ought to be worth something."

"How much are you thinking?"

"I'm thinking a dollar a day off the price."

"That's steep."

"But it gets you off the hook."

It was his turn to concede a good point. "Very true." Just to needle her a bit, because he liked the glimpses of temper that peeked through her calm, he added, "Are you worth that much?"

She folded her arms across her chest and her eyes flashed in direct challenge. "Are you really that good?"

He bit back a smile. "I'm really that good."

Every Reaper was. Killing, and the skills necessary to execute it, was the only thing they'd been trained to do. Any memory of civilized behavior they'd learned as boys had been kicked, beaten, and terrorized out of them. *They* had replaced civilization with a sense of cold, deadly purpose driven only by *Their* will. Their creators had wanted to be sure that, when the time came to strike the fatal blow, the weapons *They* had created wouldn't fail. *They* had been very skilled, but not entirely successful. In creating the evil *They* wanted to use, *They*'d overlooked the one truth that had been born with

Adam and Eve. Evil would find a way. And as surely as the serpent had invaded Eden, Isaiah and the others had found their way to freedom.

That battle had been bloody and finite. The one that followed was grueling and ongoing. It had started with the withdrawal from the drug upon which *They* had made all the Reapers dependent. For weeks the Reapers had battled agony for which the only cure had been destroyed by the Reapers themselves. Some had gone mad and killed themselves. Some had gone mad and needed to be destroyed. The experience had taught them all that just slipping back into the human world and following human laws was not going to be enough for creatures capable of what they were. They needed their own laws to punish those who lost control of their beasts. Those laws had been made. The punishments determined. And the Reapers had dispersed.

It was hard to make a life when they didn't know what they were, let alone who they were. Without the daily infusion of the drug, fragments of memories started to emerge. Bits and pieces of who they once were. With the knowledge of who they had once been, what they had lost, more Reapers had gone mad. As elected by the other Reapers to a member of the council, it had fallen on Isaiah to judge those who fell prey to the evil within and to permanently relieve the pain of the insane. It was the hardest role he'd ever assumed. Those were the hardest kills he'd ever performed. Each one taking a chunk out of the soul he was trying to build. Each one feeding the doubt that lived within. Would he be the next to lose his mind?

"Well?"

The question brought him out of the past. Addy was standing in front of him, waiting. For an answer, he realized. The tendency to drift into memories made it hard for him to hold conversations. One of the reasons he preferred his solitude. But he was getting better. The time alone had built his control. His fuse wasn't so hair trigger now. The noise in his brain tended to stay in the background more.

A movement caught his attention. She was drumming her fingers on her arm. She was waiting for an answer. Shit, he couldn't remember the question.

"I'm waiting."

Addy's mouth set in a firm line, the pretty pink color fading to pale at the edges as her eyes narrowed with the anger she was trying to hold back. She was always holding back her emotions as if she feared, if she let them go, something horrible would happen. He knew what that felt like, too. In many ways they were a lot alike. "Do you want the job?"

Oh yes—she wanted to hire him. "You gonna pay me a dollar a day?"

"Yes."

"I need the first week up front."

"I don't have it on me right now." Her chin came up, pride waving like a banner, daring him to question her integrity. "I was caught a bit unaware."

Yes, she had been. "I'll be wanting it as soon as we get to town."

"That's understandable."

"You agreeing?"

"Yes."

"Good." He took the pelt from around her shoulders. "Are you settled now?"

"What do you mean 'settled'?"

"Have you addressed all you need to address?"

"Why?"

"Because I'm tired, and I want to go to bed."

She looked at the hut and back at him. "It's not even dark."

"Doesn't change the fact that I'm tired from lugging you all over the mountain."

She had the grace to look guilty. "I'm not tired."

That was a lie. The beast could smell her tiredness. The man could see it. She could barely keep her eyes open. "Then you can lie beside me and listen to the birds sing."

"I most certainly will not!"

She was nervous about lying down with him. He couldn't blame her for that, either. Catching her hand, he dragged her along behind him.

"I wasn't planning on giving you a choice."

╼ 8 ╾

OH, MY GOD. HE WAS SERIOUS. ADDY DUG IN HER HEELS AND tugged at the viselike grip Isaiah had around her wrist. "I am not sleeping with you."

No matter how appealing the thought of having relations with this man was. No matter how strong the dart of excitement that snaked from her head to her toes at the thought of all that muscle pressed up against her. She was not sleeping with him.

Isaiah cut her a glance from under his brows. "Well, I'm not giving you the opportunity to get into more trouble if it occurs to you to strike out on your own."

"I promise," she gasped out as he dragged her two more steps, hiding her shiver of arousal under a pretense of struggle. "The thought never entered my head."

She watched the flex of his buttocks under the leather of his pants. But a lot of other impossibly exciting, highly sexual thoughts had crept in. Between her legs, a sweet ache began.

"Lady, I've noticed a lot of wild thoughts pop into your head but never end up discussed."

How could he know that? "Well, that isn't one of them."

But she wished it were. This sudden onset of primal interest was uncomfortable. The foreign strength of temptation unwieldy to control. Especially as the intriguing subtle scent of . . . him . . . teased her nostrils. He smelled so good.

"And you expect me to take your word for that?"

She ducked as he entered the lean-to, trying to force her mind off the breadth of his shoulders and back onto the conversation. "Yes."

He stopped by the pile of pelts, dropping to the side the one she'd been wearing. "Does this mean you'd be interested in doing something other than sleeping?"

Horror washed through her that he might know her thoughts.

"No!" She took a swing at him. "It does not."

The blow missed. All her blows, when it came to this man, whether verbal or physical, seemed to have the same problem. She glared at Isaiah and held absolutely still since there was nothing else she could really do. He was bigger than her, meaner than her, and worst of all, more knowledgeable than her about where the hell they were. She curled her fingers into a fist at her side, suppressing the stupid yearning that wanted to be closer to him. But the odds wouldn't always be on his side.

His gaze dropped to her fist, then moved inward. His nostrils flared. The smile left his face. "Contrary to what you believe, sleeping with you isn't going to be a picnic for me, either."

She gasped, suppressing the urge to thrust her hips forward. What was it about this man that set her senses on fire and her principles to the side? She cleared her throat and asked in an almost normal voice, "What do you mean?"

His eyes narrowed and his face took on a sensual edge that hit the backs of her knees like a nudge as he sat on the pile of furs.

"I mean, I need my sleep." Setting his hat to the side, he started tugging at his boot. "And you look the type to snore."

How dare he! She clung to the indignation as hard as her gaze clung to the powerful muscles of his thighs. "I most certainly do not."

He cocked an eyebrow at her while shucking his boots. "How do you know? You stay up nights listening to yourself to make sure?"

She folded her arms across her chest. She knew for a fact that she didn't snore. Her cousins would have ribbed her unmercifully if she did. They might love her, but that didn't spare her from their sense of humor. "Ladies do not snore."

He didn't look impressed. Instead, he looked even sexier, sitting there on the bedroll like some pagan god readying himself for a night of . . . well, pagan behavior. "Ladies don't hire Reapers as bodyguards, either, but you don't seem to have any problem doing that."

"That's different. The circumstances are special."

"Uh-huh." He started to unbutton his shirt. And he was using both hands. Darn it.

Too late, she realized he'd let go of her. He'd distracted her to the point that she hadn't noticed he'd released her hand. She eyed all that hard swell of muscle that was revealed as he unbuttoned his shirt.

Her chance for escape was gone. If she'd ever had one. Isaiah was fast. She'd seen that. A top predator when it came to his domain. Another shiver went down her spine. Another button slipped from its hole. The first muscles that cut across the top of his stomach were bared to her greedy gaze. Dear God, she was a wanton. Who would have imagined?

Addy's mouth went dry. Her knees went a little weaker, and her breath caught in her throat as she waited for him to release the next button from its restraint. She wanted to see more of the muscles that slabbed his stomach. Wanted to reach out and touch the rich, tanned warmth of his skin. The anticipation was delicious. Like nothing she'd ever experienced before. It made her wonder what more this man could teach her. What more of life was she missing? She thought of her fiancé, or rather the man she'd selected to be her fiancé. She hadn't informed him of her interest yet. Matthew was a good steady man with thinning blond hair, a pleasant face, and a stable personality. He was perfect for her plans, but he'd never made her feel like this.

She swept her gaze from the top of Isaiah's head to his feet, lingering on the handsomeness between. Nothing had ever made her feel like this.

It was disconcerting to realize, at her ripe old age of twenty-five, that she had a lecherous side. It was also disconcerting to realize that she wasn't repelled by the warm, pulsing knot of feeling growing inside her. In all her life, she'd never fallen in love with a man. Never been particularly attracted to one. For a few years now she'd wondered if there was something wrong with her that she hadn't. It was exciting to know there wasn't. It was thrilling that it was this man, at this moment. Because this was possible.

Isaiah caught her eye. She couldn't control the wild blush that colored her cheeks, or the speculation that entered his gaze when he saw it. He crooked his fingers toward the pelt. "You might as well get comfortable."

He looked like a pagan god motioning to a vestal virgin. Her breath caught and that warm knot of emotion got hotter. "I'm as comfortable as I intend to get."

At least until she weighed the pros and cons of what she was contemplating.

"You're going to have a long cold night then. As soon as that sun sets behind that ridge, the temperature drops."

"I'm sure I'll be fine."

He shrugged and took the pelt she'd had around her and pulled it over his legs as he stretched out on the bedroll. "Suit yourself. But it does look like rain."

Despite herself, she looked over her shoulder. It did look like rain. Darn it. Did everything have to go his way all the time? "I'm not afraid of getting wet." She might not be afraid, but she wasn't thrilled with the idea. Her clothes still hadn't fully dried from her last dunking.

"Well, for sure, you're not made of sugar so I don't think we need to worry about you melting."

Of all the nerve! "I'll have you know, plenty of people think I'm pretty sweet."

"They must see you in a different light."

They did. But it bothered her that he didn't see her as sweet. Another surprise. She normally was oblivious to people's opinions of her. Enduring years of rampant speculation had a way of hardening a person to public opinion. But for some reason, this man brought out in her a desire to be seen as womanly. Soft. Delicate. All the things she spent her life convincing her cousins that she wasn't.

Isaiah groaned under his breath as he stretched out on the pelts, his big body looking unreasonably comfortable against the fur. That intriguing scent that was uniquely his filled the interior, teasing her nostrils, tempting her into another breath. His mouth relaxed into a sensual fullness that had her tongue sliding over her lips as she imagined how his would feel against hers. She bit back a "stop" as he pulled his hat over his face, depriving her of the fantasy as he relaxed into the pleasure.

She knew for a fact that his bed wasn't *that* comfortable, but watching him shift and hearing his whispered sigh of relief, she found her own muscles moaning in longing. And suddenly that sense of propriety that had her standing on her aching feet, six feet away from Isaiah and the comparative comfort of the bed, didn't seem at all appropriate. A stray gust of wind blew into the lean-to, heralding the evening's chill. Addy rubbed her arms. And eyed Isaiah again. Pressed up against his side as she'd have to be to share the bedroll, she'd be warm.

"The offer's still open."

The invitation, uttered in Isaiah's rumbling drawl, slipped like a secret smile from behind his hat, sneaking past her guard and snuggling up to that part of her she'd thought missing. The womanly part that went weak for a man. The part of her that wanted to do more than sleep with him. The part of her that wanted to lie down beside him and slide her fingers under the lapels of his shirt and test the texture of his skin.

The offer's still open.

She was crazy to consider what she was considering. Isaiah was wild. He was dangerous and he radiated a potent magnetism. In short, he was everything from which her cousins strove to protect her. And maybe that's what made him so irresistible. The strip of pelt on his right side beckoned. The hollow of his shoulder encouraged. The heat of his body lured. And past her well-cultivated sense of propriety came the thought, *What is the harm if I explore the temptation he presents? What is there to lose?*

This was a man with whom she could do more than sleep and no one would know. This was a man so far outside society that no one would believe that she'd invited him to her bed. This was a man she could love and leave with impunity. This was a man with whom she could explore her earthier side, without consequence. This man, in rescuing her, had provided her with the one opportunity to be the sensual woman she'd never thought she could be.

It wasn't as if anyone thought she was still a virgin after her time with the Indians, and this excursion wasn't going to help her reputation. It also wasn't going to damage her marriage prospects. Matthew Hacklebury, the merchant she'd selected to be her future husband, had reassured her multiple times that it wasn't important to him whether she was a virgin. Despite her constant reassurances that she was, he continued to tell her he didn't mind "her experiences." Which irked her. She wasn't a liar. There were even times when she'd gotten the suspicion that Matthew might actually not want her to be a virgin, which was absurd, because every woman knew that every man wanted a pure wife. But still, at times when he didn't think she was watching, she thought she caught him watching her with a certain light in his eyes that made her wonder what he really thought had happened to her during her time with the Indians.

"You've got a strange look on your face," Isaiah murmured, pushing his hat back.

Addy put her hand on her hip and tilted her head to the side, studying him in return. "That's probably because I have a strange thought in my head."

Isaiah laced his fingers together and tucked them behind his head, looking so superior she wanted to smack him. He arrogantly thought he had her over a barrel. He thought that she was the type to back down when facing an obstacle, when in truth she was the type who liked to explore her options. But there was one obstacle she needed out of the way before she could make any decision. "You need to shave off your beard."

To his credit he didn't look shocked, or call her crazy. "Why?"

"Because I will not have relations with a man who has more hair than skin."

That arrogant smile slowly slipped away as her statement sank in. "Who said anything about making love?"

She waved her hand dismissively. "Have relations, make love. I'm not splitting hairs."

"Well, I am." He sat up. "Look, lady, I was just pulling your chain. I don't have any intention of . . . having relations with you or any other phrase you want to attach to it."

That was a heck of a note. She might not be a dewy thing fresh out of the schoolroom, but she was not a hag. And as powerful as her attraction was for him, it was inconceivable that he didn't feel the same for her. "Why not? Do you think I'm too old?"

"You're not too old for anything."

At least that was encouraging. "Do you think I'm ugly?"

He frowned at her. "I think you've lost your mind."

"Well, for your information, I am perfectly within my right mind. I'm also twenty-five years old. And despite what you might have heard, I am a virgin. I've long accepted that I'm unlikely to marry a man about whom I feel passionate, but I find, intriguingly enough, that I feel passionately about you."

"And this means what to me?"

"This means you get to make love to me and it will be no one's concern but our own. When I get home, we'll just go our separate ways and it will be over."

"So I'm just an experiment?"

"Exactly."

His expression went hard. "Well, maybe I have no interest in being an experiment."

"I'm not a young girl, Mr. Isaiah. Every man is willing to be that kind of experiment."

He grunted, then asked in little more than a growl, "And what do you get out of it?"

"Hopefully, an experience to look back on and smile over for the rest of my life."

"You should save that experience for your husband, not for a—"

"For what? For the man willing to risk his life to save mine? The man who is willing to continue to risk his life for me? A man to whom I am strangely attracted? A man who sends tingles up my arm whenever he touches my hands? A man who can steal my breath with a glance? Can you name me someone who would be a better candidate?"

Isaiah didn't have a ready response. Addy couldn't tell whether that was because he was breathless with anticipation or speechless with shock. Hopefully it was the former, but just in case it was the latter, she pressed on.

"I'm not looking for forever, Mr. Jones. I'm just looking for a night of passion with a man who I think can make me see the stars."

"And I just got done saying, it's your husband who should be making you see stars."

She folded her arms across her chest. "And I just got done telling you the man I have chosen to be my husband is not likely to even cause my breath to catch, let alone cause stars to fall from the sky."

"Then why the hell are you marrying him?"

"Because he's stable, even tempered, and makes a good income and will be a good father to whatever children I might have."

"And you think this is normal?"

"Yes."

"And what if this paragon wants you to make him see stars? Do you think he's going to be happy with a woman who can't tolerate his touch?"

He was so annoying with his logic. And so irritating with his lack of ability to see hers. "Of course, I thought of that eventuality, and that would be the second benefit to making love with you tonight. I will have the experience to be able to fake the enthusiasm that will satisfy him."

Isaiah raked a hand through his hair. "Jesus Christ, woman! You are something."

"What I am is practical, Mr. Isaiah. I'm not the type to cheat on a husband, and as I'm expecting Mr. Hacklebury to propose upon my return to town, this is about my only opportunity to experience a grand passion. If there's one thing I've learned through my experiences in life, it's that lost opportunities rarely return and chances for happiness should not be ignored."

Isaiah rubbed his hand over the back of his neck and glared at her under the slash of his eyebrows. "Shit, not only do you expect me to make stars fall from the sky, you also expect me to make you happy?"

She shook out her skirt and sat down on the edge of the pelts. He didn't need to make it sound so onerous. "I expect if you succeed in making the stars fall from the sky, I'll be happy."

Isaiah scooted to the left, putting a good foot between them. "Well, I don't want to shave my beard."

"That's not negotiable. It's extremely unhygienic."

"Then I guess you have to set your sights elsewhere."

She sighed. "I was hoping not to have to resort to this."

He ran his hand down his face and said wearily from behind his fingers, "Go ahead, I might as well hear it all. What's 'this'?"

This was bribery. "I have a hundred dollars in my bank account back home. Fifty dollars I need for supplies to keep my bakery running. The other fifty is yours if you shave the beard and—"

He looked at her over the edge of his palm. "Make the stars fall from the sky for you."

"Yes."

His response was a long silence. He didn't fidget, didn't speak or give her any other indication of what he was thinking. Was he insulted at the offer of money? Thrilled? She didn't know if that silence was good or bad, but she'd played enough poker with her cousins to know when to stay silent and when to let her arguments speak for her. This was one of the silent times. She'd never had to work harder to bite her tongue. Never been more aware of the untidiness of her appearance. Especially when Isaiah rolled to his feet, stood, and glared down at her. "You're crazy."

Bracing her weight on her hands, she arched her back in a pose she'd seen on her cousins' dirty picture cards. As she'd hoped, Isaiah's eyes fell to her breasts rather than lingering on the mess of her hair.

"And you're a coward."

He slapped his hat on his head. "You'd better hope the hell I'm not."

At least he wasn't running. "Why?"

"A coward would be thinking of the consequences of taking you up on your offer."

That was encouraging, too. "And you're not?"

"I should be."

"Why?"

Instead of answering, he strode toward the ledge.

"Where are you going?"

He didn't even look over his shoulder as he snapped back, "To shave."

SON of a bitch, he was actually shaving, which meant he was actually contemplating messing with his sanity. Isaiah stared at his reflection in the water of the pool. He touched the razor edge of the knife blade to the thick mass of hair bristling out from his face just below his ear. He'd worn the beard so long that it was a part of him. A bestial mask that reminded him of what he was. A reminder of what he could never be again. Unless he went forward with this. He tested the edge against his skin. The blade inched lower, tested his jugular. He had no right to go forward with this.

But he was. He'd sworn to regain his humanity. Making love to a woman was a hell of a step in the right direction. Especially to a woman who made him feel more human than anyone ever had. Isaiah drew the knife edge up his neck and over the edge of his jaw, feeling the bite and drag on the flesh, scenting the blood of the subsequent nicks and not caring. He was fucking shaving to make love to a virgin who wanted a love-'em-and-leave-'em moment that would make her see the stars. He needed his head examined. As if he could give any woman that.

As if he could give *her* that.

Son of a bitch, why was he doing this? He had no business contemplating making love with Addy. His beast snarled at the thought. He heard it in an inward rumble that rippled along his nerve endings and set the hair on the nape of his neck standing on end. For once he and the beast were in accord. They both needed tonight with Addy. They both needed this touch of humanity.

Running his fingers over his skin, he found it pretty smooth, the blood slicked over wounds that were healing even as he touched them. Another benefit of whatever it was that they had done to him was that he healed fast, so taking care with shaving wasn't the priority it was for most men. The pain from the nicks was barely noticeable. The torture he'd endured to make him a more reliable weapon made him pretty immune to most pain. Unlike Addy. He thought of her feet. At least his saliva had healing properties that had aided the blisters.

His reflection caught his eye. He ran his fingers over his jaw again. How long had it been since he'd seen his face? He traced the hollow of his cheek, touched the slight bump on his nose. It was so familiar yet eerily not. His nose had been broken. The change didn't heal old injuries, only new ones, so the bump was a legacy from before he'd been taken. He touched the narrow scar on his lip. Had he fallen as a child? Had he been hit? Had there been someone to comfort him? Had there ever been anyone? His fingers curled into a fist. There was a lifetime in his face, and he couldn't remember a damn minute of it. His beast growled.

"Shut up."

He didn't want to hear from *it*. He hadn't wanted *it*, had fought *it*, but *it'd* been stronger than he and now he was stuck with *it*. But that didn't mean he was going to have daily chats with *it*. Or let *it* dictate his life.

He dipped the knife in the water again, making a mental note to resharpen the blade when he got back. Or maybe later. He had a warm, willing woman in his bed.

His cock thickened on a pleasurable throb as he recalled the faint scent of her arousal. Sharpening his knife was not going to be a priority. A shiver snaked over his skin as he imagined the soft buss of Addy's lips on his. They'd be softer than her touch, sweeter than her scent. And they'd be his. Just his. A growl rumbled in his chest as satisfaction washed through him.

It'd been forbidden for the Reapers to have contact with women. The penalty had been death, but all of the Reapers' appetites, especially the sexual, had been enhanced, right along with their senses. Isaiah, like the others, had had some contact with women, but not much, though it wasn't the threat of death that kept his encounters few and far between. No, that had been seeing what Reapers, in the throes of lust while under the influence of the drug, did to the women with whom they lay. If the women survived the beasts' passion, they were often left insane by the bites many Reapers invariably delivered.

Three times Isaiah had been called in to clean up the mess—killing the rogue Reapers and supposedly killing the women. Two of the women had been bitten multiple times. They had been pathetic to see—half beast, half human, tearing at themselves with their claws as the metamorphosis could not proceed. Killing them had been a mercy. The third woman had only been bitten twice. She'd been scared, but lucid. When she'd looked up at him from her bed, sleep and innocence in her eyes, he'd stayed his hand. It would have been so easy to kill her, but he . . . hadn't. To this day he didn't know what it was that had stayed his hand, made him disobey an order, but when he'd left that house, she'd still been alive.

And when he'd returned to the compound, no one had looked deeper than his assurance that he'd handled it. *They*'d never questioned his obedience at that point. *They*'d just assumed he'd given himself over to the beast that was so strong within him by then. His lip curled in a snarl. *They* had been too complacent.

He hadn't said a word as *They*'d given him his reward. Just accepted the drug and the oblivion it brought, her face and a niggling wonder accompanying him into the void. That woman haunted him. His one failure of duty. His one act of mercy. He'd even gone back to the house for reasons he didn't understand, either, except he'd needed to know something. She hadn't been there. No one had. The house had the musty smell of neglect. He'd found a tintype with her image on the dresser. He didn't know why, but to this day, every time he looked at it, he had the same questions. Had he really done her a favor? What if it wasn't the bite that drove the women insane? What if she'd only had a delayed reaction? What if. What if. What if.

Isaiah splashed water over his head before tossing it back and shaking the excess out of his hair. She was fine, he told himself for the hundredth time. The woman was fine. Sparing her life was one of the few good things he'd done, which just went to prove nothing was all bad. He stood and shoved the knife back in the sheath. Not even a Reaper.

❧ 9 ❧

WHEN ISAIAH ENTERED THE LEAN-TO, ADDY WAS SITTING where he'd left her, fully dressed, hands folded in her lap—the left over the right. She had her worry stone in her right hand. He knew this was a mistake, but the same way she clung to her worry stone, he was clinging to her. Her dress was stained, her hair a mess. And she was still the most beautiful woman he'd ever seen.

She touched her hand to the end of the sloppy braid, then moved to the lose strands hanging around her face. Her gaze was belligerent and vulnerable all at once. "I don't have a comb."

The same turbulence warred inside him. He reached out then thought better of it. It was too soon for touching. "You don't need one."

She didn't need anything but to be herself.

She blinked as his hand fell to his side. The belligerence in her expression increased as did the vulnerability.

Shit. She wanted him to make her see stars, and he couldn't even allay her concerns about her hair. The weight of all he didn't know, all he needed to know, pressed down on his shoulders, heavier than any load he'd ever had to bear. Addy was a good woman. She should have a good man. But she was stuck with him.

"I don't do too well with words."

She blinked again. Some of the belligerence faded. With the calm logic he'd come to expect from her, she said, "I may be new to this, but a skill with words is not necessary."

"You know you're beautiful."

"You make it sound like an accusation."

Maybe it was. "Beautiful women expect a lot."

"Practical women accept what they get."

"As you're accepting me as a lover because I'm the only choice you have?"

She bit her lip, dainty white teeth sinking into pretty pink flesh, leaving it white around the edges but a deeper red farther out. She reached out and caught his hand in hers. His beast made a sound it never had before, half moan, half growl. Pleasure. Her touch was such pleasure.

He froze, closing his eyes, imprinting the memory on his mind, expecting her to withdraw her hand. Wanting her to. Needing her to. Prepared to hate her if she did. Refusing to stop if that was her wish.

"You're going to have to meet me halfway."

That he hadn't expected. He opened his eyes at the tug on his hand. Her hand looked so small in his. Because she was expecting him to do something, he curled his fingers around hers. She smiled. The connection sank deep into his bones. This was his sanity. His pleasure for the night. Her fingers tucked around his. His woman.

Yes.

Satisfaction whipped through him, whether driven by beast or man, he couldn't tell. But it was enough. Her scent held a slight, acrid tinge. "You're scared."

Her smile faltered to a twitch of her lips. "A little."

He liked that she told him the truth. He knelt beside the pallet. Her breath caught on a betraying gasp. She really was afraid. "For a woman of bold talk, you aren't that sure."

"Talk can only get me so far. At some point I need experience."

"That's true." He took a swathe of her hair in his hand. It felt like silk and looked like sunlight. "Then I guess it will be up to me to get you the rest of the way."

"To the stars?"

He nodded. "I remember the deal."

"Please." Her fingers squeezed his. "For tonight? Don't mention it being a deal."

She was still holding his hand. Her fingers were so fragile against his. "You want it to be more?"

She shook her head. "The pretense of romance will be sufficient."

Even his beast recognized the longing so carefully absent from the sentence. She wanted to be romanced. For tonight to mean more than lust. Well, so did he.

Removing the tie from her hair took little effort. "Then we will pretend."

Her smile came back as he unraveled and smoothed the heavy strands. A bit shaky around the corners, but back. She was an admirable woman. Most would be on their knees right now, crying from the emotional exhaustion of their trials. Addy was assessing the situation and making the most of her opportunities. Admirable and resourceful. He'd have to keep his eye on the latter.

But for now he'd rather look at her breasts.

Isaiah brought his hand to her cheek, bringing hers along with it for the simple reason that it was inconceivable to let her go. He felt like a fool until his knuckles brushed her cheek and her eyes widened. At that point the gesture transformed into a caress as her fingers pressed subtly against his. Her scent became muskier with pleasure. And a mistake became right.

He could do this, he realized. By following the clues of her body, he could keep his promise.

Lowering his voice, he murmured, "You have your clothes on."

Her voice was just as soft, with a husky little catch that tugged his desire forward. "I didn't know I was supposed to take them off."

Truthfully, he didn't know, either. His few encounters had always been quick and semiclothed and there was nothing about tonight that he wanted to be similar to those.

"Yes. You were supposed to."

"You expected me to await you naked?"

It did sound stupid, phrased like that, seeing as she was a virgin.

"Maybe not."

"Definitely not."

"But I want you naked."

A blush rode high on her cheeks, warming the backs of his fingers a second before she lay back. "Then you'll have to make it happen."

Lust stole his breath before spearing to his core, heating his blood, rousing his beast. His gums and fingertips itched with the need to change. His bones ached to become Other.

No!

The beast would not have this. This was his moment with his woman. Isaiah closed his eyes, trapped between heaven and hell, fighting until he won.

"Isaiah?"

He opened his eyes and found Addy looking up at him, worry replacing that first hint of passion. Leaning down, the beast's howl of protest fading into the distance, he touched his mouth to hers, being careful, so careful. He wanted that passion back. He wanted it growing to an inferno that would consume them both. He wanted . . . her.

"Isaiah."

The whisper of his name blew across his parted lips. He took it in on a deep breath. Yes, Isaiah. Not Reaper. Not bastard. Not scum. Isaiah. The man.

"Addy." Her blush deepened as he gave her back her name.

"I don't know what to do."

Neither did he, but his instincts had been sound up until now. This was not the moment to start doubting them. "Then I guess you'd best let go of the worry stone and hold on to me."

"Oh."

He lifted up and to the side, letting her slip it back in her pocket. When she was done, he fitted his lips to hers. "And now hold on to me."

Her fingers touched his hip, his waist, his ribs. Those tentative touches spread through his soul like want on fire. "That's right. Touch me."

Hold me.

He didn't say that, but the hand he settled in the hollow of her spine spoke for him, pulling her to him, riding the flow of need, of desire, of years of longing, letting it flow out through his fingertips. Letting her feel what he wouldn't say. She flowed with him as he leaned forward, her lips parting on a gasp as she fell back. Her breasts cushioned his chest, her hips his pelvis, her moan his passion. All three offered him a soft landing. A place to start something new. With her. She'd been changing his life since he'd first seen her.

Cupping her cheek in his hand, he moaned, "You're a dangerous woman, Addy Cameron." He felt her smile, heard her chuckle.

"I think I like that. It puts us on equal footing."

"How so?"

"You're a dangerous man."

"Yes." There was no point arguing with that. And he certainly didn't want to argue with her right now. Not when he could smell that intoxicating scent that was uniquely hers, not when the heat of her desire coated her skin in a fragrance so addicting he couldn't resist a taste. He touched his tongue to the side of her neck. Sweet. She was so sweet.

"What are you doing?" she gasped, arching her neck, giving him better access to the soft skin beneath her chin.

He smiled, breathing her scent as it deepened with her pleasure. "Something sweet."

"Oh, don't . . ."

He paused. Had he misread her response?

A quiver shook her from head to toe and a small erotic whisper of sound preceded her words. "Don't stop."

It was his turn to shiver. It wasn't the first time he'd heard a woman make that statement. He'd gotten the impression from his few covert encounters that it was a mandatory utterance that lost its impact after the first couple of times. But when Addy said it, it was . . . the difference between real and pretend, he realized as she moaned. This woman wanted him. His cock throbbed and his breath hitched. Him. Isaiah Jones. Just as he was. Because she knew nothing about him, making this his once-in-a-lifetime opportunity, too. The pleasure froze in a moment of doubt. He had no right to take her like this, to do this to her. His beast surged forward, possessive and demanding. Isaiah barely had time to pull his nails away from her as his claws tore through his skin. He broke off the kiss, burying his face in the side of her throat as she whispered his name. He loved the sound of his name on her lips. He preferred it husky with desire.

The beast just wanted her. From the corner of his eye, he could see his claws. A pale ivory color. Many times, he'd seen them coated in mud and blood and gore. Closing his eyes, he willed them away. They would never touch her. That part of him would never touch her. The beast snarled. He snarled right back.

"Isaiah?"

"Right here." His voice was gruff.

"What's wrong?"

"You make me lose my head."

"I thought we were supposed to."

"Not yet." And him, not ever.

She stroked his back. "I don't mind."

Her voice had its mystical, calming effect. His claws retracted. His canines retreated. The ache in his muscles that proceeded change abated, and that fast, he was Isaiah again. He didn't understand how she could accomplish so easily what he'd spent a decade attempting to do on his own.

He took a breath. Her scent flooded his senses. Desire throbbed in his veins. His cock throbbed between his legs. He wanted to bury himself in her. Not just with his cock but with his mind, his soul. It scared the hell out of him. He waited for the beast to snarl its own protest, but for once it was quiet.

Contrary bastard.

Turning his head, he kissed the side of her neck. As before, she squeaked and shivered. Goose bumps sprang up under his lips. He followed them down to her shoulder. Her collar blocked his access to her neck. He lingered there, running his lips up and down the taut tendon, smiling when her shiver immediately followed, growling when her nails bit into his shirt.

"Dangerous woman."

She smiled. "We match."

"For tonight."

A blink was her only acknowledgment of the reminder. The material of his shirt prevented him from fully experiencing the pleasure of her touch. With another growl, he sat up.

Her hands clung, sliding off his shoulder reluctantly. He dragged the shirt over his shoulders, noting the widening of her eyes and the softening of her lips. He took a breath, checking her scent. No fear. A new sensation went through him as her tongue flicked over her lips, leaving an intriguing dampness in its wake. Pride. He quelled the urge to puff out his chest, but he didn't immediately bend down, either. She liked the way he looked. There was no harm in letting her look. Especially when he planned on doing some looking himself.

"You're a beautiful man."

"I'm glad you think so." He reached for the buttons on her shirt.

"What are you doing?"

"I want to see how beautiful you are."

Her hand clutched her shirt. Her eyes sparkled in the dimness of the lean-to. Another advantage of the beast. He could see in the dark.

"I'm very ordinary."

Isaiah unbuttoned two buttons before nudging her hands down. "Not to me."

She clutched the material above her breast. "Yes, I am."

He met her gaze and tugged her fingers away from the lapel. "To me you're special."

"Me?"

How could she look at him as if he were crazy? She with her moonspun hair, big blue eyes, and fingers that flicked over his skin like hot flashes of lightning. "Yes. You."

Her smile turned sultry and her hands fell away. "I think I like that."

He undid the next three buttons in rapid order, spreading her shirt, exposing the swell of her breasts and the soft fabric of her camisole. "I know I do."

For a moment he just appreciated the view. The softness of her skin.

"Am I still special?"

"Hell yes."

She chuckled, but didn't meet his gaze.

"What?"

"I've never had such high praise couched in a curse."

"I'm sorry."

Her gaze clung to his as he lifted her up. "No, you're not." He slipped the shirt off her shoulders and tugged the camisole over her head before she could think on what he was doing.

"Don't be. I'm not."

Her breasts were small, high, and firm. The nipples were a faint pink. They crinkled into hard tips as he watched. A tide of red flowed up from her chest to her cheeks. She was embarrassed and maybe even cold.

He came down over her. "Don't be embarrassed."

He wanted her passionate and eager, not cold and withdrawn.

Her hands immediately went around his neck. "I won't be for long." She said that with such purpose.

"Why?"

"Because I want to see the stars."

So did he. "Then kiss me."

She did. Wholeheartedly offering him her mouth, holding nothing back when his lips touched hers. Kissing him the way he'd taught her. It was his turn to moan. This was what he'd been searching for those times he'd managed to steal a hurried encounter with a whore. This connection. This fire that burned from the inside out. This sense of rightness. He cupped Addy's breast in his palm. This perfection.

"Oh, my God, Isaiah."

She liked that. He could tell from the arch of her back and the increase in her scent. His beast surged along with his desire. Wanting part of this. Saliva filled his mouth, carrying the taste of her scent. His gums ached.

No! He wouldn't let *it* touch her. This was between the man and the woman.

His thumb brushed her nipple. Her whole body jerked. He did it again, lingering on the pass, liking the way the hard/soft nub bent to his will. She squeaked and shivered.

"You like that?" It was only half question.

"Yes."

"Good." He did it again, and again, increasing the pressure when she stopped shivering, smiling when it came back. So that was what she needed. When she stopped reacting to the brush of his thumb, he took her nipple in his mouth, rubbing his tongue over the hard tip, nipping with his lips, sucking. Sucking harder as her fingers sank through his hair and pulled him closer.

"Oh, please. Don't stop."

"Wild horses couldn't make me stop."

"Good. Oh good."

He liked the way her voice was husky, almost a growl. He loved the way her nails dug into his skin. He adored the way she arched up into him.

"More." He needed more. More of her cries, her scent. Her taste. Catching her nipple between his teeth, he raked it gently as he gathered up her skirts. He bit and she cried out. More of her pleasure filled the air around them. She'd liked that, too. He did it again, growling when she would have pulled away, keeping her there.

"It's too much."

"No." It wasn't enough. Kissing down the slope of her breasts, he said, "I promised you stars."

"But . . ."

He looked up at her from between her breasts. She was a tempt-ress with her tousled hair, desire-darkened eyes, and kiss-swollen lips. And she was his. *Yes*, his beast rejoiced.

"Stars."

She fell back on the pallet with a choked laugh as he piled her skirts on her stomach. "Who am I to argue with that?"

Mine. His beast snarled.

Shut up!

Addy's passion perfumed the air, drawing him down. Always down. His mouth watered, his senses heightened, focused, closing out all other input—wanting, needing to know her. All of her.

He was almost there before she thought to stop him. Her hands twisted in his hair. "What are you doing?"

Lifting her legs over his shoulders, he grunted. "Tasting." He needed to taste her. To *know . . . What? What did he need to know?*

"You can't!"

It was too late. He already was. The pain in his scalp was nothing compared to the rightness of being between her thighs, the scent of her pleasure bathing his senses, so heavy, so perfect. He knew how she'd taste. How right. His gums ached in warning. His claws ex-tended. He couldn't stop. Couldn't help himself. He had to have her.

Burying his claws into the dirt beside the pelts, he held her in place with pressure on her legs before kissing the soft folds of her pussy through the opening of her pantaloons, teasing himself, teasing her, as he fought for control. His chin grazed her slit high up. She squeaked and jumped, just as she had when he'd tasted her nipples. He did it again.

She pulled his hair hard. "Oh, my God."

Smiling and gazing up at her over her belly, he asked, "Still saying I can't?"

"You shouldn't," she gasped. "It can't be decent."

He touched her with his tongue, moaning as her sweet taste spread through his being. Imprinted on his soul.

Yes, his beast sighed.

Yes, the man moaned.

Perfect, they moaned together.

"But you like it."

"Yes." The word was little more than a puff of joy that ended in a catch as he took a deeper taste. She let go of his hair and fell back— belly tight, thighs quivering.

"Oh damn, just do what you want."

He smiled against her, laughter joining passion. Another new experience. "Kind of thought I would."

A choked sound escaped her as she threw her hands over her face. Passion? Embarrassment? It didn't matter. She wasn't closing her legs against him. Wasn't pushing him away. Instead she was lying there in breathless excitement—something he could scent, feel. No woman had ever anticipated his touch as she did. It was almost as if the excitement inside him had found its match.

Yes.

For tonight, he warned his beast. Only for tonight. The beast snapped its displeasure through his mind in a discordant flux of emotion. Isaiah ignored it, forcing his claws to retract. He'd made his promise. He'd abide by it. But he wasn't going to miss a moment of it. He took another taste, reveling in her moan as his tongue touched the hard nub straining through the soft folds, focused on it, kissed it, laved it, following the twist of her hips as she cried out. He spread her with his fingers. Isaiah smiled as Addy trembled and seemed to stop breathing altogether when he caught her clit between his lips.

"Isaiah!"

Yes! That was what he wanted. Her world reduced to him, his name on her lips, her pleasure his to deliver. Yes. That was what *They*'d kept from him. The joy a man felt at pleasing his woman. The pride, the ecstasy . . . the bond.

He blinked, his lips enclosing her, his tongue just touching her. The bond was what *They*'d feared, why *They*'d kept the Reapers from females. The bond was dangerous, but to what? To her? He couldn't hurt her.

The beast surged forward, latching on to the thought in feral protest.

Mine.

No! Isaiah's protest came too late. The beast ripped through the controls he'd built through the years, shredding them with the single-minded intent it usually only exerted in battle. Too late, he recognized the power. Too late.

The beast reveled in Addy's scent and taste, taking all she had to give, feeding on her desire, taking every flinch, every gasp as its own, leading the race to the culmination with an animalistic exultation. Sucking on her clit, he brought its claws to the inside of her thigh, massaging the soft flesh, letting her feel the power. The claws dented the white flesh. She cried out.

No.

The beast ignored the order, doing as it wanted, wallowing in the lust, the power. Addy arched and cried out as he lashed her clit with a hard circular press of his tongue.

The beast snarled and pinned her hips down.

Fight. Get away.

But Addy didn't fight. Didn't try to get away. Instead, she cried his name. Not knowing, not understanding that he wasn't the one in control. Trusting him still.

Saliva flooded his mouth, blending with her taste, blending with something else, something exotic. Something uniquely them. Something man and beast savored.

Damn it, I'm not this. This isn't me.

It didn't matter. Addy cried out again, her body convulsing. The beast growled long and low. Turned its head. Opened its mouth.

No!

The protest was lost in the storm, lost in Addy's scream of delight, the beast's howl of possession. Lost in the flood of satisfaction as the beast bit the soft pad of flesh just below the seam of her hip and thigh. Addy convulsed again. The beast held on through her orgasm. The exotic taste intensified, mixing with her blood. Her pleasure.

The beast let go when she lay quivering, his satisfaction a low rumble in his throat as he rolled her over, propped her up.

"Isaiah?"

"Kneel up."

The words were thick and hot. Addy shivered but obeyed, nothing in her scent indicating fear. Son of a bitch. Why wasn't she afraid? Isaiah needed her to be afraid. Maybe then he could subdue the beast.

The beast came over her, ready to take. The man grappled with the animal, not winning the war but gentling the moment. Keeping the beast from thrusting. Easing the claiming to possession, holding Addy firmly with his hands as her pussy spread over the head of his cock. Tight. So tight.

"Oh, my God."

"Relax."

She needed to relax. He couldn't let the beast hurt her any more than he could let go of her breast. Any more than he could stop from pinching her nipple in tiny pulses that coordinated with the controlled press of his hips.

"It hurts," she gasped.

"I'm sorry," he groaned.

"But it's good, too."

Shit, why did she have to say that? The beast smiled, and damn it, even part of the man liked hearing that. He could feel the beast gathering strength. He was losing control. Soon it would be the beast. Isaiah had to prepare her. Sliding his hand down, he cupped her pussy, slipping his fingers through the slick folds. Jesus, she was wet. So beautifully wet. He found her clit, hard and still throbbing. He stroked it. She jerked back.

"Ohhh."

Too much. It was too much. Gritting his teeth, he gentled his touch, bringing her back up to the pinnacle as he pressed his cock deeper, ever aware of the beast's impatience, looking for its moment. Addy cried Isaiah's name and pressed back. Her pleasure spilled over his hand. God, she was sweet.

The beast, always the ultimate predator, took advantage in the flicker of his attention, took control, and surged deep.

The howl echoed in his head, in the lean-to. Addy screamed and collapsed. The beast followed her down, thrusting steadily, following only one thought. Deeper. His hard cock slid along her slick channel, jerking with every caress of her inner muscles, rejoicing at every quiver. Pushing ever deeper, needing to give her more. Always more. Needing her to take, to claim in return. His groin pressed against the softness of her ass. In a convulsive jerk, he pressed farther still. Enjoying the heart-shaped beauty of her ass, the perfection of his darker skin blending with the delicate white of hers. The utter rightness of taking her.

His. His.

Her pussy rippled along his cock in a prelude to release. *Yes.* Again the exultant cry came from within.

Isaiah leaned down. Addy pressed back. The curve where her neck joined her shoulder tempted him. His gums ached. More of that exotic flavor spiced his mouth, coated his tongue. His balls pulled up tight. His spine tingled, his release built. And this time when the beast bit, the man didn't protest. The lust was too strong. The woman too right. The orgasm too intense.

His.

Son of a bitch, his.

When the last spasm passed, when he could breathe, Isaiah pulled from her body, massaged her back, rolled to his side, and opened his eyes, dreading what he would see. He'd hurt her when he'd promised her stars. He'd wanted to make it perfect, but in the end he'd failed.

"I'm sorry." Such an inadequate thing to say.

"Why?" Addy asked, nestling her cheek on her arm.

"I hurt you."

She shook her head. "That was to be expected."

"I've never hurt someone like that before."

Unbelievably, she smiled. "You've never made love to a virgin before."

He brushed the hair from her cheek, belatedly checking to make sure his claws were gone. Jesus, she addled his brain. "Apparently not."

"Good."

She had no right to sound so satisfied when she should be crying.

He touched the hollow of her shoulder. The wound was already healing. In a minute it wouldn't be visible. He put his hand over it, hiding it from her. He wasn't ready to explain it. "I bit you."

"Yes." Her smile turned sultry. "Twice." Her hand cupped his cheek. "Thank you."

Two times too many. One more would have been disastrous. Thank God he'd managed some control. She shivered.

"You're cold." He reached for the blanket.

"And tired," she said, turning onto her side and scooting back against him. "Very tired."

It was the most natural thing to put his arm around her waist and pull her back against him.

"You're so warm."

And she fit in the curve of his body as if she were meant to be there. Isaiah rubbed his chin over the top of her head. "A side benefit from what *They* did."

"*They?*"

Shit. He hadn't meant to let that slip. He never slipped. What the hell was wrong with him? "Nothing."

Addy yawned. "Who are *They*?"

"Just some people I once knew."

"Knew?" She tried to turn. He kept her put. "Did you lose them in the War?"

He remembered *Their* screams. *Their* blood. The satisfaction. "Yes."

She yawned again and nestled her cheek against his upper arm. "I'm sorry."

He wasn't. Tucking her closer, he willed the memories away. *They* had no place here tonight. He didn't want anything between them except the remnants of ecstasy. He had enough to think on.

"Go to sleep, Addy."

"But . . ."

"Go to sleep or I won't make love to you again."

He smiled slightly when she immediately went still. Staring off into the dark, he rolled the night's events over in his mind, too restless to sleep. His gums still ached and that strange taste still lingered in his mouth. He'd bitten her hard enough that she should have been screaming. Hard enough that she'd have a scar, but she'd come in a torrent of ecstasy that he'd felt all the way to his soul. He checked her shoulder. The marks were gone now. He didn't know what that was about, but his beast was silent and satiated in a way it had never been before. Almost content. That couldn't be good. Son of a bitch, what the hell else could go wrong?

⊰ 10 ⊱

"JUST GOING TO SLIP INTO TOWN UNDETECTED, HUH? TAKE up as if nothing ever happened?" Isaiah asked dryly.

If she hadn't thought she'd damage her elbow on his rock-hard stomach, she would have elbowed him right then. If telling him to shut up would have had any effect beyond tickling his sense of humor, she would have told him to shut up. Unfortunately, the meeting with her cousins was going to be dramatic enough. She didn't need to be in the middle of a dispute with her rescuer as soon as they rode up. Never mind the issue that ladies didn't tell gentlemen, no matter how disreputable, to shut up, and women who wanted to give the illusion of being in control didn't lose their tempers.

"So I was wrong."

Addy watched as the riders came over the hill, recognizing her cousin's big palomino right off. Cole only rode that horse when he was out for blood.

"Uh-huh."

She set her jaw and reached for her worry stone, stroking her thumb over the smooth surface ten times before stating calmly, "This just requires a slight adjustment to my plan."

He chuckled, his chest vibrating against her side, reminding her again how little she knew about the man and all that she did know was hard and uncompromising. She watched the approaching riders, noting Cole's ramrod-straight posture.

In contrast to Cole's aggressive posture, Isaiah seemed relaxed against her, almost as if he was anticipating the coming confrontation. Nothing in his drawl indicated tension, either.

"A big change, if you ask me."

Good grief! What was it with men? Why did they always look forward to a fight? "No one asked you."

She cut him a glance out of the corner of her eye, very aware of his body behind hers, his thighs beneath hers. To anyone watching, they presented a very intimate picture. Hot on the heels of that thought came another. Her cousins would kill Isaiah if they knew just how intimate he had been with her. She'd seen enough fights to know how Isaiah would look after her cousins vented their displeasure. That was not acceptable. "Do you or do you not want me to tell them you're not my kidnapper when they catch up with us?"

That grunt could have been laughter. Contrary man.

"That's not an answer."

"I'm waiting."

"For what?"

"To see how aggravated your rescuers are before I make a commitment."

She looked at him over her shoulder. "Did you just make a joke?"

"I'm a killer. A sense of humor isn't something I brag on."

"That doesn't mean you don't have one."

"Doesn't mean I do, either."

"I think you have one."

"I don't."

He was lying. She remembered the night before, how he'd made her fly without hurting her. She touched her shoulder where he'd so erotically bitten her. And then she remembered how he'd spooned around her afterward, his concern, the way he'd stroked her arm soothingly and rested his chin on the top of her head. "I think maybe you're not so much a killer as you'd like me to believe."

"Don't chase fairy tales with me, little girl."

Gruff and hard, the order brooked no resistance. The tone irked her as much as that "little girl." "I don't believe in fairy tales."

Another snort. "You do if you think I'm anything less than a killer."

He was always trying to make her think badly of him. "Huh!"

Addy didn't have any doubt that Isaiah could kill. But to define himself as solely that? No. That she didn't believe. And darn it, it irked her that he always made himself look so bad when he'd been nothing but good to her. "Maybe I just see you as more."

"Shit."

"I'd appreciate it if you'd watch your language."

"That'll cost you more."

She rubbed her worry stone between her fingers. She didn't have any more money to spare. "Fine. Swear to your heart's content, but I'm still believing what I want to."

"You're a means to an end, lady."

Addy rubbed the stone harder at the likely truth of that, pushing away the hurt that last night meant nothing to him. "Because you want the money?"

"Why else?"

She didn't know. But she found it very hard to believe money was the motivation for anything this man did. He'd looked too settled in the barren lean-to. Too comfortable in the remoteness of his home. The riders ahead veered to the left. Cole had spotted them. "Well then, you'd better give me my money's worth when my cousins get here."

"You afraid of them?"

Cole had a tendency to yell. "Cole can be unpleasant."

The muscles beneath her thighs tightened. "Toward you?"

Did she imagine it, or did Isaiah's grip tighten, too?

How much to confess to? "Sometimes."

"Why?"

"Cole thinks I'm headstrong."

"That's not necessarily always bad—"

"Thank you!"

"But I can see a few cases where it would be," he continued dryly, as if she hadn't interrupted him.

She wasn't opening that door if he was going to leave it closed.

Isaiah was persistent. "So why does your cousin think you're headstrong?"

"He has the silly notion that I don't take the proper precautions with my safety."

"I think I'm beginning to like him already."

"It's not your job to like my cousins. It's your job to keep unpleasantness away from me."

His hand dropped to the butt of the rifle in the scabbard by her right thigh. It was a well-formed, lean, and sinewy hand. "You want me to shoot them?"

"No!"

"It would cut down on unpleasantness."

"It would also cut my family down to three."

"That your cousin Cole on that big palomino?"

"Yes." Isaiah's chin brushed her temple as he checked out her cousins' approach. For an inconsequential contact, it had too strong an impact on her pulse. "Might not be a bad plan. Your kin's driving those horses with the intent to kill."

She wished she could argue, but her cousins were riding hard. "Well, they should be happy, not mad."

"Why's that?"

She sighed and shifted, wishing it wouldn't be indelicate to rub the inside of her thigh where Isaiah had bitten her. It itched now as much as it had burned so exotically the night before. "For sure, this incident will be ammunition in Cole's arsenal of arguments as to why I should not live by myself."

She felt more than heard Isaiah's chuckle. "I'm liking him more and more."

And she was beginning to like Isaiah's dry sense of humor that he supposedly didn't have. "That won't last."

They were getting closer. Their expressions clearer. From here she could see the dark shadow of three days' growth of beard on her cousins' faces. The darker spots of sweat on the horses' chests. They'd been riding hard. Their tempers were going to be short.

She had the irrational urge to grab the reins and turn the horse and run. Cole was not going to be reasonable about this. He, Reese, and Dane might just hog-tie her and drag her back to the ranch. She couldn't let them do that. They just didn't understand how the totality of their love combined with their definition of protection was as much a prison as the one from which they'd rescued her. As much as they wanted to wrap her in cotton wool and tuck her away on a tidy shelf, she'd lived too much to be content being sheltered. Experienced too much to believe that anybody's opinion of what was right for her was better than her own. She was a woman, not a child. And she'd make her own choices.

Isaiah's fingers brushed her thigh as he reached for the rifle. Ahead of her, Cole reached for his. Addy braced her feet on top of Isaiah's and stood, plastering a huge smile on her face and waving. From what she'd seen of Isaiah and what she knew of Cole, both were more likely to shoot than wait for her to get out an explanation. A tug on the back of her skirt plopped her back down.

Isaiah was as difficult as Cole in his own way and that just wasn't going to work. She'd had enough of violence. Tending bullet wounds was bound to end in delay and she wanted to get home, back to her bakery, her house, her china, her things, her order.

She smiled and waved again to the oncoming riders. "Cole!"

Cole braced the rifle butt on his thigh. Slightly behind him and covering his back as always, her other cousins rode, sun glinting dully off the barrels of their guns. They were an impressive sight. Hard, deadly men on a mission. She shivered. Sometimes she forgot just how lethal her cousins could be. She wanted to throw her arms wide and shield Isaiah as soon as Cole focused on him.

"Put your gun away," she whispered.

"Not a chance."

"You're supposed to be looking harmless."

Another one of those grunts. His chest pressed against her back, pushing her forward. He tucked his arm around her waist and pulled her back against him.

"Nobody's going to believe I'm your bodyguard if I go lookin' harmless."

Cole was close enough that she could see the frown between his brows as his gaze dropped to Isaiah's hand on her stomach. She gave a tug, but Isaiah didn't let go. She dug her nails in. All that got was another of those contrary chuckles.

"Take your hand off me."

"Why?"

"You're upsetting Cole." She looked over her shoulder and

was just in time to catch the edge of his smile. "You want to pro-
voke him!"

"It's been a dull ride."

Elbowing him in the stomach was looking better and better. Too
bad it might cause Cole to shoot him.

"I hired you, remember? You're supposed to do what I say."

"I'm supposed to do what you say up to the point of obtaining
your goal. If you roll over and play dead now, or make me roll over
and play dead now, you're going to be back at that ranch faster than
you can blink those pretty blue eyes."

He had a point. But still, he didn't need to keep his hand so intimately pressed against her body. "Find another place for your hand."

It slid upward.

"A decent place," she clarified. They were running out of time.
Isaiah didn't remove his hand, which could only mean one thing. She
looked back over her shoulder again. She was going to have a darn
crick in her neck from doing this so often. "What do you want?"

He didn't pretend not to understand. "I want you to let me handle this."

"They're my cousins."

"Exactly."

"And what does that mean?"

"They're not going to be reasonable."

"And you will?"

"Didn't say that, either."

"Then what are you saying?"

"I'm just saying, I'm better at handling unreasonable."

Well, he probably did have a better grasp on it, seeing as how he
was the most unreasonable person she'd ever met, but that didn't
mean she was just going to roll over. "You think that means that it
qualifies you to handle my cousins?"

He pulled the horse up. "I think I've got a better shot of getting you what you want than you do."

She glanced back at Cole. His eyes were narrowed against the sun, his jaw set. This wasn't good. She knew that look. It meant he'd come to a decision. She bit her lip. In another minute he'd be close enough to overhear.

Cole cocked his gun and centered the muzzle on Isaiah. And her.

Addy dug her nails deeper into Isaiah's hand. "Then start handling it."

"THAT'LL be far enough," Cole ordered.

Their horse took two more steps before Isaiah pulled it up.

"Hello, Cole." She nodded to the other two men. "Dane, Reese."

Reese smiled. "Hey, Addy girl. You all right?"

"It's been a rough three days."

"That doesn't answer the question," Dane prodded.

Isaiah didn't take his hand from her waist. It didn't really matter. She wasn't getting down anyway. Not when Cole had that mulestubborn look on his face. Dane's horse tossed his head. The bridle jangled loudly in the sudden silence. Addy licked her lips not trusting the calm. With Cole calm was often a prelude to the storm

"Thanks to Isaiah, I am."

Dane didn't smile. Cole motioned with the rifle.

"Get on down, Addy."

"No."

She waited for the explosion. It didn't come. Cole just sat silently taking in her refusal and Isaiah's presence. Waiting.

And as always, she felt the need to fidget. To apologize. To surrender. Isaiah tightened his grip on her and she tightened her grip on her worry stone, rubbing it through her fingers faster and faster.

She'd always had a problem standing up to Cole. She could never forget how much he'd done for her, how much he'd sacrificed for her. Whenever she wanted to go against him, the guilt drained her dry.

With a sharp motion of his hand that almost qualified as a snap, Cole pointed to the ground. "We'll exchange pleasantries later. Get down."

Either Cole couldn't read her as well as she read him, or he could read her too well and saw her weakness. Closing her fist around her worry stone, she shook her head. "Isaiah's taking me home."

Cole angled the muzzle a bit higher, in direct line with Isaiah's head. "Is that so?"

It was Isaiah who answered. His voice was just as calm, just as unemotional. "That's so."

Maybe she shouldn't have told Isaiah to handle it. Cole didn't take well to being challenged.

"And just who are you to be telling me anything?"

"No one."

Cole's gaze narrowed. "Well, Mr. No One, the lady is my cousin and my responsibility—"

"Not anymore."

"The hell you say. Addy?"

She couldn't get a word out.

"Addy hired me to see to her safety." Isaiah goaded.

"We're here. She's safe," Dane cut in.

"Not according to her."

"Bullshit. Addy doesn't need protecting from us," Dane snapped.

"Addy?" Cole asked.

She didn't know what to say, where to look.

"You feeling cornered, Addy girl?" Reese asked.

Of the three cousins, Reese was the one who understood the best. Maybe because, as the youngest of the brothers, he'd experienced the weight of Cole's protection, too. Or maybe it was just because he was who he was—a Cameron with the self-confidence to see what he wanted to see.

"I've told you I can take care of myself."

"You think hiring a stranger you met God knows where is taking care of yourself?"

"Yes."

"Son of a bitch."

"Watch your language," Isaiah ordered. All eyes turned to immediately to him.

"Stay out of it," Cole ordered right back.

"Can't do that."

The muscles in Cole's jaw bunched. "Whatever she's paying you, I'll double."

"Thanks . . ."

Addy's heart stopped in her chest.

"But I like to finish one job before starting the next."

The wave of relief that went through Addy was almost debilitating.

Isaiah's hand closed over hers and squeezed once before, with a strength that had her blinking, he lifted and dropped her over the other side of the horse. "Get back."

She did immediately, her breath catching in her throat. "Don't kill him."

"Tying my hands with that, aren't you?"

She hadn't been talking to Isaiah. Before she could point that out, Cole said, "If he leaves now, I might let him live."

Isaiah swung down off his horse and handed the reins to Addy. She took them, putting her hand on his arm. "Don't."

He looked at her hand and then at her face and nodded. "No killing."

"Thank you."

Cole swung down from his horse, too. "Nice of you to make things easy for me, Addy."

"Make what? You leave him alone, Cole."

Cole dropped the reins and took a step forward. "Some body-guard you hired, that he hides behind a woman's skirt."

Isaiah took her hand off his arm, putting himself between her and Cole. "Get back."

Cole kept coming. She wanted to run. She wanted to get between Cole and Isaiah. She wanted to put her hands over her head and cower as the tension slipped past her control and found the memories always so ready to come forward, take over. She swayed. Isaiah pulled her against his chest. Her cheek rested there.

"You son of a bitch!" The snarl came from Dane, who stood beyond Isaiah.

Too late, Addy realized how the embrace had to look to her cousins, who saw her as vulnerable. In the aftermath of her being stolen, a strange man being so familiar with her had to look bad.

One second she was in Isaiah's arms, and the next she was standing alone. She stumbled and braced herself against the horse. It sidestepped and snorted. In the same instant, she saw Cole move in on Isaiah, saw Isaiah spin so fast she wasn't sure he'd even moved. Saw him catch Cole's arm and turned him about. Saw Dane and Reese bring up their rifles, take aim.

"No!"

But it was too late. In the split second before her cousins fired, Isaiah had Cole in front of him. She closed her eyes. Oh no. The guns went off. Curses flew. Dirt sprayed her skirts. The worry stone bit into her palm. She couldn't open her eyes. Was Cole or Isaiah dead? Neither was conceivable.

"Goddamn it, Cole."

That was Dane.

"Hell of a move, stranger."

That was Reese. She opened her eyes. Isaiah was in a half crouch, a knife to Cole's throat, staring at Dane and Reese.

"Sheathe the rifles."

Neither moved to comply.

"Isaiah—"

It was as far as she got. Isaiah cut her off.

"I remember my promise."

"Then I guess that means we don't have much to worry about," Dane drawled.

"In two seconds, I'm going to put this knife through his spine."

Addy gasped.

"He won't die," Isaiah confirmed.

"He just won't be able to move," Reese finished dryly.

"You're a cold-blooded son of a bitch," Cole said as if he weren't facing paralysis.

"I get the job done."

"Even when hampered by a woman's weakness." Cole nodded carefully to Dane and Reese. They sheathed their rifles. "Interesting."

Isaiah removed the knife from Cole's throat and stepped back. Cole stood, his eyes on the knife in Isaiah's hand. So were Addy's. There was blood on the tip and a few drops on Cole's neck. Her stomach heaved. Isaiah held out his hand. Without thinking, she took it. He pulled her into his side. It was natural to lean her head against his chest. Breathing his scent settled her stomach and her nerves. The spot on her thigh itched and warmed. So did the one on her shoulder. She put her hand over it.

Cole's eyebrows lifted. He settled his hat back on his head. "Where did you find this one, Addy?"

"He found me."

"Is that so?"

"Yes."

Cole looked at Isaiah. "You just stumbled upon her?"

"Something like that."

"By our reckoning, at least thirteen men rode with the bandits."

"That would be about right."

"And they just handed her over."

"We discussed the matter."

"Like you just discussed things with me?"

Isaiah smiled a very cold, provoking smile.

"Son of a bitch," Dane drawled.

"Not many men except Cole could do that," Reese pointed out.

"Not even I could do that," Cole corrected.

Yes, he could. He'd done it before. Addy had seen it. She rubbed the spot in the hollow of her shoulder, and whispered, "I want to go home."

Isaiah nodded. "Then we'll go."

Cole headed back to his horse and gathered up the reins. "We'll all go."

"Suit yourself."

Isaiah swung up on the horse and held out his hand for hers. Without a qualm, Addy put hers in it. He might be the kind of man who could sever a man's spine without a blink, but he was also the man who'd sworn to keep her safe. When Isaiah's gaze met hers, she gave him a tentative smile. He didn't smile back, just lifted her up.

"She doesn't have to ride in your lap," Cole growled.

"You're wrong about that." Isaiah pulled the horse up when it drew even with the brothers. "And you're wrong about something else, too. She's not weak."

⊰ 11 ⊱

THE FRESH SCENT OF YEAST AND LEMON OIL WELCOMED Addy back into its embrace as soon as she renetered her kitchen after changing her clothes. She breathed deeply, letting the familiarity sink in. The dough she'd prepped before changing because she'd needed that reconnection with normal would almost be ready. Orders were no doubt piled up outside the front in the box set there to collect them. Wood needed bringing in and the stove needed firing but she was home. Inside calm, slowly blossomed. She was home.

Hard to believe after the events of the last three days, but looking around it was almost as if she'd never left. The bright blue flowers in the wallpaper, chosen because they didn't remind her of blood, shone brightly against the pale yellow background. She'd paid her cousin dearly for the paper. He'd bought it off the wagon of a peddler from back East who'd misjudged the wealth he'd find along the way to the gold mines of San Francisco. She'd never regretted the expenditure.

She loved the paper. She loved her cousin. She'd even begun to love the life she'd made for herself. But now, because someone had a grudge against Cole, his guilt was kicking in again and her lifestyle was in danger.

She sensed more than heard Isaiah come up behind her.

"It's just the way you left it."

Was it her imagination, or was there a question in that statement? She looked around the room. It wasn't exactly as she'd left it. She'd been drinking her tea when they'd taken her. She remembered it spilling, her panic at the thought of the teacup breaking. Her cup wasn't on the table, however. Instead, it was on the counter on the towel beside the sink, the handle facing inward so it wouldn't get broken. Exactly the way she always left it—the way she would have left it if she hadn't been kidnapped.

A chill went down her spine as she stared at that cup. There was only one person who could have done that. Reaching for her worry stone, she rubbed it between her fingers. "Just how long have you been watching me?"

Isaiah didn't answer right away. And when she turned around, he was eyeing her carefully. That didn't bode well. She remembered how he'd slipped through the darkness like one of the shadows, how he'd had those horrible evil bandits shaking in terror. She remembered how he'd stood up to her cousins, how he'd saved her, how wonderfully he'd made love to her. She took a shallow breath and squeezed her worry stone between her fingers. Maybe it didn't matter how long he'd been watching her, maybe she had a better question to ask. "*Why* have you been watching me?"

His expression went totally blank. That was an answer he didn't want to give her.

She considered pushing for a response, but she took in the breadth of his shoulders and that wild look in his eyes that never really went away, and she reconsidered.

As good as Isaiah had been to her, he was still an unknown quantity. A man likely broken by the War. A man of unstable temperament. Pushing the subject could make him react badly—or worse. She looked around her little kitchen, the haven she'd created for herself. He could leave. And if he left, her cousins would find out and one of two things would happen. Either they'd place one of their own guards on her or they'd drag her kicking and screaming back to the relative safety of the ranch. The ranch wasn't all they'd cracked it up to be, but it was the land over which they had dominion.

She looked around the kitchen again and then looked at Isaiah again. Sometimes a woman had to take a chance. Beneath that rough exterior perhaps was a man damaged by war, but he was also a man with a will of iron and she'd hired that will of iron to be her muscle. Whether Isaiah was unstable, or whether other people thought he was appropriate, deep down, she trusted him to give her what she wanted. That was all that mattered. She sighed. That was all she had.

Addy held up her hand. "Never mind. I don't want to know."

His eyebrow went up. As always, he seemed to say more with the flick of an eyebrow, or twitch of a lip, than most said with a thousand words. "Why?"

"I've decided it doesn't matter."

"Why?"

Always he was asking "why." It annoyed her. "Because whatever happened in your past is the past, and right now, I need you to be exactly what you are." Walking over to the cupboard, she got her cup and opened her tea tin. The lid rattled as she set it down. She picked up her kettle and gave it a shake. It was too much to hope there'd be water in it.

Isaiah held out his hand. "I'll get you some."

"Thank you."

As he took the kettle, his fingers brushed hers. Heat shot up her arm. She couldn't contain her start. The bite on her shoulder gathered the heat before sending it shooting to her core. She shifted her position as the mark on her thigh heated, too. What was it about the man that made him a match to her flame?

Isaiah stopped at the door, his expression inscrutable, and asked, "What am I to you?"

It was just a look. Nothing to make her nervous, but her breath caught anyway, and her pulse kicked up a notch. And the hairs on the back of her neck rose. Addy didn't dare lie. "A means to an end. Why?"

"Just curious." He turned and walked through the door, closing it quietly behind him.

And it was her turn to wonder why. Again.

ONLY after he got to the small stone well did Isaiah realize he probably should have grabbed the bucket, too. Addy was going to need more water than this today. After her excursion, she was going to want a bath. A long, hot bath. He eyed the distance from the kitchen to the well, calculated if he had time to get in and out before she noticed, and decided not. He'd have to slip in later and get the bucket. She should have her bath.

The back door creaked. Addy stepped out onto the porch and bent to gather kindling from the small supply there. As with everything, she did it with elegant control. He admired the graceful arch of her back as she bent—the elegance of her neck, the fineness of her hands. A scratch on the back of the left glared red in the sunlight. Anger rumbled again deep inside. They'd had no right to touch her. She straightened the kindling riding her hip.

The light flickered from bright to dark. Time slipped from Isaiah's grasp as reality wavered like an image viewed through a glass of water, expanding and contracting, slowing until he could almost see the woman. Almost see the stick in her hand, almost feel the blow. Birds still sang but he wasn't there. He knew that. On some level, Isaiah knew this was the past. He braced himself for the pain. The anger. It flowed over him in a torrent he couldn't stop. Along with it came helplessness. The protective growl started deep inside, building on that unfathomable rhythm until it found his pulse. His racing pulse. Closing his eyes, Isaiah focused on his heartbeat, struggling to slow it as he fought the memory and the emotions. He wasn't sure, but he'd theorized the beast's power subsided with his pulse rate. It was worth a try. Anything that could stop the transformation was worth a try. He might never be human again, but there had to be a way to fake it. As his pulse slowed, so did the image. The beast faded to the background. With the fading image came composure and reality. He looked at the rusted iron pump.

Water. He was here to get water. Holding that chore as his anchor, Isaiah pumped the handle several times before he remembered he needed to prime it. A few minutes later, he felt the pressure that signified water was coming. Almost detached, he watched as he snapped the kettle under the spray before the water could hit the ground. He had a memory, a quick flashback of the past, of a time when— He didn't know when it was. Just a time when fetching water had been difficult, when spilling it was an offense. An image of a bucket tipping. *Past.* Water poured over his hand, cold and wet. *Present.* Water had spilled then, too, splashing on the ground, the stain in the dust spreading right along with his terror.

Trapped in the past, he glanced at the house, seeing instead of the neat two-story wood frame structure, mud and thatch, a dark hole in the ground, a place of terror haunted by the shadow of an angry woman and the child who'd just wanted a home. He tried to focus on the memory. It was the past, maybe even his past. He shook his head as the memory faded. Or maybe it was just something he'd heard—a tale from a book. There was so much confusion whenever he reached for who he was, who he'd been before the dark time. Inside, he felt the beast stretch and howl, responding as it always did to tension. He slammed the door shut.

The beast didn't belong here. Here he needed to be a man. Water sloshed in the kettle as he jerked at the thought. He had no business thinking like that. He was what he was, and whatever that was, whatever it meant, he wasn't human anymore.

Pouring the excess water out of the kettle, Isaiah headed back to the house. The sounds of his footsteps marked his progress while a strange feeling churned in his blood. Excitement, he realized as he climbed the two steps to the back porch. He was excited to be with Addy. He shook his head, trying to understand it.

Excitement was something he was used to feeling while he waited for the opportunity to complete a mission. To kill, he admitted to himself, tired of dressing up what he'd been. The beast enjoyed killing with a primitive intensity. He paused, hand on the door, drawing a deep breath. Checking. The beast was unpredictable. He didn't want to risk it mistaking this excitement for the excitement of a kill.

Addy's scent came to him, sweet and hot. A sound, almost a purr, hummed in his head. Isaiah relaxed. One thing was clear. The beast didn't want Addy's blood. At least not that way. His cock throbbed as her scent sank deep into his being and he remembered the pleasure of tasting her.

He took a moment, beating back the beast's rise that accompanied anticipation, fighting the appearance of his canines and his claws, wondering why he even bothered. The change came when it came. There was no controlling it. To the best of his knowledge, no one had ever managed to control it. But then again, none of the Reapers had much knowledge about what they were. They'd been taken to the dark place, injected, tortured, trained, released only to accomplish a purpose, and then brought back for the drug that offered them peace from the beast's ravings. At least they thought it'd been peace, but it had only been a form of subjugation. When the Reapers had realized that, they'd rebelled.

He smiled, remembering that night. The revenge that had been taken for the lives they'd lost, the hopes that had been dashed, and a future rife with uncertainty had been bloody, thorough. Beasts turning on masters, claiming for themselves an uncertain freedom. The Reapers had taken their lives back that night and then they'd headed west. In their wake they'd left the physical prisons, but the mental ones they carried on their backs, each man with his own demon to battle. They didn't know what they were. What they were capable of. What to expect. They just knew that in the wildness of the new West they might find a home for what they'd become. Maybe in that vast, lawless land they'd find a way to free themselves from the pain, the death, and the killing.

Pain in his hand alerted Isaiah to the fact that he was crushing the doorknob. He didn't know how the others were faring, but he hadn't found much peace.

With a steady pull he bent the knob back to realign it. He gave it a test twist. It would work, but it wouldn't fool Addy. She'd notice the discrepancy. She noticed anything amiss in her world. With that as a fact, Isaiah still hadn't figured out why she'd let him in, despite what she'd told him.

A means to an end.

From his standpoint, it wasn't much of a reason, but he wasn't a woman with no muscle and no leverage. The door opened. Addy stood there, a slight frown on her face. Inside, there was that start of recognition he always felt when he looked at her face, followed immediately by the sense of excitement and anticipation. He took a breath, inhaling her scent, making it a part of him. The aroma of flour and yeast blended with her essence. She was baking. He belatedly noticed her yellow apron tied over the yellow dress she'd donned when she'd gotten home.

"Oh good, you've got the water."

"Yes." He didn't think he'd blacked out for long, but time could be elusive while trapped in the memories. He waited to see if she was annoyed.

She smiled. He liked the way her teeth were white and even, with the slightest bit of overbite that added a sexy edge to her smile. "The pump can be stubborn."

"I didn't have a problem."

Her smile faded. He'd been too abrupt. She stepped back and motioned him in with a flour-coated hand.

"Could you pour some of that into the pot on the stove?"

She wanted him to go into the room. Such a small thing. Such an impossible thing. He stared at her outstretched hand, focusing on the faint lines etched into the palm, counting them. One, two, three, four . . . The walls bulged and retreated. The wallpaper blurred at the edges. No. He set his jaw. Not now. Not now. The tang of copper filled his mouth as his canines cut anew through his gums. His fingers itched as his claws prepared to extend.

"Isaiah?" The softness of Addy's voice cloaked the beast in a tempting lure, lulling it into a softer prowl. "Are you all right?

Goddamn it, he would be. Isaiah switched his focus to Addy's face, the curve of her cheek, the strength of her jaw, the softness of her lips . . . The mirage retreated and once again it was just a room with pretty wallpaper and scrubbed floors.

He nodded his head as Addy took a step back, making room for him to pass. If she knew what he was, what they'd made him, she wouldn't be inviting him in. But she didn't have a clue. Somehow, he looked normal to her. "I'm fine."

"Then come in." Her fingers brushed his as she motioned him forward again. A tingle of awareness went down his spine, and from the catch in her breath, she'd felt that awareness, too. Her "It's getting chilly out" was a bit breathless.

He made it two feet into the room before the walls started closing in on him.

She moved past him to the worktable. "I need about a cup of water in that small pot before you put the kettle on the burner."

He could do that. He was sweating before he finished the maneuver, though. Who the hell knew how much water was in the pot? A cup, a gallon. The kettle settled on the back burner with a clank. When he looked over his shoulder, Addy was fussing with a bowl. In his peripheral vision, the walls started to move. Shit. He needed something new on which to focus. The only thing in sight was Addy.

"What are you doing?"

"Making bread."

It was late in the afternoon. "Now?"

She shrugged. "It soothes me."

She rubbed her cheek on her shoulder. "Could you check the water in the pot? It should feel uncomfortable but not too hot on your finger."

She wanted him to stick his finger in the water. He could do that. It was manageable.

"It's hot, but not too hot."

"Good. Could you bring it here?"

His beast roared "yes." He wanted to be close enough to breathe in her scent again. His human snapped "no." The beast won. In five steps, he was at her side.

"Pour it here." She pointed to a well in the flour as soon as he got close enough.

He poured, breathing the combination of her scent, flour and yeast, and a hint of . . . honey? The combination was . . . soothing. He didn't move away, just watched as she stirred the mixture together.

"What does the water do?"

"When combined with the honey, it wakes up the yeast."

"What happens then?"

Her smile caught him by surprise, flashing past his guard, finding and stroking his beast to life. Or was it the man? It was getting harder to tell where one left off and the other began.

"Magic." Covering the bowl with a cloth, she put it in the side oven and took another covered bowl out. As she straightened, she asked. "Want to be part of it?"

Yes, he realized with surprise, he did. "Sure."

She removed the cover. More dough. She divided the dough in half before nodding to the daisy print apron to the side. "You might want to put on an apron."

He eyed the feminine garment. There were limits to how far he'd go to stay in that kitchen and near that illusion of peace she offered. "I'll risk getting dirty."

She grinned. "There's no one to see."

She looked so pure in the afternoon sunlight. So clean. So . . . perfect. "There's you."

She went still and her smile took on that tension of someone unsure. He motioned with his hands. "I need to wash up."

"Go ahead. I'll wait."

He bet she would. The woman had the patience of a saint when she wanted to. He poured a little of the water from the pitcher by the basin over his hands and quickly scooped some soap into them. She seemed to be waiting for something. Belatedly he remembered to say, "Thank you."

She didn't look away as he'd expected, just watched him wash up. The hairs on the back of his neck stood on end as she watched him come back with an unconscious hunger in her gaze. He hadn't been mistaken. The attraction between them was mutual. And stronger since their "one night only." Yet another complication in an already complicated year. But at least he could control this one.

"Are you ready?" she asked when he got back to the table.

"Yeah."

She moved over, making room for him beside her at the table. "They call this 'kneading the dough.' If you do it right, your bread will be light and airy."

"And if I don't?"

"It'll sit like a rock."

"I've had a few of those loaves."

Her smile was natural as she scooped flour from a bowl and sprinkled it on the table. "Well, if you don't want to make one of those, you should knead it until it feels soft and stretchy."

"And I'll know this when I feel it?"

"Yes, if you have the heart of a baker."

He liked to think he could have the heart of something besides a killer. But he wasn't sure a baker was it. Then again, he didn't know much about himself. Or what he was capable of. He touched his finger to the dough. It stuck.

"Flour your hands."

Of course. He copied her movements, floured his hands then the space on the table before dropping the ball of dough on it. It landed with a soft splat. Flour poofed outward.

"Now knead it."

He watched her hand movements. Fold, press with a rocking motion of the heel of her hand, and then a quarter turn of the dough and repeat. It didn't look hard or particularly soothing, but when Addy glanced at him expectantly, he followed her movements. And to his surprise, as the dough absorbed the flour and began to take on a bit of resistance, he fell into a rhythm unique to himself, one that quieted the racing of his mind and offered a soothing peace. The muscles in the back of his neck relaxed.

"How long do we do this?"

"For me it's about eleven minutes but it may be more or less for you."

Eleven minutes of peace. It sounded like heaven. He kept kneading. Press, rock, turn, fold. Press, rock, turn, fold. And as he did, the peace spread. It was almost with regret that he felt the tension in the dough reach a level that just felt . . . right. He forced himself to stop. Looking up, he found her watching him.

"I think mine's ready."

"All right." She reached beneath the table to the lower shelf and pulled up a round wooden pan. "Here. Put it in here. This is a brioche pan."

"A what?"

"A decorative pan that will give your loaf of bread a nice shape when it's done."

The pan had grooves carved into the edges, like the petals of a flower. He could picture a loaf of bread with a fancy top like that. He liked it that something he did would end up pretty. He started to put his dough in. She stopped him with a hand on his forearm.

"I'm sorry. We have to oil it first."

He understood. "So it won't stick."

"Yes."

"What do I oil it with?"

She pushed a clay jar toward him. "Butter."

He scooped a handful and spread it around the bowl.

"Then sprinkle it with flour. Just put a handful in the middle and shake it all around. But not too—"

Too late. The big shake he gave the bowl had flour flying up in his face. He coughed and waved away the dust. "Not too hard? Was that what you were going to say?"

She chuckled. "You were too fast for me."

He probably had been, but at least his bread wasn't ruined. He put his dough in the pan. "What do we do now?"

With the edge of her apron, she reached up toward his face. His first instinct was to jerk back, but this was Addy and he was trying to be normal. He held perfectly still. She wiped flour from his cheek. "We let that rise."

"Rise?"

"As warm as it is now, it'll probably only be about an hour."

He looked at his dough sitting in the fancy bowl. "And when it's done? What then?"

She smiled at him as she spread butter around her own pan. One not as fancy as his, he noticed. "We take it out and then we eat it for dinner."

"Do you do this every day?"

She nodded. "I like running a bakery. I like baking bread." She shrugged. "It sells well, it soothes me, and it gives me a level of independence. Not much there not to like."

"You like feeding people?"

"Well, there is something very satisfying about watching people enjoy what you've prepared. It's a happy thing."

It was that. Isaiah looked at his pan as she covered it with a wet towel. Providing food for people was a far cry from taking away their lives.

Despite the other pan being ready, she didn't put her dough in. "You're not doing yours?"

She shook her head and reached toward her pocket before catching herself. She rubbed her neck instead. "It's not ready yet. I need to work it more."

From the way she was rubbing the hollow of her neck, he was willing to bet *she* wasn't ready. Unfortunately, his dough was done and he had an hour to kill.

"Are you going to open the bakery tomorrow?"

"I have to." She grabbed a box from the counter behind them and dumped it on the table. Pieces of paper spilled out. "These are orders that people need filled. I'm behind as it is. If I wait much longer, I won't have any customers left. While you were getting water, I went out front. These are orders people left."

"They were expecting you back?"

She shrugged. "I like to think they were optimistic, but likely Cole kept it quiet as long as he could so people dropped off their order in the box like they always have."

"You think they still want them?"

She shot him a grin. "If not, I'm going to pretend they do."

He decided he liked this side of her. "You need the money?"

"I've got to pay you, don't I?"

He couldn't very well deny that. With the tip of his finger he dragged one of the pieces over to him. Muffins.

"How do you make muffins?" He'd never thought about preparing his own food that way. Eating had been a means to an end, but he had a vague memory of eating muffins. It was a happy memory, he thought. The concept of making his own muffins became more intriguing.

"They're quicker than bread."

"Good."

"Well," she said, "if you're going to keep baking, you really need to put on an apron."

Isaiah looked at the pink gingham apron hanging on the hook. "I don't think so."

"Your clothes are going to get ruined."

"I'll wash them."

"All right."

She spun a piece of paper toward him. "Mrs. McGillicuddy wants apple bread. It's something she has every spring when her daughter visits from back East."

"How do we make that?"

"Well, first we have to peel the apples. She brought us some from her cellar. They're in that sack by the back door."

He could do that. Isaiah pulled a knife out of his boot. He was good with a knife. "I came prepared."

Addy looked at it and shuddered. "I usually use a kitchen knife."

He felt stupid as he put it back in its sheath. "Of course."

When civilized people prepared food, they probably used different utensils than the ones used for killing people. Addy handed him a small knife.

"You can use this." He tested the edge on his thumb. It wasn't sharp. "It'll take me forever to peel anything with this."

"Sorry. I'm not very good about remembering to sharpen."

"Do you have a whetstone?"

"On the back steps." Wiping her hands on her apron, she hurried to the door, scooped up a burlap sack, and handed it to him when he reached her side. Sunlight spilled in through the opening, catching her hair and giving her that halo look. He loved her hair—he could look at it all day. He'd spent so long in the dark that the play of light in her hair was irresistible.

He curled his fingers tightly around the apple and stilled the purr of the beast. *Addy isn't for me.* He repeated it four more times before he found the whetstone. He grabbed the stone and, with vicious strokes, started sharpening the knife she'd given him.

Just one more thing to lay at *Their* feet. He whipped the knife down the stone. A life with no future.

⊰ 12 ⊱

ISAIAH WAS HALFWAY THROUGH SHARPENING THE KNIFE when he heard the approach of hoofbeats. He stood, deciphering the information. Two horses, more than likely Cole and Reese. Cole because he needed control. Reese because he was a peacemaker and his protectiveness toward his cousin took a different form than Cole's. Dane struck Isaiah as a man who preferred to stay back and control from behind the scenes, hence his not coming along on this ride. Which was just as well. Two Camerons were enough with which to deal.

The Cameron brothers had the reputation of being a fighting team that was as lethal as it was impressive. Isaiah had had a taste earlier when he'd taken down Cole. It hadn't been as easy as it should have been, seeing as Isaiah was a Reaper and Cole a human. However, the man had the reflexes of a cat, and if Addy hadn't lunged forward at the moment she had and distracted Cole, he might have succeeded in getting free and the other brothers would have gotten off a shot.

Isaiah set the whetstone on the rail of the porch and stood. The front door slammed. Addy no doubt going out to meet her cousins. He would have preferred that she wait for him. Cousins or not, she should've waited for him regardless of who showed up. He was her bodyguard, but she was hell-bent on independence from her cousins and him. His beast snarled at the latter. Isaiah frowned. The beast's possessiveness was getting out of hand.

Walking to the side of the house, Isaiah listened to the rumble of their voices, picking up the intonations while waiting on the words. All three speakers sounded tense. His beast rumbled its displeasure at Addy's distress. Isaiah shot back a growl of his own. He could handle his woman's problems. He didn't need any help from *it*.

Son of a bitch, when had she become his woman? Isaiah strode along the side of the building, the turmoil inside matching the turmoil he was walking up on.

"I know what he is. I know who he is, and I still want him here," Addy said in a tight voice.

"It's not decent." That was Cole.

"Neither are your Saturday trips to Dolly's place but I don't lecture you on them."

"How the hell—" Cole cut off his words. "You know that's different."

Addy huffed, the way she did when she was confident of winning her point. "I know you'd like to think it is."

"No decent woman lives with a man not her kin."

That helpful tidbit was inserted by Reese. Addy had a response for that to. Isaiah was beginning to believe she always had a response. "You know what's not decent? Me not being safe in my own home. What's not decent is raiders breaking into *my* kitchen, disturbing *my* tea. What's not decent is those men kidnapping *me* because of . . ." Her voice trailed off.

Isaiah was surprised Addy drew the line there, as mad as she had to be at Cole's interference.

"Go ahead and say it," Cole said, his tone tight. "It was because of me you were kidnapped."

Addy's response was too quick to be anything other that emotional.

"We don't know that, Cole."

Isaiah shook his head. It was a foolish response and would cost her her edge. Guilt was too powerful a weapon to throw away. She'd been right to hire him. She was too soft to be hard.

He cleared the building and, squinting against the setting sun, took in the scene with a glance. Cole and Reese sat on their horses in front of the small building, leaning on their elbows against their saddle horns, looking nonchalant, but everything from the set of their shoulders to the narrowing of their eyes said they were itching for a fight.

Isaiah cracked his knuckles. He wouldn't mind giving it to them. They should have protected Addy better, done what was right rather than what she wanted. As he intended to do.

All three turned as he approached. It was an easy four-foot leap up from the ground, over the front porch rail, to where Addy stood. Easy for a Reaper. It would be harder for a human, but he wasn't aiming to look human for the Camerons. He wanted them to know exactly what he was. A threat.

Cole's eyebrows rose. Addy gasped. Reese nodded.

"That's what I figured."

Isaiah took a position a little in front of Addy.

"Just what did you figure?" he challenged.

"Nothing I wasn't supposed to, I'm sure."

SARAH McCARTY

"I won't have it, Addy," Cole cut in.

Addy put her hands on her hips and took a step forward, neatly sidestepping Isaiah. "What won't you have, Cole?"

With a jerk of his chin, Cole indicated Isaiah. "You staying here with the likes of him."

"It's going to grate then, when I tell you that you don't have any say in what I do."

"I'm your cousin, your oldest living male relative."

"But you're not my father and not my brother, and even if you were, I'm not a girl. I get to make my own decisions."

Cole's hands fisted on the saddle but he didn't take his gaze from Isaiah. "Not if I have you declared incompetent."

Addy gasped. He wasn't sure what Cole's threat meant, but it put the fear of God into Addy, and that was enough for him. Isaiah tucked his fingers around her upper arm and pulled her behind him. She trembled beneath his touch. He sighed. If she would just let him do what she'd hired him to do, she wouldn't be so shaken.

"Next time, stay where I put you."

She shook her head, tears in her eyes. His beast roared in his head. His gums ached and the skin on his fingers burned. He slid his hand up her shoulder until he could tip her face to his, remembering the feel of her skin beneath his touch, remembering how she trembled then. How it had pleased him. How it had pleased them both.

"What is he threatening you with?"

She shook her head again.

"He's calling her crazy," Reese supplied.

Declared incompetent. That had an official sound to it.

"She's not crazy."

Cole snorted. "From the outside looking in, she is. If all her rituals weren't enough, her behavior from before would seal the deal."

164

"I can't believe you're doing this," Addy snapped.

Cole shrugged. "I could say the same thing about you."

Isaiah had the gist of it now. Cole was threatening to call Addy crazy so he could have control over her, which only went to prove that nobody could be trusted.

Except her, the beast whispered.

Shut up.

"You want I should kill him now?" he asked Addy while keeping his gaze locked with Cole's.

Addy didn't answer right away. Cole's saddle creaked as he shifted his weight.

"Are you going along with this?" she asked Reese.

He shook his head. "No—"

"Shut up, Reese."

Reese continued as if Cole hadn't interrupted. "But I can't agree with you taking up with a man who'd kill your cousins over a minor disagreement."

"Cole's threatening to lock me up."

"He's frustrated."

"So am I."

This time it was Reese's saddle that creaked, another betrayal of the emotion that swirled around in an incomprehensible influence. Isaiah let it flow. The emotion didn't concern him. The men and their overprotectiveness did.

Reese tipped his hat back and motioned to Isaiah. "But you don't have to go to extremes."

To Isaiah's surprise, Addy put her hand on his arm. Support? A strange warmth went thought him. Pleasure.

"You said you wanted me to have someone who would do anything for me, put me first. You always said I deserved that."

What am I to you? A means to an end.

The warmth shattered, the void filled by a bitter self-mockery. At some point he'd learn.

"You do," Cole countered, "but I also want a man who knows how to love you and this one is a stone-cold killer."

Addy's fingers stroked up and down his upper arm in tiny touches. Isaiah steeled himself against his response. She was just nervous.

"And you know this how?"

It wasn't his imagination that she stepped in front of him. He covered her hand with his and removed it from his arm.

She cut him a glance and blushed. Cole glared. Reese frowned.

"Just a shot in the dark."

"Do you want them dead?" he asked again.

A floorboard creaked as Addy shifted her weight, but still she didn't answer. She might not want them dead, but the beast did. Cole was a threat. To her. To them.

Isaiah shook his head to clear it of images flashing dark then light, hazy then clear. Images of sharp instruments approaching, then being drawn away. And pain. Always pain where he loved. The images shattered in a moment of clarity in which all he could see was Addy putting her slender body between him and a threat. *Shit.* He couldn't love her. Everything he tried to love died—the dog, the odd woman.

"Should I want you dead, Cole?" Addy asked in a very civil tone of voice.

"Hell, no."

"Then what should I want?" she asked softly. Too softly.

"You should want what every woman wants. To be protected and loved by a man strong enough to hold you."

Isaiah almost jumped when she turned and her blue eyes met his, seeing far more than he wanted, asking for something the beast wanted to give, but couldn't. She reached out, palm up. Asking again.

He couldn't. The beast snarled. He shook his head. Cole swore. The confidence in Addy's eyes faded and her hand dropped to her side, but she held her ground. The woman was damn stubborn. Isaiah almost felt sorry for her cousins. They had no concept of how deep the Cameron blood ran in Addy's veins. She could outstubborn the lot of them.

"I am protected," Addy continued. "Just not by a man of your choosing."

"His loyalty is questionable."

"His loyalty is to me."

Cole snorted. "That isn't reassuring to me."

Her braid rustled against the cotton of her dress as she shook her head. "Then you'll have to adjust."

"No."

"You can't stand the thought of anyone else having control over me. You never could."

"I know where I found you."

"So do I, but that's the past, Cole, and it wasn't your fault. Just like if anything happens to me here, it's not your fault."

"The hell it's not! They took you because of me."

Addy's scent changed with her emotions, grew more acrid. She was afraid. Fear Isaiah knew how to handle. Catching her hand, he pulled her to his side.

"They won't again."

Cole's gaze locked on his hand. Just to irk him, Isaiah slid his hand up to Addy's shoulder. Cole reached for his gun. Isaiah smiled and pulled her closer. The gesture started out as provocation, but it ended as something more when Addy leaned into his side. She felt good there. Right.

"You have no say in this," Cole countered.

"Addy gave me that right yesterday and as you're upsetting her—"

"Like hell she gave you anything."

Addy pushed at Isaiah's side. It was surprisingly easy to keep her there. "Everything about her is my business and you won't upset her anymore."

"The hell I won't."

Cole might be used to that glare of his intimidating humans, but Isaiah was a Reaper. "You won't."

"You're serious about being her protector?" Reese asked, interrupting the argument.

Isaiah didn't look away from Cole. The man needed to understand where his control ended and Isaiah's began. "Dead serious."

"Good. Then you won't mind a little help."

"I don't need help."

"Everyone needs help."

"What the hell are you up to, Reese?" Cole asked.

That was what Isaiah wanted to know.

Reese motioned to the surprisingly complacent Addy. "That's our cousin, whether you like it or not, Cole, and we're not going to just hand her care over to a stranger."

"Uh-huh."

"I trust him," Addy interjected.

Cole's "I don't" was succinct and to the point.

Isaiah smiled at the Camerons. "Learn."

Reese smiled right back. "Likely I will, as I'll be staying to help out."

"What?"

"No."

Cole drew his revolver. "I was hoping you'd be difficult."

Addy stepped away from Isaiah. "Shoot away."

Cole snorted. "Looks like she's not that fond of you."

Isaiah growled. "She's fond enough."

"Addy," Reese asked. "What are you doing?"

"I'm calling Cole's bluff."

"I'm not bluffing."

It was Isaiah's turn to smile. No, he wasn't.

"What the hell do you have to smile about?" Cole bit off.

"It's my lucky day." Isaiah relaxed his muscles and his hold on the beast. It growled and stretched with anticipation. "I get to kill you after all."

"I'm the one with the gun."

"And I'm the one who can get to you before you can pull the trigger."

"Shit. Put your gun away, Cole," Reese said.

"The hell I will."

"The hell you won't," Reese snapped. "The weather's been miserable for grave digging."

"No law says we have to bury him."

"But it'd look bad if we didn't bury you."

Isaiah stepped to the side.

Addy sprang forward. "Oh my God. Isaiah, don't."

"Goddamn it, Addy!" Cole shouted and jerked the barrel up.

"See, even Addy knows he can do it."

"Even *I* know?"

Isaiah sighed and pulled Addy out from between him and Cole. "Don't do that again."

She turned on him. "I hired you. I give the orders."

"Not in this," Cole snapped.

Addy yanked at her arm. "Let me go!"

"No."

Her braid slapped across his arm as she spun back to Cole. "Since when do you side with him?"

"Since he makes sense."

"A minute ago you were going to kill him."

Cole took aim again. "I still might."

Isaiah snorted.

"You might want to give up on that idea, Cole," Reese said.

The muzzle didn't waver. "Why?"

"Remember my telling you about those men I've been studying up on."

"Yeah."

"He's one of them, and trust me, he can do what he says."

"You're a goddamn Reaper?"

This was getting out of hand. Protecting was a lot messier than killing. "Whatever I am, I'm going to rip your heart out before you can pull that trigger." Isaiah was used to men cowering when his beast showed its presence and he knew it was showing. He could feel it in the ache in his bones, in the intensity of his focus. Cole didn't twitch. He might even have been described as "intrigued."

"You really shouldn't put it like that," Reese said. With a motion of his hand, he indicated Cole. "The man is completely unable to resist a challenge."

So he could see. Isaiah tightened his hold on Addy's arm again. "I'm beginning to get that impression. He might even carry it to the point of stupidity."

"I wouldn't say stupidity, but it's been close a time or two."

"Why aren't you afraid?" he asked Reese out of curiosity.

"You're not threatening to rip out my heart." Reese shrugged. "And besides . . ." A hammer cocked. "You might be able to get to him but you can't get to me, too."

"I thought of that. The way I figure I'll handle it is, while I'm ripping his heart out, I'll slice your jugular."

"With what?"

Isaiah smiled. He wondered if it looked as cold as it felt. "That would be telling."

Abby's nails dug into his hand. "These are my cousins!"

He ignored the outburst. This was between them, and it needed to be settled, but maybe not right now. The scent of Addy's fear and distress was strong.

"Now, gentlemen, if you've satisfied your curiosity as to whether I can protect your cousin or not, I need to get back inside."

"Why?"

That "why," combined with the implication of Cole's frown, was insulting. And he wasn't the only one who picked it up.

"Not for what you're obviously thinking!" Addy gasped.

Isaiah steered Addy toward the door. "I have bread to bake."

"Bread? Shit!"

Reese broke into laughter. "Son of a bitch. She's turning him into a goddamn baker."

Cole pulled back on the reins. His bay tossed his head and pranced. "Sometime in the future, you'll have to decide, baker or bodyguard."

Isaiah shrugged. "When the time comes, I'll make up my mind, but in the meantime, I have apples that need to be peeled, and Addy has orders that need to be filled."

"You're opening the bakery tomorrow?" Cole asked.

Addy nodded. "I want my life back to normal as fast as possible."

Reese swung down off his horse and untied his pack from the back of the saddle. "Understandable."

Isaiah nodded to the porch. "You can make your bed here."

Reese cocked an eyebrow at him and then looked at Addy. If he was looking for a softer response, he was doomed to disappointment. "I hope you brought a bed roll."

On that she turned and went in the house. The screen door slammed behind her. Isaiah stayed a couple seconds longer, just to enjoy the cousins' consternation, and then he smiled. Guarding Addy was turning out to have some unexpected benefits.

ISAIAH came in as silently as he did everything, a whisper of sound stilted by motion, but this time Addy heard him. Her nerves were so jangled that everything seemed louder. Outside she could even hear her cousins talking. They didn't sound as if they were shouting but they had to be for her to hear them all the way in the kitchen.

She poured a bit of water into the basin, scooped up some soap, and washed her hands, scrubbing them over and over. Isaiah came up behind her. His scent reached her first, that purely masculine, musky, addictive aroma that just pleased her to the core.

"I'm sorry they put you through that," she murmured.

His arms came around her and his hands covered hers, separating them. Before she could protest, he took up the washing, except his efforts were softer than hers, gentler and focused more on the muscles in her palms, relaxing them.

"It wasn't anything I didn't expect." The soft rumble of his drawl blended with the soothing massage.

"They threatened to kill you, for heaven sakes."

"And I threatened to kill them back. Seems to me that makes us even."

She gave in to the urge to lean back against him. "Cole's not usually so unreasonable."

"He feels guilty, and worse, there's nothing he can do. Plus you called his bluff and blocked his play. That's pretty much guaranteed to get a man riled."

She closed her fingers around his hand. "They've got to let me go."

"They can't."

"Their love suffocates me."

He lifted her hands from the water, and poured some fresh water from the pitcher over them, rinsing the soap clean, then he pulled her back against him and held her. She should protest, because instinct told her that her cousins' possessiveness was nothing next to Isaiah's, but she couldn't. It felt so right. The spot on her shoulder burned and tingled. She put her hand to it.

His lips touched her hand. "What's wrong?"

"It feels funny."

"Where I bit you?"

"Yes. How did you do that?" she asked, looking up at him.

"Do what?"

"Bite me and not make it hurt."

"I don't know, but however I did it, I'm glad."

"Me, too. I'm even hoping you'll do it again. It was . . . exciting."

Her gaze was butter soft, her lips parted, her scent tempting. *Shit.* The one thing he could never do was that again.

"I think I'll keep my teeth to myself."

"That was our deal."

He turned her in his arms and backed her against the sink. He heard her breath catch. He scented her desire. His cock went hard, and when she spread her legs that little inviting bit, he nestled between them. "But I'm making no promises about my mouth."

"Our deal was only for one night."

"Then maybe we'll just make a new deal."

"My cousins will kill you."

"Your cousins already think we're sleeping together."

"We are."

"But it was just that one night."

"It doesn't have to be."

No, it didn't. She was a woman grown. She slid her hands up his chest. His wonderfully hard chest with that light covering of hair that felt so delicious against her nipples.

"My fiancé might not like it."

"You're not marrying that dolt."

"You don't even know him."

"I know, if he was any kind of man, you wouldn't have been begging me to make love to you."

Shame started in her toes and worked its way up, one humiliating inch at a time. She shoved at him. He didn't move. She shoved again. He blinked and frowned. "You're mad?"

"Of course I'm mad. You just called me a whore."

"The hell I did. I called you more woman than that man that you think to marry could ever satisfy."

She shook her head. "I don't need to be satisfied."

"Really? Then what was last night all about?"

"Knowledge."

"Bullshit. It was about satisfaction. For you and for me. For us."

She pushed him again, wiggling against him, moaning when his cock nudged her clit. It might be wrong, but it felt so good.

"And what is this about?" she demanded, furious.

He shook his head and she suddenly understood that he didn't know any more than she did what it was about and he was just as helpless as she was when it came to the emotions between them. And somehow that made it right, that they were lost together in it.

"I don't know."

"But it's good," she said, because she had to hear him say it, too.

She didn't get her wish. Instead, there was a flash of something in his blue-gray eyes, and his hands on her shoulders broke the intimacy. "It is, but it won't end well."

She didn't try to hold him when he stepped back. There was no point. She recognized determination when she ran up against it even when she didn't understand it. Licking her lips, she stood there, feeling awkward and exposed, not sure what she wanted to say, just knowing the urge was strong to say something that would bring him back again. And he just stared at her while she struggled. He stared at her with the same intensity, yet he took a step back. Where did he find the strength?

The mark on her shoulder heated to uncomfortable. The one on the inside of her thigh burned with the same erotic fire. In her mind she remembered the moments when Isaiah had placed those marks upon her and her knees almost buckled. His nostrils flared. His eyes narrowed. She took a breath. As she did, she noted his scent was different, spicier somehow. Better, more addictive. She licked her lips again. Isaiah stopped breathing. The spicy scent intensified.

A knock came at the door. Addy jerked. Her hand bumped the pan on the stove. It rattled loudly in the silence. The door opened and Reese stuck his head in.

"I'm settled out here. Do you all need something?"

Addy shoved her hand in her pocket. Her worry stone was there. Like a friend, it settled into her palm. Rubbing it between her fingers, she waited for the coolness to become warm. Isaiah didn't move, but somehow he had managed to give the impression that he was between her and Reese. How did he express so much with so little effort?

"We're fine, thank you," Isaiah answered.

Reese's didn't miss a beat as he ignored Isaiah and focused on Addy. "How about you, Addy girl?"

Isaiah folded his arms across his chest and waited for her to answer. Forcing a smile to her dry lips and words past her tongue, which felt too thick to hit a consonant, she said, "I'm fine."

Reese gave her a dubious look. Isaiah shot him a dirty one. "She said she's fine."

"Nevertheless, you need anything, you holler. Don't you be worrying about any repercussions, you just holler."

"Thank you."

He nodded again. "And Isaiah, I know how to take out a Reaper."

Addy could tell from his start that that was news to Isaiah.

"You think you do."

"Do anything to make my cousin uncomfortable, and you'll find out the truth of it."

The door closed. Addy rubbed her hands up and down her thighs. "I'm sorry again."

"They're the men in charge of taking care of you. I wouldn't expect anything less, but now we have a problem."

"We do?"

"I have to find a place to sleep. I was planning on sleeping outside—"

"Why do I hear a 'but' in there?"

"Reese stole my spot."

"You just don't want to give him the satisfaction of your leaving."

"You've got that right."

"What's your solution?"

"How much do you want to irritate them?"

"Enough that I don't want you sleeping outside." It might be petty, but it was the truth.

"Where's the bedroom?"

She motioned to the stairs in the foyer. "Upstairs."

"There's only one?"

She nodded.

"All right."

"What does that mean?"

"Not much."

Addy looked around the kitchen. There really weren't many options. "I'd suggest the sofa in the sitting room, but it's really not even
that comfortable for sitting."

"I'll be fine."

"Maybe I could—"

He cut her off before she could finish. "I'll be fine."

From his pocket he pulled the paring knife. "We've got to get
going on those apples if you're going to get some sleep tonight."

"That's true. And we'd better make an extra loaf."

"Why?"

"Reese loves apple bread, and if we don't make him one, he'll
steal one."

"Not if you don't want him to."

She shook her head at his tone. "My cousins may be irritating,
but I love them, Isaiah, and that's what you do for people you love.
You spoil them with little things."

"Like apple bread."

She smiled. "Like apple bread."

Isaiah picked up the apple and efficiently stripped the skin from
it, though some of his pleasure of before was missing. One of the
loaves was going to her cousin. Because she loved him. He resented
that affection.

"What's wrong?"

"Nothing."

"We're still making apple bread."

He shrugged, ready to hate the man for having her love. Hell, no
wonder *They* had forbidden emotion. It addled a man's mind.

"He's a good man, Isaiah." She hesitated and then said in a rush,
"He and Cole rode into certain death to save me once."

Did she think he didn't know about her capture and rescue from the Indians? There wasn't anyone in the territory that didn't know about that. Not many captives made it home. Not many families kept up the hunt long enough to find them. The story made the Cameron brothers heroes and Addy notorious.

"Couldn't have been that certain. They're both still alive." It was a petty thing to say and he felt petty saying it, but he didn't like that she did so much for others.

And nothing for him.

The knife gouged into the fruit. A chunk fell onto the table. *Shit.* He was getting as bad as the beast.

"They both have scars from the arrows they took. We almost lost Reese. His wounds got infected. I owe them a lot."

"Because they saved you?"

She shook her head and started making up the batter for the bread, her lower lip between her teeth, the memory of fear lending a faint, acrid tinge to her scent. "Because they never once gave up on me. In the two years it took them to find me, they never gave up. And when they found me, they did what they always promised to do. They brought me home."

"I guess I can't hate them then."

"No." She hesitated with a spoon midstir. "And maybe you could not kill them when they get too provoking?"

"How about I just agree to do my best?"

"I'd feel better with a promise."

"I'd feel better with a hedge."

She supposed he would, and considering all she knew of him and what she'd heard of his kind, it was the best she was going to get. "Thank you."

"You're welcome." He looked up, catching her looking at him. His eyes darkened and dropped to her mouth. Heat arced from him to her. She braced her weight on her hand, lips parted, nails biting into the tabletop as she waited. She swore she could hear his heart-beat, feel his breath. Oh Lord, her knees went weak.

He held up a peeled apple. "Now, what do I with these?"

It took her to the count of twenty to regain control. Her hand barely shook as she handed him the grater. "You shred them."

⊰ 13 ⊱

HE ENDED UP SLEEPING AT THE FOOT OF THE STAIRS. IT wasn't overly comfortable, but he'd slept in worse places. Tonight none offered a defensive position as well as this. All the air in the house funneled through there, carrying the scents from inside and out. It also had excellent acoustics, along with the advantage that anyone trying to get upstairs would have to step over him. That would never happen.

Settling his hat over his face, Isaiah leaned back against the railing. Closing his eyes, he took a calming breath, ignoring the beast's restless prodding that he go upstairs and find Addy. The scents of the house seeped into him along with a drowsy contentment. Yeast, cinnamon, honey, and Addy. Contentment was as foreign a beast as the one that was his constant companion. He didn't trust it any more than he trusted the calm before the storm. The latter, if one fell for it, often led to disaster.

But this is different.

No it wasn't. It was never different. There was only the illusion before the pain.

This is Addy.

Yes it was. He recalled the heat of her skin, the taste of her passion. His cock went hard and his pulse kicked up. The beast purred and growled before stretching lazily, confident in its power to please, anticipating the pleasure that awaited if Isaiah enjoyed the illusion for as long as it lasted. Isaiah shifted against the balustrade, a reckless energy joining contentment. Living for the moment was what he did. There was no reason he couldn't enjoy it with Addy. She seemed willing enough.

Because she doesn't know what you are.

So what? Neither did he.

He swore. His conscience prodded. The beast snarled. His cock throbbed, and damn it, his fucking heart hungered. He glared at the zucchini bread earmarked for Reese, sitting on the counter. For the softness Addy so easily offered others. For her smile, her company. With her, he felt human. What the hell was wrong with that?

Nothing, rumbled the beast.

Everything, snapped his conscience.

SHUT UP! he told them both. He was tired and all he wanted to do was enjoy what others took for granted. A bit of peace before he went to sleep. Was that too much to ask? He mentally elbowed the beast aside when it snarled an answer.

No one asked you.

HE woke in the middle of the night, his instincts screaming a warning. Lying quietly, not opening his eyes, he scanned with his senses. From upstairs, he could hear Addy's deep, even breaths. She was asleep. No sound of footsteps. No scent of fear or danger. On the front porch, Reese snored rhythmically. Neither of those sounds had woken him.

He lay for two minutes listening, and still nothing, but the hairs on the back of his neck stayed raised and his beast was snarling a warning. There was only one thing that caused that reaction in a Reaper. Another Reaper.

Very carefully, he rolled to his side and reached for his gun. Emptying the chamber, he reached into the pocket sewn into his shirt and pulled out the special bullets. If Reese really did know how to take out a Reaper, he'd have some of his own.

The bullets were heavy, cold, and glowed dimly in the dark interior. They were made of silver, worth more than their weight in gold. One of those, lodged in a major organ, would poison a Reaper in minutes. Anything less than a kill shot and it would only give him a nasty, soon-to-heal wound.

Crab crawling backward, being careful to not scuff his feet or hands on the floor, he moved to the darkness of the hall. Still he could hear nothing, but every sense screamed alarm. The Reaper could only be here for one of two reasons—for him or for Addy. Since there was no way the Reaper council could know of his relationship with Addy, it wouldn't be because of her. Not this soon. No one had been close enough to catch her scent on the way to town. He would've known that, which meant they'd come for him. Isaiah looked at the black beyond the window. Since they'd come for him, if he left the house, Addy should be safe, but Reese wouldn't be. Any Reaper would take him out as a precaution.

Working his way to the front door, Isaiah opened it slowly, glad that Addy was the particular type who hated squeaking. Still, if a Reaper was close, he'd hear it. But that was just as well. Isaiah wanted a battle outside.

He slipped into the darkness and made it the two steps to Reese.

When he reached to cover his mouth, Reese's hand touched his. Reese was awake. Isaiah held his finger to his mouth, unsure if there was enough light for human eyes. He heard the rustle of Reese's hair as he nodded. Bending down, he put his lips close to Reese's ear and whispered in a voice barely more than a breath, "Upstairs."

Catching Reese's hand in his, Isaiah placed the two bullets in his palm, folding his fingers over them. "Heart shot only."

Reese nodded and weighed the bullets in his hand. He mouthed the words, "And you?"

Isaiah set his hat on the porch and smiled. Leaning down again, he murmured, "Going hunting." Reese nodded when he straightened. With almost the skill of the Reaper, the other man stood and disappeared inside the house. Satisfied that Addy was protected, Isaiah blended into the shadows, searching for the scent or sound that would give the other Reaper's position away. It was quiet, without the occasional bark of a dog or even a cricket to break the stillness. Crickets were always a giveaway to a Reaper's presence. Crickets and birds. The two always seemed to sense the danger humans could not. Being easy prey for so many, they were not willing to betray their hiding places. Not to the devil's own. But their silence revealed the Reaper's location. He was around the back of the house.

Isaiah headed that way, staying upwind. It took longer, but any advantage was needed. He paused at the back corner, pressing into the rough shingles while he surveyed the yard. There, by the well. A shadow slightly deeper than the others. It shifted but not with the wind. Isaiah made his way forward carefully, palming his knife, walking toe to heel, feeling for any betraying stick or stone with his toes. The beast inside fought for the rule, wanting dominion in this fight for survival, for which it was so ideally suited. Breathing slowly, he fought for balance, tempering its impetuous nature with rational calm. Another advantage he'd spent years perfecting.

When he was ten feet away, the Reaper came for him. No control, just feral instinct backed with massive muscle. In full wolf form, longer than a man was tall, broader than a man, more muscular than an ox, with jaws gaping, dripping saliva, the beast leapt out of the shadows. Isaiah held his ground, held his beast, until the last instant and then ducked, striking upward with his knife. Vicious claws raked the air above his head as the silver-coated blade sliced along the beast's abdomen. The copper scent of blood filled the air, blending with the scent of poisoned flesh. Inside Isaiah, his own beast howled victoriously at drawing first blood.

Premature, Isaiah thought. Not a killing blow. Not even a particularly weakening one, though the silver blade would cause the other to bleed excessively. Enough of that type of wound, and they would add up. The other Reaper snarled, dropped, and spun, coming back.

Isaiah smiled as he squared off against the wolf, straining to maintain his partial human form, keeping the advantage it gave him. Wolves knew how to kill wolves. They knew how to kill humans. They didn't know how to kill a wolf that fought like a human. "That get your goat?"

The Reaper snarled and bit the air with jaws big enough to crush his head.

It would have been easier for Isaiah to just shoot him, but then he wouldn't have the opportunity to grill him. Something the wolf wouldn't understand. He waved the knife in an invitation. "Then this is going to really annoy you."

The Reaper came in, lunging low, going for his hamstrings. Again Isaiah waited, letting the other get close, anticipating a last-minute lunge upward, ducking low, catching it with his shoulder, flipping him over, slicing out as he did. He managed to cut a hamstring, again not a mortal wound, but even for a Reaper it took a couple days to heal a wound like that. This time, when the wolf spun around, he stopped. His left rear foot dangled uselessly.

He motioned again with the knife. "Want some more?"

A low rumbling growl was his response, but the Reaper didn't charge back in. He was learning.

Isaiah shifted his position so his back was to the tree. From here on out, it was going to get tricky. The wolf was big and strong, and like any Reaper, well trained. Isaiah didn't recognize him, and with the distinctive half mask, he should. That was a concern. He'd heard stories of other Reapers held in other locations who'd fared worse, as hard as that was to imagine. So hard, when discussed, they were written off as myths, or threats. Something *They* held over the Reapers' heads to keep them in line.

The breeze shifted, bringing the scent of blood closer. Isaiah's beast lunged within, breaking through his control. His canines cut into his mouth. His claws extended. The knife dropped from his hands. From the other came a bark that could have been a laugh.

Isaiah pointed to the ground. "Surrender, Reaper, to a Guardian of the Council."

The words came out guttural and malformed owing to his wolf shape, but they should've been understood. The wolf's response was an indecipherable, guttural sound. Inching away from the tree, encouraging the Reaper closer, Isaiah studied him. If a wolf could smile, the other Reaper was smiling, revealing yellowed teeth. Another oddity. Reapers were always in excellent health.

"What the hell are you?"

No answer, but as he studied the other, Isaiah realized its energy wasn't right, either. It was erratic and excitable and it lacked the focused intensity he was used to seeing in Reapers. Had the other been freed before his training was complete? Was he still—

The beast lunged. Isaiah met it halfway, chest to chest, fang to fang, claw to claw. There was only one way through a Reaper. That was death. The battle was vicious. Claws raked down his thigh, tearing open his flesh. Teeth bit into his shoulder. His own claws sank into the animal's belly. His teeth into its neck. His beast roared victory, but the other was strong, the way a crazy man was strong. It tore free, blood gushing in its wake. Isaiah grabbed its neck and fell backward, flipping it as he went. Blood covered his chest. His own beast went wild, raging for the kill.

There was a scream from the house and then two shots in succession followed by an unearthly howl. Dirt sprayed beside his face. The Reaper raced into the woods. Isaiah fought the change as he looked up to the second-story window. Reese stood there, rifle in hand, Addy holding on to his arm. She called his name, distracting him. The beast broke free of his control, the change came against his will. As his bones morphed, he dove into the shadows and ran. Again he heard Addy call his name. *Shit.*

He ran like a thief in the night, dropping to all fours as the beast took over. Isaiah let the beast run. He couldn't let her see him like this. The woman who'd taught him to bake. The only woman who'd ever seen him as a man. For the first time in his life, he felt like a coward. From behind he heard the sound of his name fade, as if Reese had pulled Addy back inside and closed the window. As well he should. The dubious safety of the house was the best place for Addy.

He stopped running as soon as his thoughts clicked past the beast's panic.

That might not be the only Reaper out there.

Shit.

And because Reese had interfered, Isaiah didn't even know why the Reaper had been there. If he'd been hunting Isaiah, it didn't make sense that he'd been hiding by the pump. Why would he hide there?

Reese had been on the porch. He'd been in the foyer. That meant all scents had been to the front, yet the Reaper had been around back.

The beast snarled in Isaiah's head. Isaiah echoed the sound. He closed his eyes and willed the change back to man, but the beast was too strong, and with the more primitive intellect of the beast in control. it was hard to hold a logical thought. The beast thought in terms of permanence, possessing, killing, eating. And when threatened, it was all-powerful. The rage that someone could be hunting Addy kept the beast to the fore.

The beast circled the town, hunting for a sign. He scented no other. Isaiah fought with the beast as it made its way back to Addy's house, following the other's trail. He had no luck. The beast wanted its mate. Son of a bitch. It was powerful, his evil half, but not his stronger half. He'd vowed that it would never be stronger. He managed to temper the urge so it settled for creeping up to the edge of the woods by the back pump. Reese and Addy were there, kneeling by the fight scene. Blood formed a black pool on the ground.

"Where is he?" Addy asked.

"I don't know," Reese answered. "Likely chasing that wolf."

"So much blood." Abby's eyes glittered like pale blue jewels in the moonlight. "Some of it's his."

"From the way he was moving, any wound was a long way from his heart."

Addy bit her lip. "You don't know that."

"Trust me, I know."

She pulled her wrap tighter around her. "I don't want to lose him, Reese. He's not like the others."

Reese took her arm and pulled her back from the scene. "What others?"

"The ones that think I'm used goods because I was captured by the Indians."

The beast growled.

Addy turned in his direction. "What was that?"

Isaiah could see the tears on her cheeks.

"Likely a dog drawn by the commotion." Reese pulled her into his side and stared hard in Isaiah's direction. "Trust me, he's nothing like the others, but if he knows what's good for him, he'll stay away from you."

So that shot had been meant for him.

"No."

Reese bent and picked up a rock, chucking it in Isaiah's direction. It bounced off his shoulder.

"Yes."

Addy shoved at Reese, moonlight rippling over her braid. "Leave the dog alone."

Both beast and man wanted to pull her close, shelter her. Instead they had to watch another take her in his arms and hold her safe. The beast gathered its muscles for the kill.

Mine!

Though this time there had been no sound, Addy looked in his direction, her cheek resting on Reese's chest, her gaze tortured. Her fingers twitched. He knew she was looking for her worry stone, because she was worried. About him. This time, the beast's growl was more of satisfaction.

"Sounds like that wolf's back."

Addy shook her head and touched her shoulder. "I don't think so, but just in case, you might want to buy more bullets."

He steered her toward the house. "You buy them."

"Why me?"

"Because I let Cole sucker me into playing cards again."

"When are you going to learn that he never loses?"

"He cheats."

"How?"

"The man has a sixth sense, I tell you."

Isaiah snapped to attention and followed as they made their way back to the house. The beast allowed it because Reese was close to Addy. A threat.

"I swear, he knows what the cards are before they're up."

"You know that's not possible."

"No, I don't."

Reese huffed. "Either that or he reads minds. Hell . . ." He opened the screen door. "For all I know, he does both."

Inside the body of the beast, Isaiah thought, *Interesting.*

ADDY woke up to the aroma of freshly baked bread. Yawning, she stretched, opening her eyes. From the light in the room, the sun was high in the sky. *Oh crap.* She'd overslept. Addy jumped out of bed and grabbed her wrapper, tied it around her waist, and went downstairs. When she reached the foyer, she heard pans clanking on the stove and smelled coffee brewing. Who the heck was in her kitchen?

Another few steps and she had her answer. Isaiah. He was dressed all in black. His brown hair was tied at the nape of his neck, revealing the strong lines of his profile. No shadow of a beard darkened his jaw. No bulk of bandages showed through his clothing. No wounds marred the sun-browned skin visible through the open neck of his shirt. By all accounts, he was perfectly fine. She remembered the pool of blood, the size of the shadowy wolf that had attacked him. It just wasn't possible.

She watched him from the doorway. He moved easily between the stove and the counter, showing no sign of injury. As she watched, he bent and opened the door, pulling out four perfect-looking loaves of bread.

"Good morning," he said as he straightened. With a kick of his foot, he closed the oven door.

She blinked and looked around. Everything was in its place. It was still her kitchen, yet not.

"What are you doing?"

"Getting the day started."

"Why didn't you wake me?"

"You were tired."

There was no logical response that didn't sound petty and mean, but she felt petty and mean. He was in her kitchen and he was taking it over. She looked at those perfect loaves of bread. "How did you . . ."

He smiled a real smile, not that tight tug of the lips she was used to seeing. "I found your recipe book."

"And you did all this?"

"You're a good teacher."

"No one is that good."

His smile faded. "You're mad."

"I don't like being played for a fool."

He pulled a basket of eggs out from the lower shelf. "Neither do I."

"So you really did make these after just one lesson?"

"I like baking."

So did she, and if she thought back, it had seemed to come naturally to her, too. She'd just never seen it come naturally to a man. She pushed her hair off her face. "I'm sorry. I'm not used to having anyone in my kitchen."

It irritated her when they left a mess or moved things around.

"I kept everything in its place."

So he had. One less thing to complain about. She forced a smile. "Thank you. The bread looks good."

"Uh-huh." Taking a knife, he cut off the end and then another slice. Slathering the slice with butter, he put it on a plate and slid it across the counter to her.

"Thank you."

Grabbing the eggs, he turned back to the stove. There was absolutely nothing to indicate that he was nervous, but she had the strangest impression he was. She rubbed the spot on her shoulder. Grease sizzled as it hit the pan. She took a bite of the bread, braced for the worst. What she got shocked her to her toes.

"Delicious." The truth just popped out, muffled by her mouth being full.

Isaiah turned, the same calm expression on his face, and this time she wasn't fooled. The man *had* been nervous, just as he was now pleased.

"You like it?"

She nodded, chewed, and swallowed. "It's . . . perfect, darn it."

To her surprise, he laughed. A genuine laugh. "You wanted yours to be better?"

"Of course."

He moved the pan off the heat and grabbed the coffeepot while motioning her to the chair. She felt awkward as he held out the chair.

"Sit."

She didn't immediately. He frowned. "I know this isn't your regular routine. I've disturbed things."

"Just a little." He poured the coffee.

I feel like tea. The words stuck in her throat. Not only because they were churlish, but because Isaiah had that suppressed excitement her dad used to have at Christmas when he was doing something big. And while she still felt awkward and unsure, she didn't feel so mean anymore.

She took another bite of the bread, humming in her throat

while it melted in her mouth. "So what else have you been up to this morning?"

"Besides baking?"

"Yes."

He brought her sugar and cream. "I'm sorry I disturbed things."

He had. Yet she hadn't reached for her worry stone. She looked at her empty hand.

"As soon as I have my coffee, I'll take you to task for it."

He actually chuckled and went back to the stove. Metal scraped across metal as he put the frying pan back over the heat. "Mrs. Mc-Gillicuddy came by for her apple bread. She gave me the money. I don't know if it's the right amount. If she shortchanged you, we can talk to her."

"Please? Talk to her? Mrs. McGillicuddy is an eighty-year-old woman. One doesn't talk to an eighty-year-old woman about discrepancies in an apple bread purchase. She's not an outlaw."

Isaiah looked at her over his shoulder. He looked so confident, so powerful, so utterly male. Her womb clenched. She took a quick swallow of coffee.

"She doesn't get to cheat you."

"We definitely have to talk after coffee."

"All right."

"About a lot of things," she added. "Like what happened last night. Where did you disappear to?"

"Finish your coffee."

She put the cup on the table. "I've changed my mind. I'd like to hear that story while I'm waking up."

He shrugged and pulled a bowl of dough out of the oven. How many loaves of bread did he intend to make?

"Where did you disappear to?"

"I went down to the lake for a swim to clean off."

"It was cold last night."

"I don't see where the cold has much to do with it."

She didn't believe his explanation and not because it didn't make sense, but because, through the scents of yeast and coffee, she could also smell . . . the lie.

"Were you hurt last night?"

"I'm fine."

That wasn't exactly an answer. "The fight sounded awful."

"Did it?"

She nodded.

He cocked an eyebrow at her as he cracked an egg into the pan. "Have you seen a lot of fights?"

"Not really." At the Indian camp she'd been kept sequestered and her cousins had been careful to keep her away from violence those first few years. She'd been very fragile.

"I see. Well, rest assured, I wasn't hurt."

She wasn't assured, because the nagging sense that there was more than what was before her eyes just kept prodding her.

"How do you like your eggs?" he asked, clearly changing the subject.

"Over easy, please."

She silently counted as the eggs sizzled. When she reached twenty, she began to twitch. He was leaving them too long.

"I don't mind cooking breakfast."

"I'll let you cook lunch."

She pushed the chair away from the table. "Let me at least work with that dough."

He turned quickly. "No. You just sit there and wake up. Your eggs are almost done."

"I'm not used to sitting."

"Then we're even. I'm not used to spoiling."

Spoiling? He was spoiling her. "Oh." She couldn't think of anything else to say to that.

That's what you do for people you love. You spoil them with little things.

She froze, coffee cup in hand, bread halfway to her mouth, staring at Isaiah's back as her own words came back to her. Did he love her? He couldn't love her. They hadn't known each other long enough. The spot on her shoulder burned.

He's been watching you for a year, the mocking voice from inside said. *He could be infatuated with you seven ways from Sunday.*

She waited for the nervousness to come that always accompanied a man's emotional interest, but with Isaiah, it just wasn't there. Maybe because he was so clueless as to what he was doing. Or maybe it was because he was so sincere in what he did. But whether he cared for her or loved her, he'd gone to a lot of effort this morning to make sure she felt special. She wished she knew why. And that she could trust the reason he gave, but she knew she wouldn't, couldn't, but still she asked again, "Why did you let me sleep in?"

He shrugged. "You were tired."

"So were you."

"I don't need much sleep."

"You need more than you're getting."

"So do you," he countered.

"How would you know?"

"Your scent."

As fast as the answer came out, his face closed up.

"Are you saying I stink?" she gasped.

His "no" was tight.

"What did you mean?"

He scooped the eggs into a plate and brought them over. The plate settled on the table with a faint click. His gaze met hers. "Let it go."

She did, not only because he was a bit scary when he looked that intense, but also because her stomach rumbled just then. She was actually quite hungry. She could always come back to the subject later. And it was awfully sweet of him to try spoiling her.

She caught his hand before he could step away. "Thank you."

He looked down at her hand on his. Tension arced between them. The spot on her neck tingled. His eyes narrowed. She saw in his eyes, before he made a move, that he was going to walk away. She didn't want that. No one had ever spoiled her before. It deserved a better ending than a fight and a threat. She stood, bringing her body up against his. Sliding her right arm up his chest, she pressed. He went still, but his eyes—oh, his eyes—got hotter than a summer day and steamier than an August night.

"This isn't a good idea."

"No, but it's a pleasant one."

For a heart-stopping moment she thought he was going to push her away. Humiliation built, but then his arm came around the small of her back and lifted her into the descent of his mouth.

She held her breath, waiting, anticipating, wondering. Could it be as good as before? And then she didn't have to wonder anymore. His lips touched hers gently—once, twice—tender touches that were enough to tease, but teasing wasn't what she wanted.

She didn't recognize this man bustling around the kitchen. She didn't recognize herself, sitting there, letting him take care of her. She needed to know that he was still he and she was still she. Parting her lips, she touched her tongue to his lower lip, tracing as lightly as she could. He made a sound like a growl and his grip switched to the back of her head and he was pulling her toward him.

Oh yes, she gripped his shirt in her hand. This she remembered. She parted her lips, accepting the thrust of his tongue, shivering as he made that rumbling noise in his chest that was as sexy as all get-out. Passion swept over her like a runaway wagon as he kissed her like there was no tomorrow. As if he might never see her again. He kissed her as though she were the only woman on the earth, the only woman for him. And she kissed him back the same way, because in truth, she couldn't imagine another man touching her. But when he let her go and stepped back, holding her up with his hands on her waist, he didn't smile.

"Your breakfast is getting cold."

She huffed and pushed at his hands. "The rest of me is pretty hot."

He looked startled and then shocked.

"The bread needs tending."

She sat and grabbed her napkin. "Second place to a loaf of bread."

He turned around, that same serious expression on his face. A quick glance down showed that he wasn't unmoved. He caught her looking. She blushed. "What do you expect, Isaiah, when you're nothing but a tease?"

He came back, those long legs of his making nothing of the distance. His finger hooked under her chin, tipping her face up, revealing her hurt and embarrassment. And likely her desire. His thumb smoothed over her lower lip, and his eyes, shadowed with a pain she didn't understand, met hers. "You're second place to nothing."

⊰ 14 ⊱

FOR A WOMAN WHO WASN'T SECOND PLACE TO ANYTHING, she was spending a lot of time playing catch-up. Addy adjusted the apron around her waist and pushed her hair off her temple. Today was just another example of the frustration she'd been enduring all week. As usual, Isaiah had not woken her up, and as usual, despite her best intentions, the alarm clock was mysteriously missing from her bedstand, and she'd slept in. And if Isaiah hadn't ignored her the rest of the day, she would have enjoyed the spoiling he lavished on her in the morning. The extra sleep, the baked goods, a pot of coffee and tea, not to mention the way he always left her kitchen exactly how she liked it. But for all his efforts, he wasn't giving her the one thing she needed. Him.

She sighed and lifted her blouse away from her body. The day was going to be a scorcher. Being hot and sweaty just added to her misery. She touched the bite on her shoulder and played with tendrils that escaped from her bun. Maybe she'd read too much into that morning when Isaiah had kissed her hotly enough to burn the soles of her shoes. Maybe it'd been pity and not lust that had had Isaiah telling her she was second to none. Maybe he'd heard the rumors that always floated around town about her. Maybe he'd decided another woman would suit him better. Because he hadn't touched her since. Not once. That was not acceptable. If she wasn't going to marry her first stable choice, then she needed another candidate. And she'd already decided Isaiah was it.

She gave the loaves of bread, so neatly lined up on the counter, a shove. They didn't make a sound, absorbing her anger rather than satisfying it. Damn it.

Humid air swept the room as the door opened.

"Morning, Addy girl."

Reese. Try as she might, she couldn't put any cheer into her return greeting. As far as she could see, nothing was going to make today better than yesterday. "Morning."

"Woke up on the wrong side of the bed again?"

She straightened the loaves she'd disturbed, unable to tolerate the disorder. "I woke up just fine. It's when I got to the kitchen that things went downhill."

He came up beside her and pushed one of the loaves askew.

"Why not just tell him you don't want him baking?"

Isaiah's baking wasn't the problem. His baking and then disappearing was. "You've seen the man. Do you want to be the one to tell him that he can't do what he wants to do?"

Reese snorted and grabbed a coffee cup. "I'll give you that he's a big son of a bitch, but you have an advantage I don't."

"And what would that be?"

He smiled and motioned with his hand. "Curves."

She snorted. "Not enough for him, apparently."

Reese sighed. "Not that I want to see you with the likes of him, but there's nothing wrong with your shape."

"Uh-huh." She took a cup for herself. "That's why I have so many suitors lined up outside my door."

"The lack of suitors might have something to do with your temper."

"Or my lack of chastity."

Reese's perpetual good humor disappeared in a flash. "Has someone said something to you?"

"Not to my face, but I've heard the whispers over the years."

Reese's smile had vanished. She almost didn't recognize the man looking down at her with such cold purpose. "Tell me who."

"No."

"Why not?"

"Because killing people won't stop the gossip."

"I think you underestimate the impact of a few corpses being lined up."

Addie walked over and got the coffeepot. The talk would never stop, corpses or not. "I think you underestimate human nature."

She put the pot on the table.

"I thought you preferred tea."

"There are days when coffee has its place."

Reese held out a chair. "Because of Isaiah."

What was the point of denying it? "Yes."

"He's not what you think he is."

She sat. "So you keep telling me, but if you're not going to elaborate, you might as well stop hammering that point."

"So who's been bothering you?"

"No one." She waved her hand dismissively. "I'm just being foolish."

"Foolish how?"

Addy felt like rolling her eyes, stomping her foot, and maybe just slapping her cousin. He might love her, but sometimes he just didn't understand that though she was his cousin, she was also a woman. "Did it ever occur to you that I might like to be courted? That I might like to go to dances? That I might like to have a man bring me flowers and say silly improbable things in my ear while we walk in the moonlight?"

"Uh . . ."

"Never mind." She poured herself some coffee before handing the coffeepot to Reese. "I can see from the expression on your face that it hasn't."

"I'm sorry, you just don't seem the type."

"There's a type? Being female isn't enough?"

"You're just so self-contained, so always in control."

"I know. But sometimes I get silly like every other woman out there. And sometimes I want the same things every other woman wants."

"You talking children?"

She almost choked on her coffee. "I'm still working on the courting part."

"I thought you were sweet on that Matthew guy."

He was being deliberately obtuse. "Tell me, Reese, if a girl wanted to get your attention, what would she need to do?"

"Oh I don't know, maybe tell a joke when I'm near. Wear a pretty scent. Maybe put her hair up in a cute way."

Good heavens. Her cousin was easy. "That's all it would take?"

"Truth be told, men aren't all that complicated, Addy girl." Reese took a sip of coffee and his expression went from amused to astonished.

She groaned. "Not you, too."

"What?"

"Everything that man touches comes out perfectly."

Reese chuckled. "What can I say? That's good coffee."

"I taught him how to make it."

"Then it must be galling that his tastes better than yours."

"It does more than that." She got up and grabbed a loaf of cinnamon bread off the counter. Plopping it down in front of them, she handed Reese a knife. "Try this."

She waited impatiently while he went through the ritual of cutting, buttering, smelling, and tasting, and then finally chewing. She wanted to slap him when his expression melted to bliss. "Darn it."

"I'm sorry, honey, but your student has the magic touch that takes your wonderful to fantastic."

It wouldn't gall so much if Isaiah took that magic to her bed, but for some reason that he wouldn't share, Isaiah was keeping his distance.

"It's aggravating, but I can't complain, business is booming."

Reese cut off another piece. "But that's not why you're mad at him."

"It's reason enough."

"But it's not *the* reason."

"No." She sighed. "I don't even think he sees me as a woman."

For a long moment Reese didn't speak. He played with his piece of bread rather than eating it, a sure sign he was debating. He tore the piece of bread in half and pushed back from the table. "He's a Reaper, Addy."

"Do you know what that means?"

"No, I don't, and neither do you, but the scary part is, I don't think he knows, either."

"Reaper" was just a grandiose term for a man with skills. "He's a man."

"No, he's not. I've been studying them since they came here, and if they ever were just men, they aren't anymore."

"Well, while you've been studying them, I've been studying Isaiah."

"And?"

She turned her coffee cup between her palms. She didn't know how to say what she had to say. She put her fingertips to the spot on her shoulder where he had bitten her. Though the wound had healed, the tingling remained. It tingled worse whenever she thought of him. And she was thinking of Isaiah now. Of the sadness in his eyes. Of how handsome he was when he smiled, truly smiled. How hard his muscles were to her touch. How soft his lips could be against hers. How great her world felt when she was in his arms. "I say he's mine."

"An 'Addy mine' or a 'Cameron mine'?"

It was a standing joke among the Camerons. A regular "mine" meant "God help the one who tried to take it away." A "Cameron mine" meant "the Devil better watch his back." "A Cameron mine."

"Jesus Christ, Cole is going to have my hide."

"Isaiah is none of his business. Tell him that."

"I'm not telling Cole that." He took a bite of cinnamon bread and washed it down with a sip of coffee. "I like my head attached to my shoulders, thank you very much."

"Then spin him a tale."

Now that the cat was out of the bag, there was no reason for her to pretend any longer. "Where does Isaiah go, Reese?"

He didn't pretend to misunderstand. "Hunting."

"What?"

There was a suspicious pause before he answered, "I don't know."

He knew. "But you have an idea."

"Ask him."

She had, but he hadn't given her a better answer. "I'm asking you."

"And I already answered."

Tears stung her eyes. Try as she might, she couldn't blink them back. "Damn you."

"Aw hell, don't cry."

She didn't know what was wrong with her. She never cried, but the more Isaiah stayed away, the more emotional she became. It didn't make sense and it wasn't like her, but she couldn't help it.

"You made her cry?" The question whipped into the room with the snap of a lash. The energy that followed it was almost as deadly. The mark on Addy's shoulder tingled, the spot on her thigh burned, and as she watched Isaiah cross the room with that predator's grace, her knees grew weak. But the tears wouldn't stop.

"No." She turned her head and pretended an interest in a robin outside the window. She might be pathetic, but she didn't have to show it. Reese stayed surprisingly quiet.

Isaiah looked from Reese's set expression to Addy's averted face. She was crying. Her blue eyes were dark, the lids reddened. A tear hovered on her lashes. With a finger under her chin, he tipped her face up to his. She resisted, but he persisted. As her gaze met his, he brushed his thumb just above her cheekbone. Just under that tear. He looked at Reese, his beast clawing at the cage he'd put around it.

"What did you say to her?"

Reese snorted. "She's not crying because of me."

"The hell she's not."

Reese finished off his coffee. "The hell she is. You're to blame for those tears, not me."

He was to blame? Isaiah shook his head. He hadn't done a damn thing. He hadn't taken advantage of the situation. He'd kept his distance. Except in the mornings. After a night spent fruitlessly searching for the other Reaper and the pack from which he must've come, Isaiah had not been able to resist the lure of the dough and the small peace it brought him. The tear quivered on the edge of her lashes. Any minute it would fall. "Is it about the kitchen?"

Reese's "no" came at the same moment as Addy's "yes."

Isaiah didn't need the contradictions to know that Addy had lied. Deception was as strong in her scent as her sadness. Shit, he didn't like to see her sad. It made his beast pace with a restless energy that echoed his own need to make right whatever was wrong.

He tipped her chin up farther, forcing her head back a little more, forcing the tension within her to focus on him. "I won't tolerate your lying to me."

Reese's chair scraped across the floor. "You talk to her again like that, and you'll have a problem with me."

Isaiah stared hard at the other man. *Leave.* He'd never had the mental powers of other Reapers, but sometimes he had the ability to influence.

"Stay out of this, Reese," Addy said.

"Funny thing about that. When a man twice your size starts threatening you, I have a problem with it."

"I won't hurt her and she knows it."

Leave. She's safe.

"You know, when you say it in that tone of voice, it is just not believable."

Addy caught Isaiah's wrist in her hand. Her fingers looked so delicate against the bigger bones of his body. He couldn't bear the thought of her being afraid of him. The world could be afraid of him, but not Addy. "Are you afraid of me, Addy?"

She shook her head. "No."

"Satisfied?" he asked Reese.

"No."

"What more do you need?"

"For you to step away from her and ask her again."

"No."

That was from Addy. Isaiah caught the tear on his thumb, letting it dissolve away before it could fall in reprimand. "Do what he asks."

"No."

Reese put his hand on his gun. Isaiah didn't doubt he had it loaded with silver bullets. "I guess you're at an impasse then, Reaper. Ask him, Addy."

She stared up at him, nothing he understood in her gaze. "Why?"

Mine, his beast whispered.

Mine, he echoed.

Shit, he needed to be taken out back and shot, but he was helpless to resist her. He dropped his voice to a low whisper, "Because I need you."

It was nothing less than the truth. He'd fought the beast and himself for a week, but when he'd stood outside that door and heard her say what she felt, he lost the reason for his resistance. "And I'd like the chance to court you."

The blush that flooded her cheeks was violent red. "How long were you standing outside the door?"

He smiled, liking the modesty mixed with her strength. "Long enough."

Addy shook her head. "You have lousy timing."

"Funny. I thought it was about perfect."

She huffed a "You would" before turning to Reese. "Leave."

"No."

Isaiah glanced at Reese. He understood the man's stubbornness. If Addy were his cousin, he wouldn't want to leave, either, but in this Reese didn't have a choice. Neither did Addy. Neither did he.

Leave.

"You heard her. I've got courting to do."

"Yes, I did. But so did you." Reese grabbed his coffee cup and swallowed the last mouthful, a slight frown on his face, as if he didn't understand why he was doing what he was doing. "She wants it done right."

Leave.

"I heard." Isaiah had no idea how he was going to deliver, but to see that hope in Addy's eyes, he'd do whatever it took.

Leave.

The door closed behind Reese and then it was just Addy and him, and the power of the attraction between them.

ADDY couldn't believe Reese had left.

"How did you do that?" Not for a minute did she believe Isaiah wasn't behind her cousin's strange acquiescence.

"I'm a tough man."

She snorted. "So is my cousin."

Isaiah brushed the hair off her face. "But I'm a Reaper."

She searched his face. "What exactly does that mean?"

There was a long pause in which the backs of his fingers slid over her cheek in a rhythmic caress that sank deeper than her skin. A caress that felt a lot like tenderness.

"It means I have . . . abilities that are different."

"How different?"

He leaned in. His lips skimmed her cheek, her ear. "You want to hear about that now?" He caught the lobe between his teeth and bit gently. "Or?"

Her breath caught in her throat. What was it about this man that could steal her reason and drive her wild with desire? Because she was wild. Her heart was beating faster than normal, her skin felt too small for her body, and she needed his touch. She so needed his touch. "What's the 'or'?"

He smiled a smile that didn't reach his eyes. "Me."

"For how long?"

A shadow crossed his face. "I only know now."

A strange way to phrase it, Addy thought, but it made sense. Isaiah never spoke of a future or talked of the past.

Addy forced a smile that felt very shaky at the edges. "Now is good."

He cupped her head in his palm and pulled her close, brushing a kiss over her right lid. And then the left. "Very good."

That rumble was back in his voice. It slid along her nerves, stroking them into life until she swore she could feel every individual hair standing on end in anticipation.

"Do you want your worry stone?"

She smiled, remembering how he'd told her to hold on to him the first time. "I'd rather rub on you."

His growl of approval was sexy. It was even sexier when he swung her up into his arms. She smothered her squeal against his shoulder. The last thing she needed was Reese to come charging in. The last thing she needed was anybody coming in. She'd never felt this way about a man. Never felt like she was dying a slow death without him. She didn't even know she could feel this way about a man, but with Isaiah, she couldn't imagine feeling anything else.

"Where are we going?"

"Upstairs."

She had to know. "To bed?"

"Where else?"

She had to ask. "To sleep?"

She loved that he could take the stairs two at a time even with her in his arms.

"Hell no."

That was also a relief.

He paused on the landing. "You afraid I'm going to change my mind?"

"You've been distant all week."

"I was a fool."

"Yes."

His chuckle was as sweet as his growl. "But not anymore."

She smiled and nipped his chest through his shirt. "No. Not anymore."

Swearing, Isaiah stopped dead. "Do that again."

She did. He groaned. She smiled, power blending with desire. He was as affected by her as she was by him. She pressed a kiss against the spot she'd just bitten, holding the thought, the desire, while he carried her those last three steps into the bedroom. As soon as the door closed behind them, he let go of her legs in a controlled glide. The friction of her thighs against his was torture. The bunching of her skirts between them, unwelcome.

His mouth bit at hers as he backed her toward the bed. "You have too many clothes on."

She was already unbuttoning his shirt. "So do something about it."

He laughed. "What happened to my shy little virgin?"

"She's too hungry to be shy."

His whole body snapped taut, and for one horrible moment, she thought she'd gone too far. "I'm sorry. I don't think sometimes."

"Shit. Don't be sorry." His fingers tunneled through her hair. "Just say it again. Now."

She did better than say it. She showed it, raking her fingers through his hair, tugging the leather thong out, freeing it to fall around his face. She grabbed handfuls, wrapping them around her fingers as she pulled him to her, rising up on her toes to meet him halfway, seeking his mouth with blind impatience.

Isaiah. His name was a chant in her mind, a need in her soul. The bite on her shoulder burned, the one on her thigh seared, and between her legs, her pussy ached. Oh God, she ached.

His mouth came down on hers. With a hungry growl, he parted her lips. On her next breath she told him what she wanted, whispering into his mouth, "I'm starving for you. Make love to me, Isaiah. I want you."

His hands clenched on her skull. His mouth bit at hers as he moaned and sat on the bed. She smiled against his lips. It was nice to know she could make his legs weak, too. Letting him take charge of her weight, she fell against his chest, straddling his groin. His cock pressed against her pussy. Hard. Hot. Ready. Oh God, so ready.

Isaiah.

He was so strong, so hot, so perfect. She'd hungered for him so long. This week. This life.

Mine.

The spot on her shoulder burned for attention. The spot on her thigh even more so.

She got four more buttons undone before she lost patience. Buttons popped off and scattered on the floor as she ripped his shirt open, exposing all that hard muscle to her touch. Isaiah was such a beautiful man. Broad shouldered, lean hipped, with a stomach ridged with muscle. His chest was covered with a fine mat of hair that narrowed to a thin line that disappeared beneath the waistband of his pants. She licked her lips, tracing the line with her fingertip. There was a strange tingling in her gums and her fingers itched. She rubbed them against the rough material of his pants, finding his erection and rubbing that, too.

He caught her hands and flipped her over, pinning them above her on the bed. "Hell, woman. Slow down."

Addy didn't want to slow down. She wanted Isaiah in her, as hard and as fast as he could be. She'd been so long without him and she needed him. Just needed him. Twisting beneath him, she rubbed her groin against his. "Isaiah, please."

"Oh, I'll please you, sweets, but not like this. Not with me so wild I could lose my head."

She didn't care if he lost his head. The thought of him losing his head, going wild, made her moan. He let go of her arms to shrug out of his shirt. Wrapping her legs around his hips, she raked her nails down his back. He swore and twisted, grinding his cock against her pussy. Close. She was so close.

The copper scent of blood blended with the scent of passion. She should have been repulsed. Instead, she was excited.

Isaiah.

"Fuck yes." Isaiah thrust against her as her nails raked down his back again. The passion flared, taking her higher, tossing her mind against his, her heart against his. Isaiah tore at her pantaloons. Addy pulled up her skirts.

He paused. She moaned, caught on the edge of anticipation, wanting to tumble over, needing to.

"Are you holding on, sweets?"

She bit her lip, nodded, and clung with her thighs, her hands. "With everything I have."

In more ways than one. She didn't know how Isaiah had become so important to her, but he had. And she had to have him. Now!

"I'm ready."

Remembering what he liked, she turned over. He caught her arm and eased her back. When she opened her mouth to question, he shook his head. "No, baby."

His thumb stroked across her cheek in a butterfly caress before his lips brushed hers. "This time, we do it right."

"I had no complaints before."

His smile was as soft as butter. "This time I want to see your face as I please you."

There was no hiding the shiver that went through her. It was scary, it was embarrassing. It was erotic, and when she thought about it, she'd like to watch him, too.

"I'd like that," she whispered right before his mouth found her breast. She expected him to go straight for her nipple. Instead, he sprinkled tantalizing kisses around the curve, kisses that felt like fire. Kisses that blossomed to nips. Nips that had her twisting with a wild impetuous need. Nips she expected to turn to one of those erotic bites. His mouth turned into her breast, opened. The moist heat of his breath caressed her. The edge of his teeth grazed her.

She arched and waited. "Oh yes."

"No," he groaned, wresting his teeth from her skin. "Damn it, no."

"Isaiah?"

"It's all right, sweets." He groaned against her breast. "It's all right."

She gripped his hair, holding him close. "Why?"

He shook his head. His hair spilled over her breast in a whisper-light caress.

"I won't do that to you. You can trust me."

She did. With her life. Her passion. With herself. His hand under her back lifted her up into his kiss.

"Isaiah."

"Addy."

She twisted closer. Arched higher. "Please."

His lips closed around her nipple, drawing first soft, teasing forth the fire, then harder, fanning the flames until they burned out of control. Until she burned. For him. She couldn't scream, couldn't breathe, could only ride the maelstrom as it tossed her this way and that.

He rubbed the sensitive nub with the rough edge of his tongue, delivering a torrent of sensation, awakening a flood of need, sending her racing toward the peak with a hard nip.

"Please!" She'd never felt like this. Never knew she could be this wild, but she loved it. "I need you."

He was already pulling her thighs apart, lifting one over his shoulder.

"God damn, yes!"

Turning his head, he placed a kiss on the spot he'd bitten before. She cried out. She couldn't help herself. He did it again, laving the sensitive spot with his tongue, tempting them both. She spread her legs wider, inviting him in. Only him.

Isaiah!

Sliding his hand down her other thigh, over her knee, down to her ankle, he lifted that leg over his shoulder. For a moment, vulnerability banked desire, but then his weight came over her, blocking out the light, the uncertainty. His cock fell against her clit, hot and throbbing. Another shiver whipped through her. His hips pulsed once, twice, driving that thick, hard length along the sensitive nub. Addy cried out. Isaiah laughed, holding himself high against her before settling his cock into the well of her vagina.

For a second, she stopped breathing, digging her nails into his back. Anticipation welled along with passion. He swore. She begged, lifting with her hips.

"Now, Isaiah. Please, now."

He didn't make her wait. Maybe he couldn't. Maybe even the same passion was tearing through him that carried her. He growled low and deep. To her surprise, she found a growl of her own. She lifted her hips for his thrust, biting his biceps to smother her scream as the perfection of his possession took over.

This was what she'd been craving. This was what she needed.

What she'd always needed. His cock speared deep, erotically gliding along her sensitive channel.

"Shit."

"More," she whispered against his arm.

"Yes," he groaned. "I need more."

He gave it to her in slow, deep thrusts that gradually gathered pleasure, gathered momentum, until he was driving into her and she was screaming into his shoulder. Her body convulsed around his cock, clenching with rhythmic entreaty, wanting, needing him to come.

Isaiah.

His body jerked once, twice, and her pussy was flooded with warmth. Her world shattered in an explosion of sensation. From afar, she heard him calling her name with the same sense of wonder and completion that settled over her. Wrapping her arms around his neck, she pulled him down. It was good. It was very good. It was the way it was supposed to be. Burying her face against the side of his neck, she whispered, "Isaiah."

THE aftermath of passion was sweet tenderness. Addy snuggled into Isaiah's side, running her fingers through the hairs on his chest as he stroked her arm with the same idle contentment.

"Will it always be like that?"

He kissed her forehead. "I hope so."

"Me, too." When he reached back to plump his pillow, she noticed the faint white lines on his neck. She reached up. He caught her hand before she could touch them.

"What happened?"

"It was a long time ago."

She believed that. The scars were flat and pale. Turning farther on her side, she asked, "How did you get them?"

"Your cousins would say because I'm a hardheaded son of a bitch."

"They'd probably say more than that, but that wasn't what I asked."

Bringing her fingers to his lips, he kissed the backs. "I don't want to talk about it."

If it was going to hurt him, neither did she. This peace was too fragile. Too new to disturb with questions about things he was trying to forget. But . . . she had to ask.

She cupped his cheek in her hand. "How did you become a Reaper?"

"That's not something you need to know."

"Yes." She touched her finger to a corner of his mouth where the remnants of his smile rested, entertaining the notion that she could hold it for him, them. "It is."

"Why?"

"Because it's a large part of who you are."

"It's not who I want to be."

He was evading. "Just answer the question, Jones."

He gave her a fake smile designed to mislead as he came over her. "Getting awfully bossy, aren't you."

She didn't answer, didn't smile back, just waited. He sighed and kissed her forehead.

"It's not a pretty story."

"Neither is mine, but you know it."

He didn't have a counter for that. She didn't give him one, just waited.

"I'm not going into detail."

She waited. He frowned down at her. "You are one stubborn woman."

She nodded and switched her touch to his shoulder. And waited.
An overview would do. For now.

Holding her gaze, he gave her what she wanted. "I'm told when I
was fourteen, I was kidnapped by some men who wanted to create a
private team of assassins."

He said it so carefully the ramifications took a few seconds to
catch up.

He'd been just a boy!

"How long ago was that?"

"Years."

"How many?"

He shrugged her hand off. "I don't know, all right?"

She put it right back earning a bit of his anger for herself. With that
force of will she so admired he brought himself under control. The
tension left his muscles first, then his mouth and lastly his eyes, but it
lingered in his scent. He wasn't nearly as calm as his next statement
would imply.

"They were very good at what they did. End of story."

She shook her head. Not the end, but a beginning. Cupping his
cheek in her palm, she placed her thumb against the firmness of his
lips, and gave him the "I'm sorry" he so deserved.

"Don't be sorry, just run."

She pushed him over onto his back.

"I spent a good portion of my life running. I've discovered unless
you're running to something, there's no point in it."

"Yeah?"

"Yeah."

The graze of his fingers down her cheek was tender, the cast to his
smile sad. "And you think running to me, a broken-down assassin, is
a good idea?"

"Yes." She thought of the tintype tucked among his belongings. "Unless you've got a reason I shouldn't."

"Other than the ones you've already heard?"

"Yes."

"Like what?"

"The woman in the tintype you keep in that box."

"I wondered if you saw that."

"I did. And that doesn't answer my question."

"There are a hundred reasons I should send you packing, but she's not one of them."

"Who is she?"

She held her breath, hoping for an answer of sister, mother, cousin.

"Someone I met a long time ago."

Her heart sank. "And she just happened to give you the tintype?"

"In a way."

Tears burned her eyes. It wasn't like Isaiah to be evasive. She was more to him than an acquaintance.

"I see."

"No you don't." His finger caught her chin and drew her gaze back to his. "I don't want her."

"Of course not. You just carry her image with you everywhere."

In a quick move, which left her blinking, he swapped their positions, dominating the moment as his fingers tunneled through her hair, not letting her look away as he gave her the brutal truth. "I was supposed to kill her."

Shock held her still. She'd known he was a killer, but she'd had a naive belief that he'd only killed those who deserved it. Bad men. Evil men. Never women. Never children. She took a cautious breath. "'Supposed to' would imply that you didn't."

He shook his head. His hair fell over his shoulders, casting his face in shadows. "No, I didn't."

Thank God. "What did she do?"

"Not a damn thing."

"And that's why you couldn't kill her?"

"No. I'd killed plenty of others with no second-guessing."

He wanted her to see him at his worst. She caught his hair in her hand and secured it at the nape of his neck. She needed to see his eyes and he needed to see hers.

"But you couldn't kill her." It was a statement, not a question.

"No. She looked at me with such innocent eyes and I thought, 'Why?'"

"Why did she need to die?"

"Yeah."

"What's wrong with that?"

"I wasn't trained to think. Just kill."

"Oh." It was hard to think of Isaiah functioning with mindless obedience.

"What was the penalty for not completing your . . . job?" It galled her to realize she didn't know what else to call it.

"Torture and eventually death."

That "eventually" was said so matter-of-factly, it made her shiver. The Reapers had been assassins. They'd delivered death and they expected it as part of their day-to-day lives. Isaiah had expected it. Dear heavens, how much pain did it take to change a boy into a cold-blooded killer? Her gaze fell to the faint scars on Isaiah's neck. How much torture did it take to keep him that way?

She touched the marks, rage simmering inside. For the boy he'd been. The man he was. "What did they do to you when they found out?"

"They never found out. I came back and they just assumed I'd completed the job."

Because he'd always had before then. "They never expected you to find your humanity, did they?"

He paused as if rolling the description around his mind. "No. They didn't."

"What happened to the woman in the picture?"

"I don't know. I like to think she's happy and doing fine."

But the not knowing haunted him. There was more than he was telling her. "And the picture?"

"I kept it as a reminder."

Addy shifted beneath Isaiah, hooking her calves over the backs of his thighs, holding him to her. "Of who you wanted to be."

"Of who I could have been," he corrected.

"Of who you are," she countered, pulling him down, getting nowhere when he tightened his muscles against her. No wonder he thought she wouldn't want him. No wonder he stayed in the shadows. He couldn't forgive himself. She knew about that kind of guilt. But she also knew Isaiah. No matter what they'd done to him, Isaiah was more than a soulless killer. Of that she was convinced. He might have lost who he was for a time, but somewhere in the middle of hell, he'd found himself. She knew that as surely as she knew her name.

"Don't go making fairy-tale endings, sweets."

"I wouldn't dream of it," This time when she tugged him down, he went. She waited until his lips were just a breath from hers before confessing, "I was thinking more along the lines of beginnings."

"Shit." His mouth bit at hers. "You are crazy."

"I know." She trailed her nails down his nape and kissed him softly, feeling his desire, his hesitation, matching it with the reckless conviction inside her. Isaiah was hers. "However, the only man I want to be crazy with is you."

"Damn it, it can't work. There are things you don't know—"

"But someday it will." She bit his shoulder, his chest, arching her hips so her pussy aligned with his cock. A single pulse of her hips enticed him in that first delicious bite. "But until then, I'm willing to take it day by day. How about you?"

His growl rumbled against her neck, his teeth grazed but didn't bite. His cock surged deep, stealing her breath, her voice. She clung to his shoulders, absorbing the impact, the beauty as they became one, rejoicing when he finally, finally, gave her what she wanted.

"Maybe."

It wasn't a yes, but it was a beginning.

⇥ 15 ⇤

ISAIAH LOOKED AT HIS IMAGE IN THE MIRROR. HE DIDN'T recognize the man looking back at him. His hair was slicked back. His body was incased in a black wool suit. A starched collar threatened to choke him and, failing that, was going to drive him crazy from the itching. He was from every angle a respectable member of society about to go courting the woman of his dreams.

But until then, I'm willing to take it day by day. How about you?
Maybe.

For a week he'd been trying to dissuade himself from following through on that "maybe." For a week he'd been unsuccessful. For a week he'd been caught up in the dream Addy had held out. For a week he'd been happy. And for a week he'd been waiting for the other shoe to fall. He gave the tie a tug. It fell back in the same position as before. Looking over his shoulder at Reese, who lounged in the wingback chair by the window in Addy's parlor, Isaiah asked, "Men court in this getup?"

Reese, who'd designated himself his shadow since that night last week, leaned back in the chair and picked up his whiskey. "Every day of the week."

"Hell, all I need is a pine box and you could prop me up outside the undertaker's."

Reese took a sip of his drink. "Not a bad idea. With a Reaper on display, we could make some money."

Isaiah tugged at the stiff collar. "I've got news for you. A dead Reaper looks the same as any other corpse."

"Now that's a pity, considering how hard it is to kill one of you."

He met Reese's gaze in the mirror. "You should know. You've tried."

Reese shrugged, not denying the second shot that night last week had been meant for Isaiah. "Not as hard as I should have."

Isaiah held his gaze. He wanted to know why Reese had missed that night. A Reaper wouldn't have. "Why was that?"

"I could say a lot of things."

"How about the truth?"

"How about part?"

Something was better than nothing, until he could get it all. "Do it."

"Because I've never seen Addy as alive as she is when she's around you."

"For that you took away her protection?"

"Nah. For that I'm risking Cole kicking my ass. He wants her safe."

As if he didn't know that. "And you?"

"I want her happy."

"At any cost?"

Reese sat forward. "Pretty much."

Reese's love for Addy was a weakness that could cost her life. He'd have to remember that. "I'm not staying."

"So you've said."

"I mean it."

"Uh-huh."

"I'm a Reaper." Reapers didn't have homes. Didn't wear ties. Didn't take women to dances. He looked at his reflection. Reapers only had the illusions.

"So you've said."

"Not to hear myself talk."

"I'm not the one you have to convince." He took another swig of his whiskey. "But I'll tell you this, if I have to put my money on Addy or your beliefs, my money's on Addy."

He'd learned over the last week, when dealing with Reese, that nothing was what it seemed. "What aren't you telling me?"

Reese smiled. "A whole lot of shit you should know, no doubt."

"No doubt." Isaiah tugged at the collar again. "Don't you have somewhere else to be?"

"Nope. My orders are to stick to you like a fly on shit."

"Cole?"

"Yes."

"Does he know what a lousy chaperone you are?"

"He might have forgotten to ask a few pertinent questions."

"That doesn't sound like Cole."

"He was a bit aggravated at the time. I believe you'd just beat his ass."

Isaiah smiled with remembered satisfaction. "A fact you took advantage of."

"Yup." Reese motioned with the glass. "Stop messing with that collar or you're going to have it crumpled."

"I'd rather just take it off."

"So would every man who has ever donned one of those suits, but women love a man spiffed up, and you promised to do this courting right."

"Which brings up another question. Why didn't you stop me?"

Reese shrugged. "I didn't get the impression at the time that anything could have stopped you."

Probably not, but someone should have stopped him. He wasn't thinking straight. The beast was too strong. Addy's allure too great. "You should have tried. We're talking about your cousin."

"Being my cousin just makes her a Cameron. And when Camerons make up their minds that they want something, they get it."

Isaiah arched a brow at Reese. "You wanted me dead."

"Uh-huh."

Isaiah gave the tie a tug. It still listed to the right. The starch in the collar of the shirt still itched. And he still wasn't a man who had any right to touch Addy.

He yanked the tie off and started over. "You should have pulled the trigger."

Reese smiled that smile that could have meant anything from amusement to intent. "You never know. I still might."

The tie still listed to the right. He left it. However it was, however he was, both were going to have to do.

"Did you get the flowers?" he asked Reese.

"Mrs. McGillicuddy wasn't willing to offer them up. She's mighty particular about her first roses of the season."

He cocked an eyebrow at Reese. "You could have just taken them."

"Did I forget to mention that she's a damn fine shot?"

"You probably would have if you'd thought there was a chance I'd believe an old woman with a shotgun could dissuade you."

Reese finished his drink. The glass clinked down on the table.

"Damn, you're getting to know me."

"A casualty of you living as tight as fleas on a dog."

"That'll complicate things."

Isaiah shot him a grin that was only half forced. Reese had a way of growing on a person. "Not if you get lost."

"Uh-huh."

Isaiah grabbed his hat off the peg by the door with a sense of finality. He was as good as he was going to get.

"Where are you going?"

"To get my ass shot off." He bared his teeth at Reese in a parody of a smile. "Want to join me?"

Reese bared his right back. "Absolutely."

Isaiah jammed his hat on his head. If Reese wasn't such a pain in his ass, he could find himself liking him.

ADDY looked like an angel standing in the doorway, dressed in a gown the color of the sky on a clear spring day. Her smile radiated happiness, her appearance elegance. Her hair was drawn up in an elaborate collection of ringlets that at once enhanced her natural grace and heightened the air of vulnerability he'd always sensed beneath her strong exterior. When she bit her lip, he realized the vulnerability wasn't an illusion.

"How the hell can you be anxious?"

Addy blinked. "How can you not be? We're going dancing!"

Reese laughed. "Quite the ladies' man. A week of courting and your lady is still as nervous as a cat in a room full of rocking chairs."

"Shut up, Reese."

"Yeah," Isaiah growled. "Shut up."

Reese held up his hands. "Pardon me."

This wasn't the way it was supposed to go, Isaiah thought, with

Reese laughing and Addy covering for him. He shoved the roses he'd stolen at her. "You look too damn beautiful to be nervous."

A tinge of pink dusted her cheeks. "Thank you." She took the roses. "Where did you get these?"

"I found them."

"You found roses?"

"Yes."

She looked at Reese for confirmation.

"Don't ask," Reese advised.

Addy sniffed the roses and then angled Isaiah a glance out of the corner of her eye. Her "all right" was very soft.

From down the other side of town came the faint sounds of musicians tuning their instruments.

"Last chance for you to come to your senses," Isaiah advised, half serious, half joking. Looking as she did tonight reminded him how far Addy was beyond his reach. How far she could fall if he slipped.

Addy touched the spot on her neck where he'd bitten her. He frowned. He hadn't seen any signs of her turning, but it made him nervous that whenever he was around, she compulsively reached for that spot. Was it a new ritual or something more?

Addy tipped the roses toward her and breathed in their scent. "I think I'll chance it."

"If you go to the dance with me, your cousin Cole will know."

She rolled her eyes. "If I go to the dance with you, the whole town will know."

"Even your fiancé, Mr. Hackleberry."

"What?" Reese straightened. "When did you get engaged to that mama's boy?"

Addy's blush deepened. "He doesn't actually know I picked him."

Reese broke into laughter. "Were you going to tell him before or after the wedding? More importantly, when were you going to tell his mother?"

She buried her face deeper in the roses. "Shut up, Reese."

"The widow Hackleberry is a formidable woman," Reese informed Isaiah. "And for all the boy would have it otherwise, she's determined that her dear son remains—how does she put it—unsullied."

"That's who you wanted to marry?"

Addy glared at her cousin. "The woman can't live forever and Hackleberry would be manageable."

"I wouldn't count on the widow dying anytime soon."

"It doesn't matter now anyway, so hush."

No it didn't. But Cole did. "Will Cole make trouble after I'm gone?"

Addy's expression closed and some of her joy in the night faded. Damn it, why the hell had he brought that up now?

"Don't worry, he won't have me declared incompetent."

"You sure?"

She looked out the window. "I'm sure."

"Look at me and say that."

From the glare she shot him, his courting for the evening might involve a lot of kissing ass.

"I'm sure."

"I thought you promised her a courting, not a lecture," Reese said.

So he had. The tuning of instruments was gradually flowing into music. Isaiah motioned to the flowers. "Why don't you put those in water and then we'll leave."

"By all means, do that," Reese urged. "Before Mrs. McGillicuddy takes a look at her rose garden."

Addy stopped halfway to the kitchen. "Isaiah, you didn't!"

He shrugged, figuring noncommittal beat admitting. He wanted her to enjoy the flowers.

With a shake of her head, and a quick glance around, she motioned him into the foyer. "You'd better get in here. Mrs. McGillicuddy is a good shot."

He closed the door behind him. "So I'm told."

Halfway across the foyer she paused and looked back over her shoulder, that blush getting deeper, her expression softer. "You look very handsome, by the way."

"And you look very beautiful."

"Thank you."

He stood in the hallway, listening to her fuss with the flowers. The courting wasn't going as well as he'd planned, but he'd managed a couple of moments when he'd pleased her.

It took thirty seconds for Reese to poke his confidence. "It just gets worse from here on out."

How much worse could it get? "I'll handle it."

"I'll enjoy the show."

Isaiah lifted his lip in a snarl. "Don't you have a woman of your own to court?"

"I do my courting a bit farther from home."

Isaiah didn't court at all, except for tonight. Because it was what his woman wanted. Because it would make her happy. Because when he left, he wanted to take with him at least one memory of making her happy.

"I'm ready."

He opened the door. Addy just stood there, looking at him expectantly. Reese cleared his throat. Too late, he remembered to hold out his arm so she could tuck her hand in the crook.

"Hell, man, don't you ever court at all?"

The growl rumbled low in his chest. "No."

Addy just smiled. "Go away, Reese."

Isaiah knew he lacked social graces. He knew what he was, and what Addy really needed, but he'd be damned if he'd have her evening ruined by her cousin's mockery.

"Yes, go away, Reese." He put every ounce of persuasive power behind that command. Reese didn't budge. Instead, he settled his hat on his head. "Now what kind of chaperone would I be if I just let you go gallivanting off to the social with no escort?"

"A live one?"

Reese's hand dropped to the butt of his revolver. "Maybe."

His beast tossed Reese a mental snarl, but Isaiah didn't care about the threat. He only cared about the way Addy was looking at him now. Like he was something. As illusions went, that was pretty good.

"Ready?"

She smiled and nodded as the fingers of her free hand touched his wrist. The satin of her glove was smooth and warm. He'd rather have the feel of her skin.

"Still nervous?"

"A little."

"Why?"

"Because it's my first time out. There'll be some talk."

"About me."

She shook her head. "About my kidnapping."

As much as he wanted to give her the courting she desired, he didn't want her upset.

"We don't have to go."

She looked surprised. "Oh, we have to go."

"We do?"

She nodded. "Oh yes." She squeezed his arm. "I wouldn't for anything miss watching those jealous cats swallow their tongues when I walk in with you."

"Glad I can be of use."

Her grin widened. "Me, too."

* * *

HALFWAY to their destination, the hairs on the back of his neck stood on end. Shit. Not now.

Reese came up beside them and drew his revolver.

"What is it?"

He held up his hand and motioned Addy to be quiet. Not even a cricket chirped.

Reaper.

"Reaper?" Reese asked.

Addy licked her lips. The scent of her fear tainted the air, but her voice was steady as she asked, "Friends of yours?"

"No."

He pushed her back against the wall. There was an alley directly ahead. It would be a good place for an ambush. On the other side were a building and a shed. Behind them was the livery. And beyond that, another alley. At the far end of the town, light spilled from the barn that had been decorated for the dance. Isaiah judged the distance. Even if they called for help, they wouldn't be heard.

Reese cocked his revolver. "How many?"

Isaiah shook his head. He didn't know. There was no way to know. "Until they attack, that will be a mystery."

"Perfect. Any idea who will be attacking?"

He wished he could say, but the energy coming toward him wasn't familiar. Over Addy's head he met Reese's gaze. With a jerk of his chin, he indicated Addy. Reese nodded.

"We're going to miss your sorry ass."

"No." Addy grabbed for his arm. "I'm coming with you."

From her purse, she pulled a small derringer. Isaiah took the gun from her hand. "I appreciate the thought, but no sense getting them madder than we need to with that peashooter."

Addy made a grab for her gun. "I wasn't intending on missing."

At point-blank range that derringer wouldn't even slow a Reaper. Isaiah tucked the gun in the back of his pants. Again he met Reese's gaze. "I don't intend for you to be a target."

Again Reese nodded. The quarter moon was just enough to throw shadows against the walls. Shadows in which a Reaper could hide. They had a choice. Go back or go forward. The crowd offered some protection, especially if the Reapers didn't want to be known. With another jerk of his chin, Isaiah indicated they go forward. He tucked Addy between them.

"I'd still feel better with my gun," she muttered as they eased forward.

"And I'd feel better if you were home safe, but it doesn't look like either of us is getting our wish tonight."

"Amen," Reese said.

The beast snarled within, clawing for control.

Quiet.

He couldn't listen for the Reapers and control the beast at the same time. Reese cut him a strange look. He couldn't deal with him, either, right now. Reapers wanted his woman. Which didn't make sense. The law said the Reaper who took up with a human woman would be hunted and killed. As an enforcer of Reaper law, it was Isaiah's job to kill the Reapers who violated the dictate. But these Reapers didn't want him. They wanted Addy.

"Do you have a way to call the men Cole sent to guard the house?"

"Yes."

"Do it."

Reese reached over and grabbed the derringer out of Isaiah's belt. Pointing it into the air, he fired it once.

"That's it?"

Reese shrugged. "Cole's orders were, at the first sound of gunfire,

230

to come running." The look Reese gave Addy was disgusted. "You could have at least bought a two-shooter."

"Next time I will." Her expression said the second bullet would be for Reese.

"I'm not even sure they could hear that."

Reece shrugged. "I figured you wouldn't want me wasting the bullets in my gun."

If they were silver bullets, he didn't. And knowing Reese, they probably were.

"Good point."

Addy dug her fingers into his hand. "What are you two not telling me?"

Isaiah borrowed Reese's line. "Probably a whole lot of things that you need to know."

"You've been spending too much time with Reese."

"Maybe."

Addy walked a little faster. Her gaze locked on the lights ahead as if they were a talisman. He didn't know how to tell her that, if the Reapers wanted her, getting there wouldn't save her.

"What exactly are Reapers?" she asked.

He didn't know how to tell her that, either.

They were almost upon the alley. His nerves scraped beneath his skin, but with a warning. Palming his silver knife, he drew his revolver. The attack was imminent. He just didn't know from where. A glance back showed Reese equally ready. But there was no sign of the Cameron men. The derringer report might not have been loud enough to carry. Or worse, they might've put the shot down to the revelry.

"This would have been my first dance with a beau," Addy whispered.

He didn't know what else to say but, "I'm sorry."

He could see her hand working inside the pocket of her skirt. Her worry stone.

Rub on me instead.

Another mistake. "I'll get you through this."

He blinked as her lips drew back in what, in a Reaper, would have been a snarl. "They have no right to ruin my evening."

"No."

Reese tapped his shoulder and pointed ahead to a balcony that hung over the street.

Isaiah nodded. He'd already spotted the Reaper crouched there, a darker shadow within the shadows. Death waiting. He looked across the street. More shadows. More death. He didn't have to look over his shoulder to know what was behind him. These Reapers hunted in packs, with a pack's skill at isolating its prey.

Tapping his thigh with his hand to get Reese's attention, he told Reese how many and where. Reese dropped back and stepped out, separating himself from them.

"Isaiah?" Addy whispered.

He held his finger to his lips. She bit her lips, coming to a stop when he did, just short of the alley. Her hands fluttered against his back in silent inquiry.

"I need a gun."

"No."

"Yes."

Reese stepped close again and handed her one of his revolvers. "Aim for the heart or it won't be worth it."

Isaiah thought the gun looked ugly in her hand, which was so much more suited to bringing pleasure. At his frown, she explained, "I don't want to be a target."

Reese jerked his chin in the direction of the street. "Too late for that."

While he'd been distracted, the Reapers had been getting into position. Their focus was on Addy. Their eyes burned red in the dark. Isaiah scented Addy's fear. Reese's anger. The wolves' lust. Son of a bitch! The Reapers didn't have her marked for death. They wanted her for sport. He'd never let that happen.

He caught Reese's eye. The time for softness was over. "No matter what, don't let them have her."

Addy gasped, Reese swore, but he nodded. Addy looked at the gun, at the giant wolves slowly staking closer.

"Those are Reapers?"

He couldn't hide it anymore. "Yes."

"But you're—"

"Yes."

She shook her head and stared at him, unable to absorb what he'd just told her.

"Goddamn it, Addy, this isn't the time to fall apart."

Her "I'm not" was shaky.

Son of a bitch, he should never have given in to the beast. Never touched her. He should have kept her safe. When Addy met his gaze, however, it wasn't fear Isaiah saw in her eyes, but determination.

"I'll hold one bullet back."

With which to kill herself.

Hooking his fingers on the back of her neck, Isaiah pulled her close, pressing a hard, hot kiss on her trembling lips.

"It won't come to that. I promise you."

He'd deliver the killing blow himself before he'd put that burden on her soul. The smile she forced broke his heart.

She touched the spot on her shoulder. "I know."

Guilt flayed him anew. With all he'd done to her, she still believed in him.

Because she can't understand, the voice inside whispered.

And she never would. For as long as he drew breath, she wouldn't know the truth of the man she cared for.

Isaiah held her for a second more, breathing in her scent, imprinting it in his memory. "Thank you."

For giving him peace. For giving him normalcy. For giving him her heart.

He took a step back. Before she could realize what he intended to do, he grabbed her around the waist and bolted across the alley. Her scream trailed behind him. The revolver thumped against his side. He only had time to open the shed door and toss her in before the Reapers were upon him.

Claws dug into his back and legs, raking with lethal efficiency, shredding his skin. His beast howled a challenge, and raged forward, claiming sinew and muscle for itself, changing him from man to animal in the blink of an eye. Rearing backward, he slammed the Reaper back against the wall with enough force to break through. They fell into the livery. Horses neighed and stomped their feet. The Reaper lost his hold. In the split second he fought to regain it, Isaiah ripped out his heart. From the street there came the sound of more snarls, Reese's curse, which sounded more like challenge than surrender, and the faint melody of a waltz.

"Gave you a bit of indigestion, did I?"

Isaiah leapt through the opening to see Reese standing in the street, surrounded by Reapers, including one writhing on the ground in front of him, vomiting profusely. Blood poured from its eyes and nose.

The other wolves backed off a step when Reese stepped forward, holding up a bottle. "Anyone else want a taste? "He took another step into the street. The Reapers followed. Reese smiled as he lured the wolves away from the shed. Away from Addy.

Isaiah rushed up silently behind the Reapers, driving them toward Reese, away from Addy. He went for the weakest, the one thrown by the other wolf's spasms. A snap of his jaws at the base of the wolf's skull severed its head. Isaiah's beast howled its victory, an alpha in its glory, before plunging through the ring of wolves to take a position at Reese's back. Lifting his head, he issued an age-old challenge to the bravest.

"You've got blood on your mouth," Reese observed.

Isaiah could only rumble a warning. His beast was unpredictable. Even around friends.

"Just thought I'd point out that Addy's not going to find that attractive."

Addy wasn't going to find anything attractive about him after this. Isaiah knew that, but the beast didn't, and they couldn't afford anything that would distract the beast from the battle.

Reese feinted forward with a lunge toward a wolf that had got too close. The wolf stepped back but not as far as before. "Well, one thing is for sure, you're a big son of a bitch, whatever form you take."

Yes he was. And he was a Guardian, too. A Reaper with special powers and above-normal strength among beings who were already above normal. And if he was alone, he could probably take them all, but he wasn't alone. He had Addy. It changed the dynamics of everything.

A wolf lunged at Reese. He tossed the bottle on the ground. Glass shattered. Liquid sprayed. The wolf dropped, its body seizing in a grotesque spasm. The Reapers in front jumped back, but the ones behind closed in, cutting Reese and Isaiah off from the shed.

Fuck that. Isaiah spun. Reese was right beside him, another bottle in his hand. It hit the ground. The Reapers sprang back before it exploded, creating a hole that Isaiah leapt through. Despite holding his breath, the fumes burned his eyes. Behind him, Reese swore. Ahead, there was the sound of cracking wood, Addy's screams, and a single gunshot.

Addy!

⛧ 16 ⛧

HE THREW OPEN THE DOOR. BLOOD WAS EVERYWHERE. A small unstained section of Addy's blue gown peeked out from beneath the body of a rapidly changing Reaper. More wolves were pouring through the back entrance of the shed, stopped by their own mass. Behind him Reese called, "You got her?" In his mind he said, "Yes," but it came out a rough bark. He had to get control. He couldn't take her out like this. The wolf was hampered by his form. He needed hands. He needed feet. He needed Addy.

Closing his eyes, he did something he hadn't done in ages. If ever. He prayed to whoever or whatever was out there, ruling this hell.

Give me the power to change. Please.

It started slowly, but built in momentum as he nuzzled Addy's limp hand with his nose, breathing her scent, which was tainted with the foulness of blood and fear and gunpowder. Something hit his side as he covered her body with his. He held his ground. He took another blow on his back. He didn't move, focusing on his human form, remembering how it had been to be in Addy's arms. Wild. Whole. Human. For Addy he needed to be Isaiah. There was no other option.

Setting his jaw, Isaiah braced his shoulders as blow after blow rained down on him. *It will happen*, he told his beast, fear driving conviction. Fear for the woman they both loved. And then, between one blow and the next, it did. Half-morphed, with the jaws of the wolf and the hands of a man, he grabbed the gun from the floor. It wasn't as smooth as it would have been had he been fully changed, but it was enough. He pulled the trigger. Heart shots each. One. Two. Three. Four. The Reapers went down. Three more stood outside the door. A glance over his shoulder showed Reese going down under the Reapers out there.

There was only one way out and that was forward through the three that remained in the building with him. Hauling Addy up, he threw her over his shoulder. Her blood soaked his skin.

I'll hold one bullet back.

Guilt flayed his conscience until he remembered the dead Reaper on top of her. She hadn't held it back. She'd used it immediately. She'd fought back. He should have known she'd fight back. She was a Cameron. They were fighters to the last. So was he.

His beast howled a challenge. The Reapers hesitated and then closed in. Confident in their superior numbers. Reese backed through the door, pistols firing in a rapid burst.

"You know we're fucked," he called over his shoulder as he dropped one gun and palmed a second.

"Not yet." It couldn't be yet. It wouldn't be. Isaiah grabbed the gun from the other man before pushing Addy into his arms. He pointed toward the three Reapers, the lesser of the two evils.

"Run."

Reese didn't make it two steps before they had him, but Isaiah was on them, fighting with every skill he possessed, tapping his beast for the primitive drive to succeed beyond anything, ignoring the pain, ignoring the odds, fighting for Addy. He didn't need to win. No, he just needed to buy Reese enough time to get Addy free. Blood dripped into his eyes, filled his nostrils, spilled onto the ground. The blows kept coming and he kept fighting, buying Reese and Addy's freedom one inch at a time, striving to make that split-second opening they'd need to escape.

A new sound broke over the fray. A hoarse war cry pierced the snarls and grunts. The first was joined by another. And another. A wild Celtic cry rose above it all.

"Cole," Reese groaned, holding tightly to Addy and dropping to his knees, his breath soughing in and out of his lungs.

Isaiah threw back his head and howled an answer. A challenge to his enemies. A call to battle for his allies. A Reaper leapt onto his back. He staggered under the weight. Something hit the wolf on his back, spinning them both around before it slid off. Free of the wolf, Isaiah was able to grab the one in front, taking him by surprise. A simple twist of his head and his neck broke. A snap of Isaiah's jaws and his throat was ripped out.

Isaiah dropped the Reaper and looked around. The Camerons were making a dent. Wiping the blood from his eyes, he saw Cole caught between two Reapers. He should have been dead but he wasn't. Any other human would have been, but Cole's reflexes were lightning quick. Those reflexes, combined with his smaller form, gave him an edge. He fought like a Reaper in the body of a man. He fought for the same reason Isaiah did. This battle, they wouldn't lose. Another Reaper came barreling up. Isaiah turned and blocked the blow. *Shit.* How many were there? Why were they here?

The next time Isaiah turned, there were no more enemies to fight, just bodies on the ground, some human, some in the process of changing back to human. Everywhere was the scent of blood. Cole threw his head back and released that warrior cry. Isaiah's wolf answered, releasing his own frustration. It was crazy. It was wild. It was what it was. To the victor went the spoils. And the Camerons and Isaiah had won this battle.

Isaiah headed for Addy and Reese. So did Cole. The beast snarled a warning, but Cole got to her side first, taking her hand as Reese laid her on the ground. The anguish on Cole's face as he knelt by her side told Isaiah all he needed to know. Cole brought the gun up, and centered it on Isaiah. This time the beast's howl was of pain.

Reese shook his head. "No. No."

Isaiah stepped forward, ignoring his wavering vision, ignoring the gun leveled at him.

Cole cocked the gun. "You son of a bitch, you did this to her."

Isaiah didn't argue. Even if he was capable of coherent speech, there was no point in arguing. But if Cole thought he was going to keep her from him, he had another think coming. And if Addy was dead already, then what did it matter if Cole pulled the trigger? Her head rolled to the side. Tears streaked the blood on Cole's face, incongruous against the usual sternness of his expression. The barrel didn't waver from Isaiah's chest. In the background drifted music from the dance. Lively. Happy. Hopeful. And the crickets began to chirp.

"They were going to the dance, Cole," Reese said. "He didn't do anything."

"They came because of him."

Reese shook his head. "They came for Addy."

Cole spat the blood out of his mouth. "They didn't even know she existed."

Reese wiped his sleeve across his eyes. "Are you sure the reason she was taken the first time had nothing to do with the attack tonight? How do you know this isn't a part of that?"

"Because there weren't any Reapers there last time."

Isaiah staggered a step forward, blood loss taking its toll. He grunted, "No." It sounded incomprehensible to his ears, but Reese understood.

"There was a Reaper, wasn't there?"

Isaiah nodded, keeping his gaze locked on Addy, forcing back unconsciousness through sheer force of will.

"What the hell are you doing talking to this fucking monster?"

"Watch it, Cole. This one's my friend."

"Since when?"

"Look at him. He gave his goddamn life for Addy. And maybe you've forgotten who we are, but I'm a Cameron, and I know where my loyalty belongs."

Cole didn't lower the weapon. "If he takes one more step, I'm killing him."

Isaiah took another step, catching himself on the wall. Addy shouldn't be lying in the dirt. She hated dirt.

"I'm warning you, nothing would make me happier than pulling this trigger."

Isaiah understood that. He just didn't care. He just wanted Addy, with her quirky ways and big heart and angel-soft hair. He had to touch her one more time. Just once more. On the next step, he staggered and fell to his knees.

"Jesus Christ, Cole, can't you see he loves her."

"The love of a monster."

"The love of a man," Reese countered.

The argument swirled around the perimeter of Isaiah's mind, significant but somehow not. He coughed, blood spattered his hand. Shit. He was hurt.

"That's not a man."

No. He was more. Or was it less? He couldn't remember what *They*'d made him.

"What do you know, Cole? You're so blinded by your guilt, you can't see what's real."

"I know an abomination when I see one."

Yes, Isaiah thought, *I am an abomination.* Only an abomination would bring this down on Addy. Only an abomination would have ignored the rules. Only an abomination would've been so weak.

Reese put his fingers to Addy's neck. With a curse, he reached for the upper left pocket of his jacket. His hands shook as he pulled out a small hand mirror.

"What the hell do you keep in that coat?"

"Whatever I need." No one, including Isaiah, breathed as he slipped the mirror under Addy's nose. Reese swore and dropped his head.

No!

"She's still with us, Isaiah. Barely, but she's hanging on."

Alive. Isaiah closed his eyes as a wave of blackness rode the relief. Addy was alive. It wasn't too late.

"Remind me never again to tease you about that coat of many pockets," Cole drawled.

Reese opened what was left of Addy's dress. The wounds were extensive, gruesome. Mortal.

"She didn't shoot herself."

Isaiah could have told them that. Addy was a fighter.

"Never thought she would." Cole reached out with his free hand and touched a clean spot on Addy's cheek. "Addy's not the type to give up."

"Damn it, Cole, sometime I'm going to have to introduce you to Addy."

"Let's get her home."

"No." Reese shook his head. "She'll never make it."

Yes, she would. She'd make it if he had to carry her the whole way. Isaiah made it halfway to his feet before dropping back to his knee.

"Neither will he."

The beast growled. The man vowed, *I'll make it.*

"We can't leave her here, lying in the dirt among all this." The sweep of Cole's arm blurred out of focus. Isaiah swallowed back his gorge as the world spun.

"This mess is going to be hard enough to explain to people," Cole continued.

"I don't give a shit about explanations."

Neither did he.

"But being found amidst a bunch of dead, naked men isn't a tale she'll want following her."

No, she wouldn't. Isaiah forced himself to his feet. Addy was alive. Her future had to be protected. He stumbled sideways, not forward. Catching himself on the wall, he gritted his teeth and willed the dizziness away. As he stood there, the hairs on the back of his neck rose. Holding perfectly still, he listened. The music still played but crickets were silent.

Reaper.

He shouted it in his mind, but the warning never made it past his lips.

"Put the gun down, Cole."

"Give me one good reason."

"He's her only chance."

"What the hell are you talking about?"

"She loves him. Let him help her."

Isaiah met Cole's gaze and lifted his lip in a snarl. There was no "let" about it. Whatever Addy needed, he would provide. Cole broke the stare first.

"Help her how?"

Isaiah took another step forward. And then another. He had to get to Addy. To protect her.

Reaper. He didn't know if the warning made it past his mind.

"By getting out of the way," Reese lashed out. His fist caught Cole on the jaw. The big man went down. Reese shook his hand out. "I'm sorry, brother, but you always did have a glass jaw on that side."

Reese put the mirror under Addy's nose again and swore.

"Get over here, damn it."

Isaiah pushed the darkness away, and took a step. At least he thought he took a step.

Reese swore again. Dropping the mirror, he rushed to Isaiah.

The beast snarled and bared its fangs. Powerful muscles gathered for the strike.

No!

Closing his eyes as Reese slipped his arm around his waist and wedged his shoulder under his arm, Isaiah willed the beast under control.

"Damn, they really tore you up."

The beast snarled again, ready to strike as Reese half led, half dragged him. Isaiah snarled right back. *No!*

"Are you going to be all right?"

Isaiah nodded and dropped to his knees beside Addy, gritting his teeth as the beast struggled to gain control, its instincts demanding the death of the threat that was so close to its mate.

Leave him be.

The beast growled and clawed at Isaiah. Isaiah clamped down harder, fighting the beast's power and his own growing weakness. The darkness beckoned. He shook his head. Soon enough, but not yet. Addy needed him.

"Isaiah. Stay with me."

Yes, I have to stay.

"You need to bite her," Reese ordered. "Three times."

No, he couldn't do that. The memories of the women he'd had to kill flew at him, half morphed, eyes wild, tortured with the agony of a conversion that could never complete, caught between the world of human and Reaper, insane with the reality of it. Screaming women. Hurting women. Unable to die, unable to live. Women who chewed off their own limbs to end the madness of the third bite.

"No." He forced the word out in a guttural bark. "Madness."

"I told you, I've been watching. They don't all go mad."

He thought of the one he hadn't killed. He'd always assumed she'd avoided the third bite, but what if she hadn't? The beast howled, *Yes!* Hard, fast, and powerful, the order surged past the barrier, feeding his hope.

No! He shook his head. He couldn't do that to her. Couldn't risk it for the selfish need of the beast. He'd let her go to her God, whole, as she was meant to be. Let her live with the angels. He had the devil covered.

The beast howled a protest and clawed at its confines. As weak as he was, it was a struggle to keep it contained.

"Goddamn you, bite her. You're not going to let her die with her only memory of this life being the hell she fought her way out of." Reese grabbed his shoulder and shook him. "She loves you, goddamn it, be worth something to her. Bite her!"

A hand reached out of the hovering darkness, followed by a body. *Reaper.*

"Who the hell are you?"

Isaiah recognized the scent.

"Blade."

Blade looked around. "Hell of a fight you had here."

Reese swore. "What the hell do you want."

"I heard the ruckus."

"From where?"

Reese was right to be suspicious. Blade was an unknown quantity. A Reaper with no loyalties other than to himself.

Isaiah didn't need to see Blade's face to know the look Blade was giving Reese.

"It doesn't matter."

"What are you?"

"Reaper."

"The good kind, I hope."

"If there is such a thing."

The sound of the hammer of a gun being drawn back and Blade's low chuckle preceded the scuff of leather across dirt as Blade knelt beside him.

"You're his friend?"

The weight of Blade's hand increased as the darkness encroached further. Keeping his gaze locked on Addy's face, Isaiah held to consciousness.

"I wouldn't go that far."

Isaiah shook his head and touched a drop of blood sliding down Addy's cheek, stopping its fall. She was cold, so cold. Her image grew fuzzy around the edges, but that blood spreading over his finger stayed bright. He was losing her.

"Make him bite her."

Blade sighed. "You know they go insane."

"Not all of them."

There was a long pause in which Isaiah could feel Blade's energy gathering. Isaiah gathered the remnants of his own strength in preparation for a strike. Reese protected Addy. He needed to live.

Finally Blade answered. "I'd be interested in knowing how you know that."

"I bet you would."

"You're playing on dangerous ground, human."

"I'm not playing."

"So I see." Air swirled against Isaiah's cheek as Blade motioned to Addy. "What if she's one of the ones that go insane?"

No!

"Then you'll kill her."

"That's not a job I want."

"But you'll do it."

Yes, he would, Isaiah knew. Blade's ethics leaned toward not torturing women. It took tremendous effort for Isaiah to turn his head, but he needed to see Blade's face. The man was looking at Addy, a strange expression on his face. With a twitch of his lips, Blade nodded. "Yeah. But not for the reasons you're thinking."

"I don't give a shit what your reasons are, just make him bite her."

"I'm not sure I can do that, either."

"Then you bite her."

Blade easily blocked Isaiah's lunge. That shouldn't be possible. The thought flitted through Isaiah's mind. He and Blade were evenly matched.

Rest, Reaper.

The order slid easily under Isaiah's beast's confusion. Powerful and seductive, the command quelled the beast.

Reese brought up the gun. "I said, you bite her."

"I can't."

"Why not?"

"It takes three bites to convert a human, but there has to be at least three days between the second and third bite."

Three bites, Isaiah thought. He'd already given her two.

"She'd die before I could do her any good."

But you can save her, Isaiah's beast nudged.

Shut up.

"What happens if it works?"

"Your spying didn't reveal that?"

"Just answer the question."

"She becomes a Reaper."

"Completely?"

"I don't know." Blade leaned in. Both Isaiah and the beast snarled a warning. There was the sound of cloth being disturbed and the scent of blood increased. Addy's blood. "It's just a theory."

Easy, Reaper. Again that deft delivery of calm from Blade before he said, "He's already bitten her twice."

"How can you tell?"

"A Reaper can always tell."

"Why did those other Reapers want her?" Reese asked.

Blade's expression stayed carefully blank, but Isaiah could feel his tension. "To test a theory."

"How did they know about her?" Reese asked, keeping the gun drawn.

"Through me."

"Why the hell did you tell them?"

Isaiah's beast snarled. *Yes, why?*

Blade nodded toward the gun. "Not only is that empty, but I'd take off your arm before you could even pull the trigger, so put it down."

Reese hesitated. Isaiah found the strength to reach over and take the gun. At Reese's glare, he shook his head. Fresh blood dripped down his side. The small effort left him totally drained. Blade took the gun from his hand and set it on the ground.

Thank you. I didn't want to kill him.

I don't want to kill you.

Sending the thought back drained the last of Isaiah's strength. He listed to the side. A shift of Blade's position and he was unobtrusively propping Isaiah up.

Bold talk for a half-dead Guardian.

Try me.

"Did you tell them on purpose?" Reese asked, interrupting the mental exchange.

"That's a stupid question."

"Did you?"

"Yes."

"Why?"

"*Why?*"

"Maybe I thought my influence could stop all this," Blade snapped back. "Hell, what does it matter? We're wasting time. He's going to pass out soon."

"He fought a good fight."

"He's fought a lot of good fights," Blade corrected, sliding a hand under Addy. The move released more of her scent. The beast howled at the odor of impending death that rode it. "But I have to admit, he's never been hurt this bad."

"You're a cold son of a bitch, aren't you?"

Yes, Isaiah thought. *Very cold.*

"So I've been told."

"So are you going to help or not?"

"I believe I am." Isaiah knew what Blade was going to do before he felt the touch of his hand on his arm and the brush of his mind.

No!

Yes.

Blade could influence anyone, anyone but Isaiah. Blade had never been able to influence him.

Don't fight me, Isaiah.

It was an impossible request. He couldn't turn his Addy into a beast. He couldn't see her struggle, couldn't deal with her hate, couldn't be the one to kill her if it all went horribly wrong.

There's no point in fighting.

The order echoed in Isaiah's mind, bouncing off barriers until it found a weak spot to glide underneath. It found his beast with unerring accuracy, soothing it into a semblance of calm.

She needs you.

Insidious and debilitating, the truth wended deep.

With you, she'll have life.

His *no* wasn't as strong as it should have been.

She's your mate. It's your duty to give her what she needs.

Duty. He understood duty.

She needs you.

He remembered her smile, her fear, the way she didn't need her worry stone around him. *Yes.*

Complete the bond. It's your duty.

No.

If you don't, They will.

They're dead.

No, They're not. Without the bond, she's not safe. You have to keep her safe.

He'd promised to keep her safe.

It's the only way.

He'd never let *Them* have her.

She needs you.

Yes. She needed him, he needed her. Isaiah leaned down, or did Blade lift her up? He didn't know. He heard a groan.

"Hurry up," Reese said. "Cole's coming awake."

Addy's scent grew stronger, even through the coppery stench of blood. So pure, so perfect.

She's yours.

Yes. Mine.

She needs you to make her strong.

Strong. Addy was always strong. But she had to be stronger to fight *Them*.

Do it. Do it.

The order echoed in his head, gaining strength with every reverberation in his ears, different voices all with the same imperative—save her. His mouth flooded with that spicy taste he'd known only once before. *Now*, he thought, *now I am ready*. He touched his lips to her throat. His Addy. His sweets. He kissed the side of her neck.

In the second before he bit, he whispered, "Forgive me."

His teeth pierced her skin. Her taste filled his mouth. All went dark and then there was a sensation of being in a tunnel, buried beneath an overpowering, cloaking darkness.

Wait. The beast? Blade? He didn't know, but he waited, not trusting that darkness, holding Addy tightly. At the edge of the tunnel, sparkles of light appeared, tiny flickers that built to streaks. Around his hands more appeared, solidifying as he watched, glowing strong enough to push the darkness back. There was the impression of movement, of going deeper, yet he went nowhere at all. Another flicker of light joined the others. This one was more centered and blossomed at his approach, luring him closer.

"Addy." Her name came out in a breath of recognition.

The light flared in response, filling his vision, before flickering.

He lunged forward. The light surrounding him surged, too, wrapping around Addy, trying to hold her. Her light whooshed back down the tunnel, growing smaller and smaller. Somewhere a waltz played.

"He's a heavy son of a bitch," he heard from afar.

"Move him over before he crushes her."

"If we can get them on these horses, can you get them somewhere safe?" Reese asked.

No, he wouldn't leave Addy.

"Yes."

The last thing he heard before the darkness smothered him was Reese.

"Make sure it's far enough away that Cole can't track them."

"He'll follow?"

"Yes."

Yes.

⤜ 17 ⤛

REAPER!

Isaiah slammed into consciousness, nerves snapping taut. Keeping his eyes closed, he took stock of his surroundings. Clean air, scented with leather and wood smoke. Warmth on his feet and shaded light on his eyes. Two people—

"About time you woke up."

Blade.

Images flooded his mind. Addy in her blue dress, laughing. Reapers attacking. Blood in a pool. Addy . . . He shied away.

"Hate to break it to you, Blade, but as ugly as you are, I just didn't feel inspired."

Fingers toughed his cheek in a fluttery caress. Addy.

"How about me? Do I inspire you?"

Isaiah opened his eyes. Addy stared down at him, a forced smile on her lips. He had a vague memory of that face streaked in blood, the lips pale, the eyes closed. Reaching up, he pushed a loose tendril of hair off her cheek. His beast moaned in pleasure at the contact. He knew exactly how it felt. The man was pretty pleased, too. "For you, I'd not only wake up, I'd get up."

She chuckled. "That might be a bit ambitious. You've been unconscious forever."

Her fingers quivered against his temple. Beyond her head he saw a mesh of twigs and leaves. They were at his lean-to. Interesting that Blade would bring them here.

"Forever? I must give 'ugly' a new definition."

"You look good." Addy's smile was as soft as her touch and just as shaky.

"I was just thinking he looked about as attractive as a pig in a wallow," Blade interjected. "So if you do get him up, steer him toward the pond."

"Blade!" Addy pressed her hand against Isaiah's shoulder in the delusion that she had a prayer of keeping him down.

His beast didn't like her familiarity with the handsome Reaper. He wasn't too fond of it himself.

"Just saying my nose could use a break," Blade clarified.

"He was hurt."

"So were—"

Blade cut him off. "Well, I'm the one who's hurting now."

Isaiah cut Blade a glance. He didn't want him talking about her injuries? Running his hand over the beard on his cheeks, Isaiah sighed. "I must look a sight."

"Been sleeping like an angel over there for two whole days," Blade snorted. "You ought to look like something."

Two days. It usually only took a few hours for a Reaper to heal, unless the wounds were mortal. Two days meant he'd been near death.

"Two days, huh?" He ran his hand over his chin, rasping his nail on the rough beard. "I must have been tired."

The wind changed direction. The aroma of roasting rabbit joined the other scents. His stomach rumbled.

"Must have been, but don't think we're going to let you lollygag once you get up."

Addy gasped. "Blade, hush!"

Isaiah cocked an eyebrow at Blade. He was willing to bet that the last time the big Reaper had been told to hush was never. "Guess I can take a hint."

"Don't you dare get up."

And the last time someone had given him an order had to be never times two.

"Sweets, I need to get up."

"A bath can wait. You were very . . ." Addy's fingers dug into his shoulder in a rhythmic pattern and her gaze skirted his. Licking her lips nervously, she finished, "There's no rush."

Rub on me instead.

He put his hand over hers, not stopping her rubbing, just shielding it from view. She must have lost her worry stone in the battle. He didn't mind filling in.

"Sweets, I've been lying here for two days. There's a need."

Blade chuckled. The rubbing continued another second, hesitated, and then stopped altogether as his implication sank in.

"Oh." She sat back. Blade chuckled. Addy snapped, "Shut up, Blade."

Another chuckle. Isaiah caught Addy's hand and brought it to his lips. Something he most likely would not be able to do later. She was Reaper now, but judging from her calm, she didn't know it. When the reality hit, there'd be no more soft touches. Just hate and anger.

"And since when do you go calling a strange man by his first name?"

Her smile tightened. "Since he doesn't seem to have a last name and since he saved both our lives."

Blade turned the rabbits. "The lady is eminently logical."

And Blade liked that. Isaiah's beast snarled a silent warning. Blade tipped his hat. Isaiah bared his teeth before nodding to Addy.

"I thought his name was Billings." He shifted up on his elbows.

"He says it's not."

"Always the man of mystery."

Blade didn't deny it. "Yup. You going to lie there all day?"

"No."

Addy pressed her hand against his shoulder again and shot Blade a dirty look. "I'm not sure you're ready."

Isaiah met the worry in her gaze calmly. "I'm getting up."

She took her hand away with a huff, clearly not happy.

She fussed with the folds of her skirt. Arranging them to hide stains in the once-fine material. Folding and tugging until the tears in the fabric were aligned in the manner which, he recognized, meant she was struggling for calm. How much did she know?

He looked at Blade. Blade looked at him. Addy rolled her eyes and put her hand to her shoulder where he'd bitten her. "I've seen that look before."

"What look?" Blade asked.

"The one that says the men want to talk without the risk of upsetting the women present."

"I can see there's going to be a downside to you being raised by your cousins." Isaiah tossed the pelt off his legs, and then immediately yanked it back. "Where the hell are my clothes?"

Addy didn't even blink. "There was nothing left to save, and I don't consider being raised by my cousins as a downside."

Blade chuckled. "Logical and smart."

"Thank you."

"Shut up."

Blade's smile never slipped, but he picked up a small pail and held it out. "Addy, would you please get some shaving water for Isaiah?"

Addy stood and took the pail. The white of her petticoats showed thorough the gashes in her skirt. Black stitching held together the rips in the top. "I'll be right back."

That warning was directed at Blade.

Blade waited until she was a good twenty feet down the path before saying, "Translated, that means we won't have much time to talk."

His beast growled. Isaiah echoed the sentiment. "You two seem to have gotten very chummy over the last two days."

"It would be a waste of time we don't have for you to be jealous, Guardian."

"Why?"

Blade shrugged and tossed him a pair of pants. "She doesn't want me, and that's not a woman a Reaper can influence."

Good. "Why don't we have time to waste?"

"With word out that you broke the law in regard to consorting with human women—"

"Thanks to you."

Blade nodded. "Some information it pays to control."

"So they could come after me faster?"

Blade met his gaze. "So they'd know where I stand on the issue."

Blade had tried to alter the law. For him. *Shit.* If anyone could change Council law by simply voicing his displeasure, it was Blade. A spark of hope flared. "And?"

And died just as quickly as Blade let out a long breath. "They're a bullheaded bunch."

Isaiah slowly pulled on his pants, absorbing the possible implications. "They sent you to kill me?"

"You know I don't belong to the council."

Yes. He did know. The newly formed council would have loved to have Blade—the oldest known Reaper—as a member, but Blade preferred the title of Rogue to Guardian.

"But someone is coming."

"Yes."

Isaiah buttoned the fly. "What about Addy?"

"They don't know about her change, but when they do . . ." Blade shrugged and checked one of the rabbits before turning it on the skewer. "The law says she has to die with you, but that might change when they find out you were successful in making her both Reaper and mate. That had not been considered possible."

No it hadn't. Hell, he still didn't believe it. "Shit."

Blade nodded. "That about sums it up."

"What does Addy know?"

"Nothing about the council."

"And about her . . . situation?" *Shit*, again. He didn't even know what to call it.

"She knows she's a Reaper."

Isaiah ducked out of the lean-to. "Why the hell did you tell her?"

"I didn't directly. Apparently, she's the type to eavesdrop when she's dying and then has the inconsideration to remember what was said when she gets well."

"That *was* inconsiderate." Not to mention inconvenient. He would have preferred to have told her himself, once he found out what being a Reaper meant to her.

"I told her to come to you with her questions."

That explained the skirt folding. "Does she believe it?"

"She watched your wounds heal, so if she doesn't believe yet, she's got a good head start."

"I guess I'll go talk to her."

"That might be a good idea." Blade tossed a packet to him. Isaiah caught it. A woodsy scent wafted up from the parcel. The distinctive scent was a strange choice for a Reaper who preferred to blend in rather than stand out. "You might want to have that bath first. You do stink."

"That bad?"

"Even a human would smell you coming."

That was bad. Isaiah stopped before he left the encampment. "Just out of curiosity, why did you refuse to join the council?"

Blade fed a couple sticks to the fire. "Could be, I'm just a contrary cuss."

"Or?"

For a minute he didn't think Blade would answer, and then the other man shrugged and stabbed the last stick into the flames. "I simply believe, until we know what we are and what we're capable of, any creation of laws is premature." He looked up at Isaiah. "Like the one the Council created that says you have to die for falling in love."

WELL, how the hell could they have known a Reaper could fall in love?

Isaiah stood hip deep in the cold water of the pond, rubbing the soap over his body. The scent was pleasing, fine soap a pleasure he'd never enjoyed before. But as Blade had so brutally pointed out, there were a lot of things in life that Reapers hadn't experienced. And he was right about something else. Creating laws in the midst of that much ignorance wasn't smart. But changing those laws now? Isaiah shook his head. That would be a battle, and would not be accomplished before the Guardians came hunting for him. And Addy.

The beast snarled, and for a brief moment, he embraced it, eyeing the trail south. When they came, blood would flow, but it wouldn't be Addy's. His claws cut through the soap. He would guarantee it. Life was full of surprises, he was learning. He hadn't expected to survive his wounds. He hadn't expected Addy to survive her conversion. He hadn't expected to find an ally in Blade. And the council would not expect his primal need to defend his mate.

Shit. His mate. His sweet Addy. A Reaper. He had no idea what that meant for him to have a mate, even less what it meant for her, and she was waiting for him to explain it to her.

Closing his eyes, he willed the beast back. Damn it, things couldn't get more complicated. Picking up the soap, he looked at the gouged bar as he rubbed it over his chest in quick circles. At this rate, it wasn't going to last long. Nothing fine lasted long under the beast.

"It won't last very long," Addy said from the bank.

"You reading my mind now?"

She snorted. "There isn't that much to read at the moment."

Did that mean she could or couldn't? "So what are you thinking?"

"I'm thinking you're trying to decide how you can get out of talking to me."

"You're good."

She shrugged and rubbed her hands up and down her arms. "Three older cousins, remember?"

"Yeah. Plus Blade gave me a heads-up. For a man with a reputation of being closemouthed, he talks too much."

"I like him."

"You would."

"What does that mean?"

"Nothing."

"Didn't you have enough of a fight in town? Why do you want to start another with me, here?"

"I don't, but couldn't you have waited until after I finish my bath?"

The conversation could but this couldn't. She held up a large piece of thick cotton. "I brought you a towel." She motioned to the bank to the right. "And a clean shirt of Blade's."

"Thank you." After carefully cleaning the area around her feet, Addy sat on the bank and drew her knees up, looking as if she planned to take root. He slowly rubbed the soap over his stomach. "Now what are you doing?"

She rested her chin on her knees. "Waiting for you to get done."

"What if I want privacy?" he stalled.

"You're not going to get it."

"Why not?"

"Because I'm afraid you'll run away and leave me here."

"I wouldn't leave you."

Her eyes never left his hand as he ran the soap over his groin under the water. She licked her lips. "Apparently, I'm no longer the sweet little thing you liked to protect."

The soap popped out of his hand. He grabbed it before it was lost. Son of a bitch, he would never understand a woman's mind. Dunking underwater, he wet his hair. As soon as he broke the surface, he started scrubbing.

"In case you're wondering," she pointed out, "this is one of those delicate moments in a relationship where it can all blow up in your face."

He shook his head. There was no one like Addy anywhere, and she was his.

"I see. Could you give me a hint as to what you want me to say?"

"I would, if I could."

Great.

"What does it mean, my being a Reaper?"

"I don't know."

"What does it mean for you, being a Reaper?"

That he didn't want to tell her, but as she sat there watching him with such trust, he found the lie he'd considered dissolving, and the flat truth coming out instead.

"It's hell."

She winced and her fingers fussed with her skirt. "Why?"

This wasn't the kind of conversation a man had while standing naked in a stream. A lot could go wrong. Addy could be shocked, run away, necessitating they start over. And once he started, he wanted it over and done. He leaned forward and ducked his head underwater, letting the water block out the world. Standing, he flung his head back and shook the water out of his hair.

"Hand me the towel."

Tossing it, she muttered, "Spoilsport."

He caught it and wrapped it around his waist before wading to shore. The closer he got, the easier it was to see the nervousness in his woman's eyes.

He stopped just short of the shore. "You've had a lot of practice hiding how you feel."

She opened her mouth. He held up his hand, forestalling what she was about to say while slicking his hair back with the other. "I know, three older cousins."

"Three *overprotective* older cousins," she corrected.

"I'm beginning to see why." Holding the towel, he stepped up onto the bank. Small stones pricked his feet. The fact that it didn't hurt confirmed what he already knew. He was healed.

"So tell me what it means for you to be a Reaper."

She was like a dog with a bone. "Turn your back first." Her eyes went wide and she inched backward. He shook his head. What did she think he was going to do? He bent and picked up his clothes. Throwing the shirt over his shoulder, he shook out the pants. "I thought I'd get dressed."

"Sorry, I'm a little impatient." She turned, still sitting, until her back was to him.

"So I see."

"Blade wouldn't tell me anything."

She sounded annoyed. He guessed he couldn't blame her. "He told you enough."

"Not really. He seems to think he's clever with his almost answers," she informed him over her shoulder.

"But he's not?"

"No. Cole does the same thing. It's annoying."

Yes, it was. He stepped into the pants and pulled them up. "I agree."

"I've at least figured some things out for myself."

"Like what?"

"Well, you told me those giant wolves were Reapers."

"Yes."

"You've told me you're a Reaper."

He buttoned his pants and pulled the shirt off his shoulder. "Yes."

She took a breath and pressed the fold in her skirt flat. "Are you telling me you can turn into an animal whenever you want, too?"

"Maybe."

"Why maybe?"

"I don't know."

She slid around. "What kind of answer is that?"

"The kind of answer that says I don't have an answer, and I'm guessing."

She held his gaze. "Look. This is unbelievable enough as it is. Either you can turn into a wolf or you can't."

Despite the snap in her tone, he could see the plea in her eyes. *Tell me no.*

"Yes."

She didn't say anything right away, just looked at the fold she was pressing flat. Very slowly she ran her finger over the center, following the curve of her bent knee. Once, twice. "What part was the maybe?"

"The part about changing at will."

Her finger stopped midpress. "Oh."

In for a penny, in for a pound. "I don't have much control."

She just kept pressing that fold as she asked, "How did you come to be a Reaper?"

"All the Reapers I know came about the same way."

She frowned at the fold, changing the alignment, pressing harder, faster. "How is that?"

He shook out the shirt and shoved his arm into the sleeve. He didn't want to relive this. "I wasn't the only one taken captive as a kid. There were a lot of us, and we were all brought to an underground place. None of us remember specifics, but there was a lot of pain over a long time—"

The memory of that first violent conversion, the loss of self, shuddered through him. He tried to keep his voice flat, but something must have given him away, because Addy looked up and touched her shoulder.

"They didn't bite you?"

"No. Yes." He raked his hand through his hair. The beast snarled, gathering its power to fend off the threat. "I don't fucking know. *They* . . ." Shit, he hated admitting this. "*They* tortured us until they broke us. There's no one memory. Just a pile of hell."

She stopped pressing the fold. "No wonder you're not afraid to die."

Dying would be a blessing. He stopped himself, just in time, from saying it. Not only because of who he was talking to, but because it was no longer true. He'd gained some control over the years. Of the beast, at least.

He shoved his other arm into the shirt. "Pretty much, the beast just appeared."

"The beast?"

How to explain the beast? "The beast is primitive, unruly, incredibly strong."

"Is that what you mean when you say they're wolves. Is that their beast?"

"Yes, but the beast is always there inside me, fighting for control."

She came up on her knees. He took a step back. "If it's inside you, can't you talk to it?"

Shit. If only. "Rarely does it like what I have to say."

Like now. The beast wanted to press her down into the bank and fuck her. To reassert its claim. To make sure any male around knew she was his. The man wanted to keep her clean.

She reached out. He took a step back, not trusting the beast when it crouched like that inside, waiting for its opportunity.

Licking her lips, she pulled her hand back. "Didn't your family come looking for you?"

"None of us remember having family." None of them remembered much of anything.

"These men who took you . . ."

"Yes."

"Kidnapped you . . ."

"Yes."

She came to her feet. "Did you make them pay?"

"Yes."

Her smile was cold.

Reaper.

"Good."

Isaiah took another step back, the pain a living thing inside. *No. Not good.* The beast prowled, ready to strike, needing to strike.

Her gaze searched his. "How old were you when they took you?"

"I told you. I don't remember. I only know what I was told and I don't believe much of that."

"I don't understand."

"*They* did something to our memories. Sometimes I get flashes, but I can't tell if they're real or just a story I heard."

Addy was looking at him with a strange expression. The wolf howled a protest. Hell, he didn't know why he expected her to understand what he was saying. He didn't understand what he was saying.

"They hurt your mind."

Systematically, ruthlessly, permanently. He debated buttoning the shirt. "*They* were damn good at it."

Her fingertips grazed his sleeve. "It doesn't show."

He turned away. "Thank you."

She went with him, her hands sliding around his chest, settling on his skin. Warm. Dainty. Pure. His cock hardened at her touch and his beast rumbled its pleasure. He removed her hands from his chest. She stepped around and put them back. His fingers closed around her wrists. She stopped him with a shake of her head.

"Don't."

"Why?"

"I need to touch you."

He yanked her hands free and held them wide. "I don't need your pity."

She shook her head. Tears hovered in her eyes. For him.

"It's not pity."

The beast snarled. At him or at her? "Looks like it to me."

"That's because you can't see."

He saw everything. Her soft heart, her pain. The future he'd delivered her into. "What do you think I should see?"

Not fighting his grip, she stepped forward and rested her cheek against his chest, whispering softly, "Me."

Ah hell. He didn't have the strength to push her away. He let go of her hands. They went around his waist. He didn't know what to do with his.

She squeezed gently. "I'm so sorry."

"It wasn't your fault."

She shook her head again. Tears eased the friction of her cheek against his chest. *Damn it*, she was crying. He started to push her away. The beast snarled. At him.

She resisted the pressure. "Put your arms around me, Isaiah."

"Why?"

"Just do it."

He did. "Now what?"

She snuggled closer. "Wait."

"For what."

"Just wait."

He did, breathing in her scent, counting her heartbeats, her breaths. She was calm, he realized. It was against his nature to stand still and just let things be, but this was . . . nice. The beast stopped pacing. The pain faded, and as he rested his cheek on Addy's head, the beast calmed. A few more minutes and he felt almost peaceful.

"Better?" Addy asked quietly.

He kissed the top of her head. How did she do this to him? "Yes."

She straightened the front of his shirt, her touch as soft as her voice. "Cole taught me that, too. When I first got home, I had such nightmares and they'd stay with me during the day." Her gaze skirted his. "I used to think I could hide from them."

He understood that. He tipped her chin up, needing to see her eyes. "And?"

Her smile shook with the strength of the memory. "Cole would find me wherever I was, take me in his arms, and then he'd just hug me until the demons went away."

Like she'd found him. "Guess that means I'll have to try harder to be civil to his ass in the future."

She sniffed and traced a pattern in his chest hair. "I'd appreciate it."

They stood that way for a few minutes longer. He holding her, she holding him, the two of them together, building their own world amid the backdrop of the gurgling stream and the singing birds. Their own strength. His beast rumbled its contentment. Turning his head, Isaiah pressed a kiss to her hair. His sweets.

Gradually tension slipped into Addy's muscles. Her hand flattened against his chest. Her scent changed. He held her, waiting for whatever it was.

"Were there other women Reapers?"

She was jealous.

"Everyone taken was male."

Her fingers rubbed against his shoulder. "But you had women."

He kept his arms around her, battling the growing tension in her the only way he knew. "Women were forbidden to us."

She rested her forehead against his chest. "Blade says Reapers are very attractive to human women."

"Blade says too damn much."

She went silent, but the tension grew. He wanted the peace back.

"What are you asking me, Addy?"

"You know."

Son of a bitch. "No, I don't. In case you haven't noticed, I don't guess well."

The rubbing stopped. So did her breathing. He waited. So did his beast. Finally she turned her face to the side and whispered, "I fell into your bed so easily. Was I just one in a long line of women falling there?"

How was he supposed to answer that and keep his pride? Tell her she was the third woman with whom he'd had sex and the only one to whom he'd made love? Did he really want to look that much of a fool?

"Hesitation is never good." She tried to take a step back. He didn't allow it. They'd come too far together for running away. And worrying about his pride, he realized.

"Yeah, but probably not for the reasons you're imagining." The broken breath might have been a sob. Hell, he wasn't interested in other women. What was the point of faking it?

"We were forbidden contact with women."

"But you were with me."

"Yes."

He could actually feel the blush heating her cheeks. "You knew what to do with me."

"Yes."

"You've probably been with a hundred women."

"No."

"Fifty?"

"No."

She cut him a glance from beneath her lashes. "Ten?"

"Goddamn it." She jumped. He gritted his teeth. "Before you, I had two women, and they used their mouths."

Naturally, she looked up then. A mixture of shock, relief, and—son of a bitch—fascination filled her expression. "I could use my mouth?"

Ah, hell. His cock went hard in a rush. Fisting his fingers in her hair, he lifted her mouth to his, kissing her hard and deep before admitting, "Anytime you want."

He expected her to back off. Her gaze didn't leave his as he straightened. Little by little, the tension within her lessened. A small smile hovered on her lips.

"You were a virgin."

Shit. This time he was the one to let go and she was the one to hang on.

"So were you," he growled.

Her smile broadened, with pleasure, he realized. "Yes, I was."

He let her pull him back. "You didn't seem to mind."

She grabbed his hand and tucked it around her back. "I didn't think it could have been more special, but I was wrong."

She wasn't disappointed. He went back to hugging her. "But?"

"Knowing I'm the only one who knows you that way." She snuggled closer and kissed his chest. "That just makes it perfect."

Yeah, it did. Holding her mouth to his skin, he hummed his agreement. "It was perfect."

She gave a nip that set his senses aflame. "Are you talking about my jealousy, or the first time we made love?"

He smiled. "Both."

"I should warn you that I'm not very calm about you being with anyone else."

"Good, then you'll understand when I tell you I don't like you being friendly with Blade?"

"Blade? But he's harmless."

He stored that away to tell Blade. Sometime when he was being more arrogant than usual. "Harmless or not, the beast wants to rip his heart out when you smile at him."

She blinked and leaned back. "That's pretty violent."

"It's always violent."

"I don't think my beast is as mean as yours."

"Maybe." But he'd never heard of a kind and benevolent beast. "Or maybe it just hasn't made itself known."

She frowned at him. "Maybe I have a nice beast."

He didn't have the heart to take the delusion away from her.

She pursed her lips. "I think I'll call it Jessica."

She was going to give her beast a name?

"What do you call yours?"

"The beast."

Leaning back against his hands, she shook her head at him. "You haven't even tried to get along with it, have you?"

She had no idea what she was talking about. "Not really."

"No wonder you're fighting all the time."

"I wouldn't exactly call it fighting. More of an armed truce that kept falling apart."

"What happens when it falls apart?"

"If the beast wins, then I change."

"That's the only time you change?"

"Yes. High emotions seem to give it the upper hand."

"Can you control it?"

"To some degree."

She frowned at him. "Show me."

"I'm not a damn side show."

"I never thought you were, but it's only logical that I'm curious. You say I'm changed. I need to know what that means."

"I can only change when I'm mad."

"You can't control it?"

"I told you no."

"Then how, I mean why . . ." She pushed her hair out of her face. "Why did they even create you?"

"To kill."

"Who?"

"Whomever they wanted dead."

"If you can't change at will, how could they even know you could do what they wanted? I mean—"

"The beast likes to kill."

She blinked. "Oh."

"Exactly."

Isaiah couldn't blame Addy for her withdrawal. He couldn't blame her for her questions. He just didn't have the answers she required.

Blade's soft call slid beneath the breeze, rustling the leaves.

Addy turned her head and listened. "Blade's calling."

"You've definitely got Reaper ears."

She touched her ear. "I do?"

Nodding, he motioned toward the campsite. "A human would never have heard that."

Stepping back, he held out his hand. Water dripped from his hair in a cold trickle down his back as she took his hand in hers and turned it over. She ran her index finger down the center to his wrist, coming to a halt at his pulse. She held it there a second before meeting his gaze with hers.

"Your hands were shredded."

"Excuse me?"

She licked her lips. "I didn't wake up until yesterday. A lot of the damage had healed. It looked weird," she told him, as if he didn't know. "Like open wounds without the blood."

He knew that stage. It wasn't something he'd ever wanted her to witness. "Why are you telling me this?"

"Because I want you to understand something." Squeezing his hand, she whispered, "I watched you become whole again after I thought I'd lost you. It was a miracle." Stretching her hand flat over his, she pressed the other against the back, balancing him in the heat and strength of her touch. "Even though this doesn't feel real to me, and if I hadn't seen that, I'd be telling you now that you're insane—"

"I am."

She shook her head. "No! Awful things were done to you and maybe like the men who came back from the War, some of the memories stay and haunt you, but you're not crazy."

"You don't know what goes on inside my head."

"You're not in mine."

She let go of his hand. Again, he expected her to step back. And again she didn't. "My beast likes yours."

He blinked.

"And I like you, and I'm sure if there ever comes a time when this seems real, I'm going to be very mad at someone. But right now, I can't see it as all bad. The beast brought you back to me."

She smiled and stood on tiptoe to kiss him softly. "And for the first time in thirteen years, I don't miss my worry stone."

As her lips met his, he thought with satisfaction, *Because you have me.*

⚜ 18 ⚜

WHEN THEY GOT BACK TO THE CAMPSITE, BLADE WAS nowhere in sight. The hairs on the back of Addy's neck stood on end even before Isaiah held up a hand for caution. She looked around, saw nothing out of the ordinary, but still she knew, just knew, something was amiss. Where was Blade? Deep inside there was a stirring, the feeling of something evil coming to life. Her beast? This wasn't the time for them to be introduced. She took a step backward, against a tree. The breeze kicked up. With it came the scent of blood and . . . others. Something had happened to Blade.

Isaiah caught her arm and yanked her to him. Pressing a hard kiss on her lips, he shoved her back the way they'd come. "Run."

She went as quickly and as quietly as she could, her heart thundering in her ears, her breath catching in her chest. Reapers. Reapers were here. Images of giant wolves with bloody jaws drove her forward. *No. Dear Lord, no. Run!* They needed to run.

She stumbled as something unfurled inside, stretching and coming to life. Something alien and new brushed her awareness. She leaned against the tree, gasping for breath.

"Isaiah?" She turned around, expecting him to be right there. He wasn't. He'd told her to run. And like a coward, she had. But he'd stayed and fought. For her. From inside, there came a whisper. *Isaiah*.

Another brush along her mind. Her beast? She waited for the violence that Isaiah said went hand and hand with the beast, but all she felt was a sharpening of her senses. Isaiah had stayed behind to fight the Reapers. She had to go back.

That something inside growled.

No.

She had to either go backward or go forward. Ahead was a fork in the trail. The branch to the right went to the lake. She knew there were no Reapers at the lake. They'd just come from there. She started down that trail.

The *No* was sharp and immediate. She was stopped so fast, she lost her balance. When she tried to continue, she couldn't. In her mind the beast paced impatiently. *No.*

She reached for her worry stone, forgetting it wasn't there. Fear pushed her toward the lake. The beast pushed her up the mountain. Her hand slipped through her shredded pocket, finding nothing but air. What should she do?

Normally the question would have paralyzed her while she struggled with a decision, but this time there was an answer. A mental push to go up.

"All right," she whispered, "I'm going."

The beast grumbled its satisfaction with her obedience. Her skirts tangled around her legs, slowing her down. She had a mental image from her beast of tearing them off.

"No." She couldn't go naked, she just couldn't. Her beast was quite ruthless in its logic. It didn't speak in words, but she definitely got the impression that if she couldn't move freely, she would be dead. The beast was very good with images and emotions.

She couldn't do it. "I'm sorry."

The beast snarled its displeasure.

It was easier to climb the mountain than it should have been. Her legs seemed to eat up the distance with unnatural speed. The waist of her skirt cut into her skin. Her blouse was too tight at the neck, too binding at the wrists, irritating at her shoulders. Her hands and toes tingled. An ache grew in her gums. Her muscles twitched until she couldn't stand it. Ducking into the shadows of a pine tree, she took off her blouse, her skirt, and her petticoats, leaving on just her camisole and pantaloons. The beast wanted them gone, too, but she couldn't take them off.

"Twenty-some years of modesty don't disappear just because one develops a beast," she informed the disgruntled being in a harsh whisper as she balled up the clothes.

She stepped back onto the trail. An image of the clothes falling over the ledge flooded her mind. She looked at the bundle in her hand. The beast growled a warning. The clothes would leave a scent. Why hadn't she thought of that? Stepping carefully, she made her way off the trail and hurled them over the edge. They didn't go out as far she wanted. One of the petticoats caught on a rock a few feet down, but the rest floated to the ground far below. She turned away. The beast growled.

"Oh my God, you are a nag."

Finding a long stick, she lay down and, reaching over the edge, poked the petticoat free. It floated down with the rest.

"Happy now?"

The beast didn't answer. She tightened her grip on the stick, squeezing tightly to still the panic. She didn't have a gun. She didn't have Cole, or her other cousins. She didn't have Isaiah. She'd learned how to survive captivity. She knew how to survive rumors and speculation. She didn't know how to survive being hunted by Reapers. She listened. There was nothing anywhere. Even the birds had stopped singing. She hefted the stick. They knew what she knew. Death was about.

She searched inside for the beast. There was no sensation of anything other than her own fears, her own insecurities, her own doubts. Tightening her grip on the stick, she borrowed one of Isaiah's favorite curses. "Shit. You picked a lousy time to go silent."

She continued going up because it was only logical and that was the direction the beast wanted her to go. Of course, that might mean she was attributing a level of intelligence to the beast that might not be there, but then again, it had told her to throw her clothes away. So it had to think about something. Even if it wasn't talking about it.

The trail up took a turn to the right. She followed it. *Like a lamb to the slaughter*, she thought. It ended at an outcropping. She crept to the edge and looked down. It took her a minute to get her bearings, but below, she realized, was the campsite. The rocks that looked so imposing down there were insubstantial from here. She could see the pond. She could see the trail leading away from the lean-to. She pressed her hands flat on the rock. She could see trouble.

Three wolves wove through the trees. From the trajectory of their path, they'd come from the pond. She gave her beast—no wolf she realized watching the Reapers coming up the path—a mental pat. Had she been at the stream, they surely would have captured her. They stopped at the fork of the trail. Two looked up. She didn't move, didn't breathe while they appeared to communicate with each other. As one, they continued forward.

She rested her head against the hard rock. They knew where she was, they just weren't interested in her right now. The wolf/beast growled. Her head snapped up. Isaiah! They were hunting Isaiah. She dug her nails into the ground. Rock, she realized as they grated loudly. She was digging her nails into rock. When she looked down, her hands were not her own. Instead of the small, pink, carefully tended nails she was used to seeing, she had round, wicked-looking claws that stretched from hands still feminine but larger, and more sinewy. Claws strong enough to gouge into shale.

Panic seared through her. She reached for her worry stone. It wasn't fair, but her beast was calm, confident, ready to fight.

She shook her head. "I can't."

Her beast snarled and scented the wind. Isaiah. She was looking for Isaiah. So were the Reapers below, she realized. Three against one. Those weren't good odds. Isaiah was a good fighter, but maybe they were, too. Her beast snarled again and urged her away from the edge. She resisted the overwhelming urge, studying the ground below, making a mental map of the area. The beast tugged at her.

"Hush," she whispered. "We might need to know this."

Surprisingly, she thought she felt a sense of agreement. She stood, brushing the dirt from her hands. Her claws clacked together. Inside, horror and panic began. What was she becoming? A primitive thought broke into her panic as she studied the wicked curves.

Weapons.

She held up her hands and looked at them with new eyes. The claws were a good two and a half inches long, thick and strong. They would do damage. Some of that sense of helpless panic left. She turned her hand over. In some ways, they were even better than knives. She couldn't drop them.

The beast growled her approval, or impatience, Addy wasn't sure. But she agreed. They had to get moving. The wolves below thought she was hiding up here. Thought they could get to her at their leisure. They thought wrong. She curled her claws into her palms. The days when she waited for rescue were gone. She started back down the trail. A *No* flashed into her mind so strongly, it was like walking into a wall. She began to get a sense of why Isaiah was so frustrated with his beast. If they always worked off reaction rather than forethought, it could be a problem.

Inside her shoes, her toes ached and her gums continued to itch. More change? She looked at her hands and looked at her feet. There was no way she could sprout claws on her feet inside her shoes, but if she went barefoot, they'd be torn up.

She remembered claws slashing at her, pain, jaws opening, saliva dripping in her face. As she'd done many times the last two days, she put her hand on her stomach, searching for scars. There was nothing. It stood to reason that if those wounds could heal, that if her feet got a little torn up from going barefoot, those wounds would heal, too. She looked at the ground, the dirt, and then her shoes. It was surprisingly easy to bend down and fasten them closed. Where she expected revulsion and crippling indecision, she found only a sense of urgency pouring from her beast.

Hurry.

Yes, she had to hurry. She took off her shoes. It wasn't enough.

All.

With only a second's indecision, she took off her camisole and pantaloons, standing naked as the sun poured down on her body. Again she waited for that sense of panic. She was naked in public. She should have been horrified. All she got was a sense of urgency.

Hurry.

Picking up her clothes, she wrapped them around her shoes, and just like before, she hurled them over the edge. From below came a howl. Isaiah? One of the three wolves hunting him? She didn't know. Inside, the beast paced with impatience. Clearly feeling that she should know.

"Pardon me," she muttered, her new claws nicking her thigh as she reached for her worry stone. "I'm new to this."

The beast had no patience with her excuses. It wanted to go now, toward that howl. She wasn't so sure that was a good idea. The beast didn't care. The tingling in her toes intensified. The itch in her gums built to an ache. Her vision blurred. There was a surge of power in her mind, a blankness to her thoughts, a sensation of running freely downward, trees and rocks flying past, her mind focused with a peculiar intensity so similar to the focus she had trained herself to use with her worry stone. But there was a difference. The beast wasn't thinking of calm. It was thinking . . . blood. Battle. Isaiah.

The beast was focused on Isaiah. Through the disorientation, Addy struggled for some comprehension. She was herself, yet not. She was running, but not like she was used to. Her mind was filled with scents and sounds, processing them at a speed she wasn't used to. She struggled to see, but the wolf didn't care about what it saw. It was, she realized, relying on scent and sound first. Most of all, she realized she wasn't afraid. There was dirt on her hands and she wasn't disgusted. She was naked and the knowledge wasn't overwhelming. She had choices and she wasn't panicked.

She was going into battle, with all the courage she'd always thought she had but could never tap into. It should terrify her, that much change in such a short amount of time. Instead, it was liberating. Here, in this moment, in the form she didn't recognize, she'd found the person she had always struggled to be. Herself.

Where are we going? she asked the beast part of her, amazed at the agility of this form.

Isaiah.

That was all she got. Isaiah had been right. The beast was a little single-minded and primitive in its thought processes. Tracking their progress, she could tell from her mental map that they were heading toward the campsite. Where Isaiah was. Where the Reapers were. Her beast was powerful, her body strong, and two against one were better odds. She wasn't the victim in this fight. She was going to be a part of it. As she got closer, she heard the sounds of battle. Four different growls, four different scents. The beast/wolf rumbled in her mind.

Isaiah.

Addy stilled the rumble before it became a growl. The element of surprise was not one she was willing to give up. There was a moment of resistance in which she wasn't sure she could attain her goal, and then the wolf . . . agreed.

It was hope. Her intelligence combined with the beast's power and drive and fearless dedication to fight. They might actually be able to do something. The beast put on a burst of speed. It seemed to fly along the trail, covering the distance ten times faster than she had. The growls ahead turned to snarls. As she got closer, she could hear teeth snapping, and dear God, maybe the sound of flesh rending? Her beast snarled. So did her human. They were hunting Isaiah, the man who gave everything for her and expected nothing back. She'd been his first love, his first lover, and he'd been hers. No one was taking that away from her without a fight. The beast agreed with a snap of teeth.

The trail turned. She didn't follow it, but instead plunged into the trees straight ahead, following her nose and ears to the fight. Isaiah might have wanted her to run while he sacrificed himself for her, but he wasn't alone anymore. And she didn't want his sacrifice. They cleared the woods. Ahead she could see Isaiah fighting three Reapers. She knew him from the shade of his fur, the color of his eyes. His back was to the wall. The Reaper on his right had his back to her.

She focused on him. The most vulnerable. Silently, she whispered to the beast, *Quiet.* She needed surprise. Just a few seconds longer.

There was no hope of keeping her beast silent as it closed in and leapt. Muscles surging, adrenaline flowing, fangs bared, claws ready to rip the flesh. Primitive, feral, effective, it landed on the Reaper's back, digging its claws in, holding on as it leaned forward. The human in Addy recoiled when her beast's jaws locked in the base of the other Reaper's neck. Horror and repulsion filled her as blood pooled in her mouth and the shocking crunch of bone reached her ears. But the human wasn't in control. The wolf was, and the only thought going through her mind was, *Isaiah.*

The beast released the dead wolf and turned just in time to take the attack of the other. The ease with which it took her to the ground was disheartening. Its jaws closed over her throat. A thought thrust into her mind.

Surrender.

Her beast snarled its defiance. Out of the corner of her eye, she could see Isaiah fighting with the other wolf. It was as big as him. His fur was covered in blood from multiple cuts and bites. The same blood colored the ground and scented the air.

His howl ripped through the air as the Reaper's jaws tightened on her throat. Her beast flailed and fought, no thought of surrendering in her mind. In another second, the Reaper would crush her throat.

Beyond the beast's mind, Addy crouched, assessing the situation with human intellect. The Reaper expected her to surrender or die. It thought in terms of all or nothing. The human side of her saw the gray area between.

Relax, she told her beast. *Give him what he wants.*

The refusal was immediate. Violent.

No. Isaiah.

Yes, Isaiah. We need to help him. The Reaper's teeth tightened on her throat, puncturing the skin. The scent of her own blood joined the vicious mix filling the air.

Relax, then kill.

Her beast absorbed the image she sent. Then relaxed. The Reaper growled once more and then stood, releasing her. Too smug in its belief that she had been cowed.

Addy projected an image into the mind of her beast. An image of it grabbing the Reaper with its hind legs and sinking her claws into the Reaper's side and shoulders. In that split second, the beast pulled the Reaper down, using that second of surprise and a human form of attack to draw his neck into range before, with lethal efficiency, ripping out the Reaper's throat.

Blood poured over her face. The beast rejoiced. The human recoiled. But again it didn't matter. When revulsion threatened to cripple her, the beast took over, following through, springing to its feet, ready to attack, only to find another Reaper in front of her, just as bloody, just as victorious.

Isaiah. He was a beautiful wolf, his brown fur tipped with gold and his eyes a steely gray. His scent was different, yet familiar. He was a giant wolf, but in the way his nose touched hers tenderly, followed by the force of his reprimanding bark, she found familiarity. Her beast looked around. The Reapers were dead, their bodies slowly reverting to human. The danger was over.

The woman became aware of the dirt and blood and gore covering her beast's fur. The beast didn't care. It only wanted Isaiah. It sidled up to Isaiah.

Addy did care. She couldn't go to him with this. She turned and trotted back down the path, headed for the pond. Isaiah followed silently. Her guardian. Her mate. Her beast rumbled its satisfaction. Addy fussed with her beast, not comfortable with the images coming out of the reality swamping her. Not comfortable with this form. This was her new reality, but it wasn't her. Yet.

As soon as she got to the pond, she jumped in. The wolf didn't see the need. Addy didn't care. She wasn't coming back to human form covered in gore and blood. She had enough to deal with. Isaiah joined her in the water, but stayed at a distance. He was right to be cautious. She was feeling unbalanced. She needed normal. Standing in the water, she focused.

My turn.

The beast was succinct.

No.

Closing her eyes, Addy pushed everything out except the scent of the woods and the water, and Isaiah. Rubbing her worry stone in her mind, she gathered her will and projected one thought.

Me.

There was a disorienting pain in her muscles, tingling in her gums, and an ache in her fingers and toes. She lost her balance and pitched forward, going underwater. She came up sputtering. A glance at her hands revealed neat pink fingernails. Once again she was Addy. With all of her weaknesses and vulnerabilities. But inside she was the beast. Ready and waiting. And the beast feared nothing. She shook the hair out of her eyes and stood, smiling. The beast was freedom.

"Now there's the sign of a true Reaper. She comes out of a fight smiling."

Blade. Addy dropped down in the water and covered her breasts. "Where the hell have you been?"

"Here and there."

Something hit her side, knocking her back. The stench of blood and wet fur swamped her nostrils. "Isaiah."

Teeth snapped at her in warning. If she hadn't just come out of a battle, Addy would have been intimidated. She thunked him on the head.

"Addy!" Blade splashed into the water toward them.

"Don't tell me what to do," she informed Isaiah's beast before looking up at Blade, who was standing in the water staring at her like she'd just spun gold from air.

"What?"

Isaiah rumbled another warning and flashed those teeth at her again.

"Step away from him slowly," Blade told her in a very careful tone of voice.

"Why?"

"He's not himself."

That was bull. Isaiah was always Isaiah. "Stop upsetting Blade, Isaiah."

The beast turned and squared off in front of her.

"I can't change to protect you," Blade warned.

Who asked him to? "Then make yourself useful and throw me your shirt." He hesitated. "Then turn your back," she added for good measure.

"Hell." Blade never took his eyes from Isaiah as he stripped off his shirt. His body was covered in bloody gashes.

"Here and there?" she asked as she caught the shirt. She dunked it in the water. Blood reddened the water. Whatever Blade had been doing, he'd been fighting. Isaiah's beast grabbed the shirt in his teeth.

"Hey." When she tugged, the beast growled.

"Let him have it," Blade called.

"I am not going naked so a spoiled beast can have a tantrum," she snapped. To Isaiah, she said, "Tell your beast to let go of the shirt."

"He doesn't have any control right now." Blade waded two steps closer only to stop immediately at the beast's warning growl. "It's too soon after battle."

She looked into Isaiah's eyes. There was resolve but no insanity.

I want to kill Blade every time he gets near you.

"He has control."

"You don't understand—" Blade said, moving sideways to a better position.

"I understand perfectly."

"You have no idea—"

Addy cut Blade off again, looking at the beast, staring into Isaiah's eyes. "I understand everything."

The beast feinted forward, terrifying in its size and its anger.

"Shit!" Blade lunged. "Get away."

Instead, Addy took a step forward, ignoring Blade, her human terror, listening to her beast's whisper of *Isaiah*. "He won't hurt me."

"What the hell makes you so sure?" Blade snapped.

Letting go of the shirt with one hand, keeping the other over her breasts, she reached out. "Because I'm all he's thinking of right now."

The beast lifted its lips in a menacing snarl.

"Addy . . ."

"Just like he's all I'm thinking of."

The snarl faltered.

"He's unstable."

She shook her head. "He hasn't been, not for a long time."

"Addy."

"Shut up, Blade."

The beast didn't stop snarling and Addy didn't stop reaching. If Isaiah was going to kill her, she wanted to know it now. She touched the beast's snout, felt the reverberations of its violent nature in her fingertips.

Isaiah.

"Isaiah," she echoed her beast's whisper. "Come back to me."

The beast went absolutely still. He could have been listening or preparing for the kill. She had only her beast's conviction and her heart's belief telling her which.

"I need you, Isaiah."

Another snarl, this one deeper, louder. Even more menacing.

Shaking, scared, hoping, believing, holding the shirt and her ground, she whispered, "Please."

There was a bunching of muscle. Closing her eyes, she braced herself for teeth tearing into her arm. Tension abruptly left the shirt. She stumbled backward. Wet, hard hands closed around her shoulders, stopping her fall. Familiar hands, followed by a familiar voice drawling, "You do like to dance with the devil, sweets."

She opened her eyes. Isaiah stood before her, bloody, victorious, handsome. Hers.

"Isaiah."

Isaiah.

"Who the hell else did you expect?"

From afar she heard Blade whisper, "Son of a bitch."

She shook her head, relief taking the strength from her knees. She didn't have to worry. Isaiah didn't let her fall. "No one."

Isaiah cocked a brow at her as she clutched his arms. "You going to put that shirt on?"

She licked her lips and nodded, holding tightly as the events of the last half hour rushed forward. Terror, horror, and shock replaced confidence. Had she really ripped out a man's throat? Broken another's spine? Had she really stood naked and become a . . . beast? From deep within, the shaking started.

"I'm sorry." Isaiah's grip became softer as he tugged her forward. And she went. Needing him.

"I changed, Isaiah."

"I saw."

She supposed he had.

She dug her nails into his arms, wrestling with the reality. "I did horrible things."

"Necessary things," he corrected.

"But horrible." The shirt dropped into the water with a small splash. Drops of water flicked her side. The memories wouldn't go away.

"Aw, sweets," Isaiah murmured, drawing her in with a touch and voice so gentle neither could shatter the remnants of her composure. "Feeling like hiding?"

She nodded. "Until they make snowballs in hell."

"That's a long time."

"It's been a long day."

"I suppose it has." Another light tug on her arms. She shook her head. "Let me hold you."

"No."

"Why?"

She shook her head. The cold of the water matched the coldness in her soul. This was nothing like she'd planned. Out of control. It was all wrong.

"Why," he repeated.

She licked her lips, staring at the wounds on his chest, and shook her head. "I don't know."

His finger under her chin forced her face up to his. "Then I guess this decision, I get to make."

This time he didn't allow her to resist the pull. All it took was two steps and she was in his arms. Two steps and her cheek was against his chest. Two steps and she could hear his heartbeat, breathe his scent, feel his love. Two steps and she knew she'd guard the three with her life. Two steps was all it took to lose all regret.

His hand cupped her head; his lips brushed her hair. "Let me hold you, sweets."

"Why?"

"Because you hurt."

"Why?"

"Because I need to."

"Why?"

His lips brushed her hair, her cheek, her mouth before he finally gave her what she needed. What they both needed. The truth. "Because I love you."

Oh God, the impact of those words! The chaos of the day faded away. Addy opened her palm over his chest, over his heart. She didn't know what her future held, but she knew this. "I love you, too."

His hand fisted in her hair, holding her still for the descent of his mouth. He didn't have to worry, she wasn't going anywhere.

Isaiah, her beast sighed.

"Isaiah," she whispered.

"I love the way you say my name," he breathed into her mouth. "Like I'm some kind of dream you're happy to wake up to."

She caught his lower lip, ran her tongue over it, smiled when he shivered. "You are. My very own Prince Charming."

He chuckled and kissed her softly, cherishingly. "Complete with fangs and claws."

Tilting her head back, she gave him access to her neck, moaning as the spot on her shoulder burned hotter with each press of his lips along the taut cord. "I have some of my own."

She felt his smile against her skin then heard it in his voice. "So I saw."

She clutched his shoulders. "I killed a man."

"He was trying to kill me, and would have killed you."

Yes, he would have. And she had a right to defend herself.

"She loves you, you know."

He didn't pretend not to understand. "Mine's pretty fond of you, too."

She rubbed her fingers against his shoulder as she shared a truth of her own. "I like my beast."

The kissing stopped. So did his breathing.

When Isaiah pulled back, his eyes were dark with concern, his expression serious. She cupped his cheek in her hand. "She's part of me. The part I could never find when I was in captivity. The part I was afraid to grow when I was rebuilding my life. She's capable of defending herself."

"Yes."

She remembered the blood, the sense of victory, the power. But she also remembered her beast's inability to switch between battle and thought. "But she needs me, too. To think, to rationalize." Licking her lips, she explained, "To bring her above the level of an animal. To make her . . . human."

"Son of a bitch," Blade swore again in a mix of shock and admiration.

Addy blushed and pressed against Isaiah. She'd forgotten about him.

"Do you know what this means, Isaiah?" Blade asked.

Isaiah smiled and brushed his fingers down her hot cheek. "Yeah, I do."

Addy's breath caught as his gaze held hers, all the love his man and beast were capable of feeling, all the love she could ever desire, showing in his eyes.

"Addy tamed the beast."

⊰ 19 ⊱

THEY SAT ON THEIR HORSES HIGH ON THE BLUFF LOOKING down on the valley below. Three riders. Three different backgrounds. One Goal. Survival. Addy shook her head. How her life had changed in just three weeks. She touched the spot on her shoulder. Her beast stretched in contentment.

Beside her, Blade and Isaiah pulled their horses up.

"Beautiful country," Blade said.

"Yes."

Isaiah took her hand and squeezed. "Big enough to get lost in."

Everywhere she looked there was wilderness. To the northwest were more mountains, and beyond them enough uncharted land for a hundred Reapers to get lost in. A week ago that thought would have terrified her. Today, it was exciting.

"Yes." Fear and excitement shot through her in equal amounts.

"This is as far as I go," Blade said, backing his horse up a couple steps.

"We'd be happy to have you come with us," Addy told him. She hadn't been lying when she'd told Isaiah she liked Blade. He was sarcastic, and deadly, but he had a sharp wit and he'd proven himself a good friend.

"Thank you."

But he wouldn't she knew. Isaiah had explained the council, the laws, Blade's position. Everyone had to find their own way. Hers and Isaiah's was to the northwest. Blade's was . . . She didn't know.

"Where will you go?"

Blade exchanged a look with Isaiah. "I thought I'd drop in on an old friend."

"And from there?"

He shrugged. His horse tossed his head. The bridle jingled. "I'll see where the wind takes me."

She smiled. "Well, I hope the wind takes you our way again."

Isaiah made a growl in his throat. Blade laughed.

"Maybe, but not for a while." His expression sobered. "You need to disappear."

Isaiah nodded to the valley and squeezed her hand again. "Just let the land swallow us up."

Both men looked at her. She knew why. Unlike her, they had no ties, but she had her bakery, her friends, her cousins. Disappearing into the wilderness meant cutting herself off from everything she knew. Everyone she loved. Some days she was all right with it. On others not. But no matter how the day went, no matter how her mood went, Isaiah was always there. Ready to give her what she needed. Sometimes even before she asked. He was a good man. Her man. And she was happy.

Her beast rumbled its approval.

"Maybe someday we can go home."

"They'll never stop hunting you," Blade interjected.

She knew that. Just as she knew there was no going back. She was Reaper. Reaper law had been broken. There was a price on her head as well as Isaiah's. She squeezed Isaiah's hand. But at least she wasn't alone. Not like the woman in the tintype. And in reality, what she was doing now was no different than what her parents had done, newly wedded, heading into Indian territory facing death every day, gambling everything on the hope of building a better life for themselves. "I just like to keep the possibility open."

"Thinking that way will get you and Isaiah killed."

"Leave her be, Blade," Isaiah drawled.

"She needs to understand."

"She understands, we both do."

"It's not just the Reapers you have to fear." Removing his spyglass from his saddle horn, Blade handed it to Isaiah. He pointed to the far right corner of the valley.

"Look there."

Isaiah took the spyglass and swore before handing it to Addy. She knew what she'd see before she saw it. Coming up the path they'd traveled two days ago was a lone horseman dressed in a brown duster and a dark brown hat, riding a flashy palomino. "Cole."

"The man's part hound," Blade groused.

She slowly lowered the spyglass. "Maybe he didn't get my message."

"I delivered it personally," Blade informed her. "He just doesn't believe you'd leave willingly."

"He doesn't understand."

"He needs to," Isaiah cut in. "Or he'll lead the Guardians right to us."

"He wouldn't."

"He wouldn't know he was doing it."

Blade's gaze met Isaiah's over Addy's head. "I could talk to him again before I head out."

Addy sat up, hope blossoming. "Would you?"

"No!" Isaiah countered.

"Is that the man or Guardian talking?" Blade asked.

Isaiah looked into Addy's big eyes, seeing the understanding of what Blade's version of a talk would entail darken them with horror. She didn't have to worry. He knew what family meant to her.

"Just me."

"Reaper and man together?"

"We're working out a truce."

Blade jerked his chin in the direction of the valley. "You know leaving him is dangerous. He won't give up."

No, Cole was not known for giving up on those he loved. "Then I guess I'll have to throw him off our trail."

"You got tricks we haven't tried yet?"

"A few."

"Then you'd better haul them out."

"I hear you." Isaiah held out his hand. "Try to stay out of trouble."

Blade shook it. "Where would be the fun in that?"

Isaiah shook his head. "Nowhere, I guess."

Blade tipped his hat to Addy. "You watch your back, Addy. Don't let this big lug run roughshod over you."

"I won't."

With a tip of his hat, Blade headed down the mountain to the left toward the other side of the valley. The sound of hoofbeats faded quickly, leaving only the sound of the wind through the leaves and the birds in the trees. They were alone on the mountaintop, their future spread out before them. Isaiah turned to Addy. "You ready?"

She didn't answer right away. Instead she glanced toward the speck that was Cole. Isaiah's nerves were pulled taut, then Addy turned and her calm confident smile lit up his world. "Yes, I believe I am." She touched her shoulder. "Any idea where we're going?"

"Yes." He looked into her eyes, seeing the strength, the woman. Seeing his future. He grazed the backs of his fingers down her cheek before resting his hand over hers and smiled. "Into our beginning."

She leaned across the distance separating them, cupping his face in her hands. "I love you, Isaiah Jones."

Son of a bitch. The words shot through him with the impact of a bullet. Isaiah could no more stop himself from pulling Addy off her horse and into his lap than he could stop taking his next breath. He needed to touch her, to hold her, to kiss her. Hip to hip, heart to heart, she settled against him. She was his. The gift he didn't deserve. The gift he'd always cherish. The one he'd always love. His Addy. His sweets. He drew back just far enough to murmur, "And I love you, Addy Cameron. Today, and always, in this life and the next, long past the time when tomorrow stops coming, I'll be loving you."